SOUTH B'S FINEST

SOUTH B'S FINEST

Makena Maganjo

Published by Tablo

Published in 2020 by Tablo Publishing.

Cover photo by Julian Christ on Unsplash.

For Agnes and Bernard

There is always a maybe in our failures and a chancy sometimes in our hopes.
Maybe we will get there. Sometimes we will think that we have arrived.
Kenya @50:Trends, Identities and the Politics of Belonging|
Dr. Joyce Nyairo

CHAPTER ONE

Windsor Golf and Country Club, August 4th, 2012

This is not the beginning but when I consider it all (pictures, diary entries, recipes cut out of magazines, old receipts—I was thorough), it is this wedding photo of the Malaba Estate neighbours (ex neighbours, some of them), smiling into the camera, the years showing in their smiles, hard stares, grey hairs, that calls to me most. It is in this moment, captured by a hired photographer who delivered the pictures a full year after the wedding, that the past stretches its hand into the present and reminds it that it is nothing without the weight of events that have come before. Very well then, to honour the past, we will begin here.

~

The venue practically chose itself. Since what can only be described as the dramatic departure of President Moi a decade earlier, economic prosperity had found its way to the vacant and ghostly corridors and lawns of Windsor Golf and Country Club, and returned the once glamorous club to a sibling of its former glory. In the hall that held the wedding party, there was only the slightest hint of judgment, not unusual at these things, of course. This was not the couple's first marriage. No dowry had been paid, an agreement the couple came to unanimously. This agreement did not sit well with some of the bride's family, but what can we say?

Impressively, the food at the reception was not…bad. Now, mind you, I didn't say it was delicious, but the roasted goat meat, though not tender, was well salted, the pilau, though under-spiced, was not dry, the chapatis, though dry…no those were bad. The chapatis were, without question, bad. Regardless, the caterers had outdone themselves, delivering a lukewarm yet passable selection of Kenya's finest foods.

The Priest kept on time and on message during the mass earlier that morning. He only strayed off topic twice, the first time to deliver an anecdotal story on the power of faith in times of strife, and the second to remind the guests that an offering would be taken. Even the M.C. largely behaved, referring to the couples advanced age only a handful of times.

The gifts table was piled high with starter-home gifts—you know the lineup—the cheap glasses, one set of good china from a wealthy distant relative, pots and pans (non-stick), dining table mats and one tiny Samsung fridge. The D.J. played all the wedding classics (think Backstreet Boys and Boyz II Men), and nostalgic tunes from E-sir's *Boomba Train* to Esther Wahome's *Kuna Dawa*. The M.C. like a hype man in a rap contest brought the guests to a fever pitch and had them dancing and singing along for the better part of the reception. So far, the wedding was a success precisely because it was tinged with the right amount of mediocrity to ensure it was not memorable for the wrong reasons.

~

'If you are tired, we don't have to stay long.' Steven Kosgei touched his new wife's hand lightly. Beatrice shook her head. Tired? No. She was far from tired, instead she was overwhelmed with gratitude at how her life had turned out. It was nearly fourteen years to the day her first husband, Mr. Mathai went missing.

Beatrice was a practical woman who believed that life dealt you your cards and you either played a damned good game of poker or you lost. There was no time to bemoan the set of cards, you just got on with it. This was how she came to find herself married to a man she barely understood at the age of twenty-five and, at twenty-seven, pregnant with what I suppose would be referred to as her childhood sweetheart Macharia. Yes, these were her cards, but for the first time, they seemed to be—she hesitated to even think it—good.

~

'Betty, Betty…' Mrs. Mutiso, a long standing friend of Beatrice whom she'd met when they moved to South B nearly twenty years ago, waved a phone in Beatrice's direction as she made her way to the stage where the bride and groom sat on a lone table piled high with a floral arrangement that had given Beatrice heart palpitations when she found out how much it would cost. Nevertheless, her wedding planner, the very same Mrs. Mutiso, had persisted. Mrs. Mutiso stopped before the stage. She briefly pondered taking the steps up to join the couple then thought otherwise and stretched her hand out for Beatrice to take her phone.

'The twins are engaged? When did this happen?' Beatrice asked looking at the phone. Before her was a picture of Mrs. Mutiso's daughters holding out their left hands, ring fingers adorned with matching engagement rings.

'Yes! Just now! Just now!' Mrs. Mutiso beamed, her mouth curved into a bright, lipstick-red smile.

The girls in the picture stood side by side in winter coats, their necks and the lower part of their faces obscured by giant woollen scarves, behind them a white canvas of fresh snow. Steven, who'd also leaned in to look at the picture betrayed his confusion. It was only August. There was no snow in Frankfurt in August. Beatrice shook her head lightly deterring him from pointing out that the engagements could not have happened just-now. Mrs. Mutiso didn't wait anyway for a response. She reached out for her phone and the moment it was in hand, she swayed away, phone ahead of her, ready to show anyone else her twins and their just-now engagements.

~

'Mum, some of us want to go out after this, is it okay?' Kanyi, Beatrice's son and youngest child, jumped onto the stage, kissed her cheek and patted his new step-dad absentmindedly on the back.

'Where to?'

'Just like a ka-after party thing.' Kanyi evaded the question of "where" and took a long swig of his mother's glass of water in an effort to seem nonchalant.

'An after party for what?' Beatrice saw her daughter and eldest child, Nyambura, wading through the crowd of guests, headed for the stage. She already knew that with Nyambura, whatever the girl was going to say it was not going to be in the form of a request.

'But si-for you mum.' He winked.

'For me how and I'm not even invited? Steven, did you hear anything about a party? Me I didn't know we were going out after this. How can you celebrate someone who isn't even there?' Though she belaboured the point, Beatrice did so in an effort to prolong the conversation.

'You'll be there in spirit and you look like you need to rest anyway,' Kanyi joked as he jumped down from the stage, her "yes" a foregone conclusion.

'Hey! Watch it young man. This is my wife you are now speaking to.'

Steven Kosgei tried his hand at banter, the outcome a tepid

response that Kanyi politely laughed at. When it was clear that he was serious about Beatrice, Steven, a man who did nothing in half measures, pursued a relationship with her two children. The impetus wasn't what you might be thinking. He did not need nor was he seeking their permission to court their mother. From the time he was old enough to understand that there was this thing called fatherhood, Steven had yearned to play the role to his future children. His future children became a distant dream when, a few months into his first marriage, his wife walked into their bedroom just after the nine o'clock news and announced she didn't want to have kids. Steven, not used to speaking his mind, accepted this new reality with an equanimity that would have been puzzling if you had never met a person of his temperament.

But now life had given him a chance at a sort of fatherhood and he had taken on the challenge with zeal. Steven was not deterred by the emotional and physical distance between the two children and their mother. Nyambura was a comic living in what he surmised as poverty in New York (...at this age? Sharing a house? Why doesn't she just move back. At least here she can afford an entire apartment with what she pays for a room there. Beatrice have you asked her if she'd like to move back? Maybe if we gave her incentive to move back…), Kanyi a third year student at JKUAT who found every excuse under God's green earth not to visit (is this normal? Do other children do this? Beatrice, maybe we need to buy him a car so that it's easier for him to make the trip from Juja…).

He researched things on Google, and later Quora (...did you know Beatrice that you can ask a question on Quora and people, real people, will answer in less than five minutes…), like "How to bond with your step-children", and "Why don't children pick up their phones even when they are online?"

Before long, Steven and Beatrice had a joint family account (...for holidays and emergencies for the kids…), and Steven had added them to his health insurance plan (...Nyambura, I know you're not on one as you pursue your dreams which we pray will earn you money…). He sent the children (as he referred to them), educational emails about Kenya's history on public holidays—this one a particularly lamentable effort—but we have time, we have time, you will see why in time.

'Hey guys, I'm going out with Esther later.' Nyambura had finally arrived and even before the sentence was finished she was already weaving her way through the guests, towards her childhood best friend, Esther Karanja.

CHAPTER TWO

A Past Revisited

Beatrice watched her children as they disappeared into the crowd. Kanyi had taken after her. He was short and compact, even his movements were hers, practical movements. They didn't exert energy where it wasn't needed lest it be useful somewhere else. That was the philosophy in their stride.

Nyambura, in a case of nurture versus nature, defied reason to become a replica of Mr. Mathai. Her sensibilities so aligned with Mathai's. Beatrice couldn't think of one without thinking of the other. It was as if everything of Macharia—everything that Nyambura could have inherited from her biological father, his features, his character, his little idiosyncrasies that Beatrice had come to know so well she'd catalogued them in her organised mind (once, not any more, she reminded herself), had been excavated from Nyambura's DNA. Fate, it appeared, had refused her even this: it would not let her make a totem out of her daughter.

~

Someone came up to congratulate the bride and groom, but Beatrice's mind was back in time. Nairobi, circa 1981, the year she bumped into Macharia on Biashara Street on her way to buy Kitenge fabric she was going to up-sell for twice as much as it cost to the richer girls in her halls of residence at University of Nairobi. There had always been something between Beatrice and Macharia, even though, from the beginning, it felt more like dying embers than the sparks of a new fire.

Macharia asked Beatrice if perhaps she had time for a quick lunch, to catch up, and in the characteristic way she forgot her characteristic self when she was near him, Beatrice forgot the errand that had brought her into town. He looked good. He was studying architecture. Oh, I didn't know you liked architecture? He laughed, he didn't think he liked it all that much.

'Maybe I should have come to you for advice first. You always know the right thing to do.'

'Me?' Beatrice sounded incredulous.

Macharia was a year older than her. He was (for the neighbourhood they grew up in), a symbol of success. Everyone either wanted their children to be like Macharia or their daughters to marry Macharia. Beatrice had never stopped to consider that the self assured boy, she'd played with in her childhood was ever unsure about anything. He'd always moved with an ease and certainty about him. When his classmates dropped out of school to run their parents business concerns, Macharia was resolute about finishing his A-Levels and applying for university admission. He was the first of his generation from the whole neighbourhood to join university.

'You always knew what would get us in trouble and what wouldn't,' Macharia said.

They grew up with only a barbed wire fence separating their homes. Their families were intertwined and forever feuding, as all great neighbours must.

'That's just common sense which wasn't a strength of yours.' Macharia affected a look of hurt. Beatrice bit her lip. He made her want to giggle, she wasn't the giggling kind.

'That's fair. Anyway, how are you finding Nairobi?' The last time they'd seen each other—when was it? Ah yes! It was during an event at her parent's home in Nakuru, but Beatrice couldn't remember what it had been for, maybe her older brother's rũracio? Her memory of the event was inextricably linked to Macharia. He had offered to help her uncles roast the goat meat, a generous offer that was met with raucous laughter. In his crisp blue shirt, neatly folded up to his elbows, no one took him seriously as "one of the men". 'Nairobi has changed you,' they kept saying to him, and to her, 'don't let it change you when you go next year.'

Macharia had turned to her in surprise then.

'Next year?' he'd asked, a look that could only have been joy and relief, on his face. She too had been accepted to the prestigious University of Nairobi to study Commerce. Beatrice, ever practical, had never nursed any hope that they would continue their friendship in the capital city. Macharia was her brother's friend. He wouldn't want to spend time with her if her brother wasn't around, at least he'd never shown any inclination to do so. This is incorrect. He had shown an inclination but it was always covert and she'd thought that was meant to make the connection more special and intimate somehow.

Their friendship, yes, you know the kind I am about to speak of, friends by proxy (a brother, a friend, a cousin), with an undercurrent that is powerful, spiritual (I'm fanciful, allow me this), never spoken of but always tugging underneath until—

Macharia reached across the table in the crowded restaurant full of Nairobi's denizens jostling each other in a pretend rush to finish lunch before heading back to work. He took her left hand into his and lightly squeezed it. Sitting across from him, their hands intertwined, Beatrice forgot Mr. Mathai who had been courting her for nearly six months now. Her mind replayed that last evening at home with Macharia, underneath a full moon, their hands squeezing each other, just like this (familiar gestures are like magic spells, you are in thrall each time they are repeated), the kiss that came after, his warm breath upon her ear, 'I'm really happy you're coming to Nairobi. It's lonely there on your own.'

Beatrice blinked and forced herself to stay in the present.

'Ciku, it's really good to see you. I'm sorry I've been so busy, I haven't looked for you. But you look good—happy I mean,' Macharia was saying now.

It was the touch not the words. The way his hand felt in hers. In high school, Macharia asked her best friend out. They dated for three brief months (if you can call it that), in which he wrote Beatrice more letters than he wrote Freshia.

After lunch, they promised to keep in touch.

Beatrice waited the kind of waiting you wish never to do on behalf of anyone. Macharia never looked for her, never visited her at her halls of residence, never called the phone booth outside her halls. In the months after their lunch, Beatrice recounted their conversation like a detective looking for missing clues. Had he said he was quitting architecture? Maybe he moved to another campus away from this one that was beside the central business district? Why did she not take his address? Don't be silly you were never going to show up to his place unannounced! What if he'd come to visit her and he'd asked for Ciku when everyone in university knew her as Beatrice or Betty? Even as her courtship with Mr. Mathai hobbled along, Beatrice would catch herself wondering if maybe today Macharia was going to remember his promise to keep in touch.

He never came for her wedding.

~

The next time they met, four years later after that encounter on Biashara Street was at a mutual friend's home and Beatrice was a married woman. Mr. Mathai interrupted their reunion to ask Macharia where he got such an excellent fedora from. He then steered the conversation and Macharia away from Beatrice who was left standing next to Macharia's wife. Once or twice, she thought she saw Macharia looking at her, though she reprimanded herself each time. She was a married woman now. Looks and eyes and these things that hope surfaced did not, could not, mean anything.

~

They were in the city again when they next spotted each other across Kimathi Street. Beatrice was going to wave and carry on her way but Macharia crossed the street. He took her to Trattoria for lunch where they got a table at the balcony. They talked of inconsequential things: new music, what was showing in the cinema, their careers, childhood friends, home, and when the conversation lulled, they watched the pedestrians below in a silence that felt like a homecoming.

As the waiter took away the bread basket, Beatrice watched the basket rise and in a moment of lucidity understood what this feeling she had for Macharia was: it was as if for a moment she was suspended thousands of feet above ground with a view of valleys and lakes, blushing flamingos, bowing mountains, the Great Rift Valley endless and majestic below her and then all of a sudden she was falling.

'Why didn't you ever visit?' she asked interrupting his story about a colleague at work (he never quit the architecture degree). Macharia straightened, taken aback by the question, he ventured a look at her face then looked down to where fellow Nairobians were milling around on the street below. She watched his side profile, her heart beating hard against her chest, knowing that whatever answer she got would not improve or change anything. Yet, hopeful (again, against her character), she waited in expectation for something, she didn't know what, but something nevertheless.

'I couldn't,' He said. The shrug: an impulsive movement but also a self-defence mechanism against a feeling. It succeeds in isolating and belittling at the same time. Which was how Beatrice came to find her absurd hope dashed against the absurd shrug.

'What do you mean? Macharia, when we left…I don't know, I just thought, I thought that maybe you'd keep in touch or even write a letter like you used to.' Beatrice hated how she sounded, she hated that she was giving her cards away, that he knew she had waited.

'Ciku, I don't have many friends. I didn't want to lose you and I knew then I wasn't ready to be with you in that other way.'

'What other way?' Beatrice asked, knowing the answer but wanting to hear him say it anyway. Let him reveal his cards too!

'You know,' Macharia said with a quietness that made it sound grave and sad. Odd. A man could love you and it could be grave and sad and not enough.

'Who was asking you to be with me like that?' she asked, feeling like cauterised rejection.

'Ciku, before we were kids. It didn't matter then but now—'

'It didn't matter?'

'No, you know what I mean. It wasn't serious.' The waiter arrived with their food. They could have been eating bricks for all Beatrice cared.

'So you never came because you didn't want to be with me, which is what you think would have happened?'

Macharia's eyes never wavered from hers as he said, 'Yes, we don't know how to be without being something else. I was going through things and I knew…if I came I was going to keep coming and then…then I was going to stop. And I didn't want to hurt you.'

'Wait—' Beatrice put up a hand. 'So, you preferred never to speak to me again but still call me your friend?'

'Ciku…does it matter now?' The unsaid: We are married.

'No, I guess not, only you never gave it a chance to matter.' And then, throwing caution to the wind and that absurd hope again: 'And after…when you…you were ready? Why didn't you come then?' The unsaid once more…

…

Macharia's brows furrowed. By now, there was no longer any pretence at eating. Beatrice started to say something again. She stopped. The waiter came and took their plates away, asked if they wanted their food packed (both shook their heads no), asked if they were interested in dessert (a no from the pair once more), it was getting late, they needed to return to their lives.

When the waiter returned with the bill, they reached for it in unison. Their hands grazed and Beatrice was soaring again. It might have been the intimacy of the touch, their inability to be without being something else, whatever it was, instead of parting ways when they got to the street, they walked in complicit silence to the Hilton Hotel just round the corner from the restaurant. They stayed there till seven p.m that evening.

~

'Betty?' Steven was looking at Beatrice as if he'd been trying to reach her for some time.

'Oh, sorry, sorry, I'm just…I'm just, I don't know Steve. I don't know how to tell you. This…everything…' she gestured towards the wedding guests below. 'This is more than…I don't know…' she shrugged and shook her head. He kissed her forehead.

Beatrice had told Steven bits and pieces about her first marriage. Never straight on. Never "I wasn't happy" or "I loved another man" and definitely not "I had an affair and Nyambura is not Mr. Mathai's child". She'd told him about the long hours at work, building the family business from a tiny car spare parts shop to owning a BMW dealership as well as several other businesses. She'd told him about Mr. Mathai (though the man's reputation preceded itself so Steven knew a lot about him either way), his chronic people-pleasing ways, his penchant for dipping into company coffers, his affair. Steven's life appeared less complicated. His wife passed away from a brief bizarre bout of Tuberculosis sometime in the late nineties or early two thousands.

'People are starting to say we are acting like high school lovers. Let's go mingle a bit,' Steven suggested. They descended from the stage as the DJ remixed Sauti Sol's *Lazizi*, joining their guests who for the most part had abandoned their seats, socializing around or on the dance floor, at the buffet table, balancing plates and drinks as they exchanged stories.

~

Beatrice's last wedding had triple the attendance of this wedding. Of course, that was during the time when weddings were held in the village and even people from the surrounding villages came "just to see".

And her first husband? Mr. Mathai had a joviality that was

intoxicating and addictive. To spend time with him was to see the sun and live to tell the story. She was marrying the sun. The sun had deemed her worthy of his eternal light and warmth—at least that's what her friends from university said. The question many had and some were tactless enough to voice when Beatrice and Mr. Mathai announced their engagement was, "How did you do it, Betty? How did you convince Mr. Mathai to settle down with you?"

The early days of her first marriage were not anything Beatrice was in a hurry to remember. Somehow in the chaos of unrequited love for another man and the blinding light of the sun, she'd not formally met her husband. That is to say, they were veritable strangers to each other.

Yet, to forget those early years would be to forget the love that surrounded her today. Perhaps, Beatrice reflected, it was just as well the memories would not let go of her.

CHAPTER THREE

Malaba Estate, January, 1991

New neighbours in Malaba Estate were treated like curios, their lives, prior to Malaba, a puzzle that the incumbent residents enjoyed assembling until it was as complete as possible. Seldom did a stranger move into the estate. Perhaps Mama Sally referred one of her friends, or maybe the referral came from the Shahs who'd already bought three houses next to each other, knocked down the walls in between the houses and built hallways connecting them.

A neighbour would hear that so-and-so's friend had moved into house thirty-two and from this, one could reasonably deduce that if the new resident was so-and-so's friend and it was clear so-and-so was of questionable character, then it only stood to reason that the new resident was also highly suspect. A judgment that held until such a time as such and such proved they were not.

There were allies and enemies and peace treaties over tea, intermarriages, deaths and divorces, playground fights, tribal wars, harambees, all-night prayer meetings, dowry celebrations. In short, Malaba was a city unto its own. A fine one at that. It was a clean little estate on twenty acres that housed fifty-seven, three-bedroom maisonettes.

To get there you'd take the number eleven *matatu* at the Gill House bus-stop in town. At the time, they were the loudest matatus. The graffiti on their bodies (political satire meets pop culture meets animated cartoon characters), the most elaborate, and their makangas, the politest on any route in Nairobi. Malaba Estate was within the South B area, a twenty shilling ride from Gill House.

Each of the Malaba houses sat in the middle of an eighth-of-an-acre plot with squat identical black gates. At the centre of the estate was a community centre cum shopping complex that never quite took off, and a large ovalish field with a balding brown spot in the middle where grass refused to grow.

At the shopping centre, there were at different times, a hair salon, a video store with a Sega and Nintendo you could rent for an hour at a time; a supermarket; a gym; a restaurant, and one or two other entrepreneurial ventures (most of which were owned, operated and bankrupted by Mrs. Mutiso). Within the estate walls it felt as if time moved irresponsibly slow until, of course, it sped up and moved recklessly fast.

~

The Mathais came by way of Annabel Oluoch. The beautiful Annie, the Annie who studied English Literature at University of Nairobi and later went on to Oxford for a masters in History of Art. In the second year of undergraduates, Beatrice and Annie lived across from each other in Hall Twelve. In their third, they were roommates.

'When you know the history of the art then what?' Beatrice had asked Annie when, in the space of the first few hours of their meeting each other, Annie had given her a thorough rundown of her past, present and future. The English degree sounded ridiculous in the first place. Beatrice couldn't think of a career, other than teaching, for a person who studied English and teaching was a wholly underwhelming existence as far as she was concerned. She grew up the daughter of two teachers.

Her friends' parents had experienced upward mobility in a way her teacher-parents simply would never experience.

Her family went from being among the wealthiest in her neighborhood to being a lower-middle income home as inflation surged and teacher incomes stagnated. Even after her father was promoted to Headmaster of the high school he taught at, it made little difference to their financial situation. Beatrice grew up with the conviction that there must be more to life than the mediocrity of *just* making it, *just* meeting an income-class threshold, *just* about putting food on the table.

Annie studying English made no sense in Beatrice's world because according to her, wealthy people (for Annie was the kind of wealthy you wrote home about), only applied themselves to activities that would increase their wealth. As far as she could see, there was nothing about English Literature that was wealth-creating and, certainly, the same could be said of History of Art.

'You know most of our art is in foreign museums, and we just keep letting it go because we don't understand its importance. Those works of art are our history and it just breaks my heart that we don't care and worse still, we are forgetting.'

'If it's our history you want to learn, why do you need to go to Oxford to do that?' Beatrice asked.

'It's the best department.'

'For our history?'

'No! No, to learn how to understand art in the context of history or the other way round as well, actually.'

'So you need to go to a white man to learn how to interpret your ancestors' art?'

'No, it's not like that. You don't get it.' Annie was irked by Beatrice's disregard of a topic that was her life's passion.

'Me I think it doesn't make sense but it's your life,' Beatrice capitulated after the taut exchange. It wasn't the kind of conversation that one would imagine a friendship would sprout from, but as luck would have it, they got on with each other better than they did with the other girls on their floor and as it often the case is in youth, that was enough incentive for them to conduct a friendship.

~

Annie met her husband on the first day of her master's program at Oxford. She was the kind of person who believed in the importance of serendipity. She had spent the last three years examining minute details in literature, say for example how a word, or a tone or even an eyebrow raised at the wrong time could change the course of a character's life. Such a microscopic study of human nature, fate and language, rendered Annie unable to think rationally in the real world where she applied the same skills she used to analyse a text to analyse the events of her life. Where there was only a commonplace occurrence, she saw poetry, where a person mistakenly brushed her hand, she read intent in the way a writer can alliterate to draw an attentive reader's attention to a particular idea.

They slammed into each other just outside her college gate. He was the first Kenyan she'd met since arriving at Oxford weeks earlier, he told her she was also the first Kenyan he'd met. She was lost, he showed her to her first lecture. A master's degree and a child later, they were married. Lucas Oluoch was half Congolese, half Kenyan and fully godlike, except for the little matter that he was a degenerate and a womaniser, but he had high cheekbones and dark smooth skin you see, so it was inevitable that Annie fell for the spell wrought by that firm jaw which she had encountered so many times before in Jane Austen's romance novels.

They separated three days before Christmas. By New Year's Day, Lucas had officially moved out and Annie, whose house was a wedding present from her parents, found it difficult to live in it any longer.

~

The Mathais came to see Annie's house together. Upon arrival, Mr. Mathai did not waste time in asking for a cup of tea. He kept Annie busy in the living room, regaling her with story after story, her cooperation in the conversation irrelevant in ensuring his enthusiasm. Beatrice went through each room cataloguing its size, attributes, issues, weighing them up against her vision of what they should have at this stage of their lives. Three bedrooms, master en-suite. No visible signs of mould. Electricity and water were dependent on greater powers, there was only so much one could do about those. The house would come with the furniture.

Beatrice's pleasure in Annie's home was derived from what it meant for their lives. The house was a symbol of a principle she lived by: forward motion. Every decision Beatrice made was influenced by her desire to keep moving forward. Without forward motion, she would be her siblings who'd never left Nakuru, she would be her parents who were still teaching and furnishing their home with crocheted seat sleeves.

Back downstairs, Mr. Mathai had moved on from general gossip to recounting the newspaper's main articles of the day. Tension simmered just under the smooth shin of a growing economy. The country's prismatic state, suited Mr. Mathai's personality to the hilt. You could watch the news with him and he'd still choose to recite it to you again and you'd prefer his version of events no matter the lack of veracity in his accounts.

'What do you think Betty? Is it nice? I did a fresh coat of paint for you. You can move in as early as tomorrow. I'm ready to go.' Annie looked tired but still ethereal, as if even pain suited her.

'Are you sure about the furniture? What will you use?' Beatrice never answered questions directly. Do you like your job? It puts food on the table. Was the pregnancy difficult for you? She is healthy, we thank God…

'So,' Annie clapped once signalling the end of the tour. 'When do you want to move in? You know, I'm just so happy that it's my best-friend renting the house not a stranger. Can you imagine someone you don't know using the same toilet as you?'

Beatrice was about to speak but Mr. Mathai, who didn't do well at the periphery of conversations interrupted and changed the topic:

'Annie, can I just ask you, where did you get those knives in the kitchen from? They look first rate!' The women turned around, one surprised by the turn in conversation and the other irritated by it. Beatrice knew Mr. Mathai had no real interest in the house itself or the matter of how they were going to afford it. He took it for granted that they would because there had always been this forward motion with Beatrice. Who was doing the pushing was not his concern. He did not wait for Annie to respond to his question.

'I was reading the other day about these knives from…where was it?' he snapped his fingers trying to recall. 'It must have been Germany. Si-they are the ones who make good cars?'

Beatrice squinted wondering what knives had to do with cars, but this was Mr. Mathai, ladies and gentlemen.

'They are so sharp they can slice through a wooden board.

In fact, I was telling my wife,' this was the first Beatrice was hearing of this, 'I was telling her that we should start importing them and selling, we can make a killing in the business and…'

The moving date was agreed upon. In two weeks, the Mathais would be the newest residents of Malaba Estate. Annie saw them off, standing shoeless in the heat of January's unyielding sunshine, her feet getting burnt by the hot concrete of her verandah, as if this early disappointment in life had somehow dulled her other senses.

~

On their way out, Mr. Mathai kept up a steady stream of one sided conversation. He noted the potholes on the road that looked like they'd been filled up quickly awaiting a proper date to fix the road that, as yet, had not arrived. The bitumen holding the road together like a bandage had cracked in on itself, the friction worsening the original potholes. The handsome maisonettes were gently wrapped around with a riot of colour in the form of bougainvillea fences of all varieties; white, red, lilac, orange. The colours, intertwined or in block formation, looked as if an artist had sprayed the petals onto the shrubs creating a visual masterpiece.

On their way to Annie's house, they had driven straight down from the gate taking the long route round to the house. From Annie's house they continued straight on to complete their tour of the oval-shaped estate and it's homes. At the other end of the estate, just before the main exit, the bougainvillea fences came to an abrupt halt for three houses on the right hand side of the road. The fences had been replaced with stone walls and the black gates guarding the houses had metal carvings on them, painted in gold. Each stone wall had broken soda bottles and glass jutting out at the top, the glass pieces so close together you couldn't find a surface to place the palm of one hand flat.

When he noticed these homes, so different from the others, Mr. Mathai slowed down, peering into the verandahs. He noticed the long corridor connecting each of the three houses together. Just outside the last house, two boys and a girl played a game of hopscotch, further ahead of them on a red velvet sofa, sat two grandmothers and not far from them were two house-helps peeling potatoes as they balanced their bottoms on overturned buckets.

'We've made it! We're sharing an estate with people that rich?' Mr. Mathai pointed a thumb backwards as he drove off, shaking his head in disbelief. According to him, all Kenyan Indians were wealthy and the idea that he would be living in the same estate as them was titillating.

~

Just outside Malaba's gate stood several kiosks garishly painted red with Coca-Cola scrawled on their bodies. Whilst the estate had been quiet and serene, the kiosks were an industry of activity. At once, you were overtaken by loud conversation, the sight of people lying idly on the grassy knolls leading up to the kiosks, chewing miraa and dozing off in the midday sun, house-helps strolling from one kiosk to the other in search of garlic and gossip, bicycles piled high with crates of soda stopping to unload here, cycling a little further to unload there.

The Kiosk directly across the estate gate looked to be the busiest. Whilst several people stood at the window of The Kiosk to make purchases, others sat around it's direct vicinity on tiny wooden stools or plastic chairs people watching, talking amongst themselves, shouting down from time to time to someone walking past (a greeting, a rebuke, a reminder then laughter again). It was as if they had been transported to the markets in their respective home villages by this sight, so uncharacteristic of the Nairobi they'd come to know. Nairobi was already becoming the type of city where conversation was a luxury and time a finite resource, but here across from Malaba Estate stood a world that was far removed from the city that stretched beyond.

Though they had driven passed the kiosks on the way in, they'd both been preoccupied with the impending tour of Annie's house (for different reasons as you can imagine by now). This time, they watched with fascination, Mr. Mathai trying to picture himself inserted into the on-going narrative before them.

'I think we need to buy some water,' Mr. Mathai said. Before Beatrice could protest the decision, he'd parked the car on the side of the knoll and jumped out to begin his ascent to The Kiosk. Though the people around The Kiosk kept up their conversations, their attention was drawn to the stranger who was presently making a show of greeting everyone as if they were long time friends.

Ng'ang'a, The Kiosk owner and unofficial arbitrator of conversation around his Kiosk, asked the question on everyone's mind: Who are you and where are you from?

Now, it must never be forgotten that Nairobi was, as capital cities go, brand-spanking new, an afterthought of a city, a miracle if you will allow. Unlike other African Capital Cities, Nairobi had no rich deposits of minerals to speak off, no sea or ocean to flow out of. In short it had no obvious advantage save for its national park, and lions do not bring in the same revenue as diamonds or oil. Nairobi was a city anchored on luck and the Great British Experiment: The Lunatic Express.

And yet!

My to have seen it then. It was as if they spun money out of air, industrialisation out of a vast nothing. Nairobi's beauty was in its alchemy, how it conjured riches from what had always been a swamp.

In the 1990s, most of the city's inhabitants could not trace back their roots in Nairobi beyond one generation. The overwhelming majority were new. Some came running down from the highlands, afraid of a life of endless farming. Others came by way of the Great Rift Valley, hungry for a chance to become Nation Builders. Others still, crossed borders, desirous of a new life in the metropolitan heart of East Africa. Then there were those who came carried along the Tradewinds of the Indian Ocean, singing that here, in this city they were destined to find Love and Wealth. To be a Nairobian was to be struck with the ravenous lunacy that plagues only the alchemist.

CHAPTER FOUR

A Series of First Encounters, February, 1991

Packing up their thirty-five square foot cube of a flat took no time at all for the Mathais. Beatrice took little with them. Most of their clothes, furniture and even photo albums were handed down to relatives. The past, sticky as it is, cannot be conveniently handed down but Beatrice's belief in "forward always backwards never" did not allow for the possibility that you couldn't hand over a memory just because it didn't fit in with Annie's Italian furniture in the new house.

The rent? How could they afford this move up in the world? Their business selling care spare parts was thriving as the city council operated Kenya Bus Services collapsed and got cannibalised into inefficiency, pushing up the purchase of cars significantly. Many of these new car owners were not versed in how to take good care of their cars. As a result, they needed spare parts as early as six months into owning their 'new' cars. The business had its moral angle to it though. The spare parts—not all—but a number, were stolen parts from cars left unattended and promptly raided of everything but the engine.

Regardless of the questionable provenance of some of their products, this little shop at the bottom of Kirinyaga road was Beatrice's shrine. The shop was the only place where she felt that the person she was, was right and necessary and enough. Here, she'd spend her days in her own version of bliss: quiet consistent labour towards a future of plenty. What a disappointment for Beatrice when, even after all these years—whether she was ringing up an order, or waiting for a supplier to pick up the phone on the other end—in those brief caesuras of life where a quiet moment was unexpectedly snatched and the clock ticked the seconds a little louder than those that came before—an image would slip into her mind seductive and unbidden.

Macharia that last afternoon they spent together. Even after repeatedly rinsing him from her mind, bleaching the memories that hurt most, the smell of his skin was like a favourite perfume you don't wear anymore because it reminds you of that time. If she concentrated, she could smell him in those pockets of halted life.

'But you know this has to stop. What did you think? We would keep doing this for all our lives?' she was four months pregnant that last afternoon though it didn't show. Was there a moment she wavered and considered sharing the news of her pregnancy with Macharia? Does it matter anymore?

~

Their daughter, Leslie (Mr. Mathai's idea), Nyambura Mathai was declared the fattest baby to come out of the Aga Khan Hospital Maternity Ward the day she was born. The nurses had no scruples about nicknaming the baby Kanono. The diminutive stuck long after Kanono and her tired mother (who was now saddled with the equally unfortunate diminutive Mama Kanono), were discharged from the ward.

Mr. Mathai sang *Mwanamberi* on the drive to the hospital to pick up mother and daughter and he kept up the same song along with the same enthusiasm on the way back to their home. Mama Kanono sat in the back seat, rocking the sleeping Kanono, staring out of her window at April's torrential rain, wishing Mr. Mathai would not drive so fast or with such little keenness for the road. Every hundred meters, he'd pick up a stale blue rag from the dashboard and wipe the windshield in front of him in vigorous circular motions to clear the mist that kept fogging up the window. Not once did he let up the singing throughout this exercise.

'She looks just like me!' Mr. Mathai stood over Mama Kanono watching attentively as she changed Kanono's nappy. Mr. Mathai was a tall man, Masaai blood ran in his family, he always said whenever people remarked on his height. His forehead was partly obscured by an afro that flopped forwards, his eyes slanted down towards his cheeks that were almost always kicked up in a grin. Mama Kanono said nothing in response to this statement. When Kanono was gently placed in her arms for the first time, she'd expected something of Macharia's to be present in her daughter. No, it was useless thinking about such frivolous thoughts now. Kanono looked nothing like her father. Very well. These were her cards.

~

On their first Sunday in Malaba, the Mathais were on the way to church when they met the Mutisos. It was a busy morning in the estate. Cars crammed with more people than their size allowed, pulled out of driveways and zipped down the road, shouts of "don't forget this" and "don't forget that" ringing all around.

Of the fifty-seven households represented in Malaba Estate, fifty-one had ticked Christian under 'Religion' during the 1989 National Census. The hubbub of activity that Sunday was enough to convince anyone that, at least in theory, no one had lied about their religious beliefs.

Mr. Mathai came out of the house first with a cup of tea in hand that he planned to keep drinking on the way to church.

Mama Kanono hurriedly passed him with Kanono waddling behind her. Church started promptly at eight a.m. They were thirty minutes late already.

The Mutisos emerged from their home just as the Mathais were getting into their car. The Mutisos had an air of refinement to them. The Patriarch in a fitting dark blue suit with a gold tie, his shoes twinkling in the morning sunlight. Matriarch pumped, stockinged, and in a dress designed to show off all her finer qualities, but still managing to be church appropriate. The dress was a sunflower yellow whose colour so matched her complexion that she appeared to have a halo surrounding her. Her dark skin shown, luminous against this dress. Behind her was a house-help dressed in a chequered white and blue uniform with a matching cap, a child on either side of her. The girls, twins, wore yellow dresses identical to their mother's, white stockings with lace trimming, and pumps with a slight heel!

The Mutisos looked like those pictures that come in photo frames that you're supposed to remove and replace with your lacklustre excuse for a happy family photo. Every estate has that one family that is revered for the excellence with which they live their lives, their wealth (both purported and real), and their compounded beauty. The Mutisos were that family for Malaba Estate. They were, to be plain about it, the finest family in Malaba and with an ushago in Karen to top it off!

The families took in each other. The Mutisos saw a dishevelled but handsome Mr. Mathai, a thin Mama Kanono with her braids severely pulled back against her face, a chubby little girl by her side.

Good etiquette recalled, it was Mrs. Mutiso who began the introductions.

'You're the family that's just moved in?' Mr. Mutiso asked

interrupting Mrs. Mutiso.

'Two days ago in fact—' Mr. Mathai bounded forward to greet Mr. Mutiso.

'What a beautiful baby!' Mrs. Mutiso offered, smiling at Kanono. 'If only mine could agree to eat as much as her.'

'But look at yours, they are so well behaved. And the matching dresses…' Mama Kanono returned.

Their first conversation was a dance of half sentences, polite remarks and appraisal. The basics of each family were gleaned. The Mutisos had moved into Malaba a few years earlier, it could have been six as per Mr. Mutiso's recollection, but Mrs. Mutiso was adamant it was only five. Where had they come from? Here the details got scarce. Mr. Mutiso mentioned he had grown up right here in Nairobi, Mrs. Mutiso agreed he had grown up in Nairobi but didn't expound on her background, as if in marriage, she had assumed her husband's past. The party agreed to organise a Sunday lunch once the Mathais had settled in though neither of its members felt convinced that the lunch would ever materialize and now, come to think of it, the two families never did enjoy a meal together as a complete unit.

~

Mama Kanono could not countenance the embarrassment of walking into church an hour late, as a result, the Mathais got back home at twelve p.m. having waited in the church parking lot for the second service to begin. As Mr. Mathai switched off the engine of their Nissan, he informed Mama Kanono about the lunch party they were to host in a matter of minutes for their friends, who (his words), couldn't wait another day to see their new house!

'Nyambura! Please! Enda ucheze mahali pengine. Can't you see mummy is cooking?' Mama Kanono and her daughter were standing in the corridor just outside the kitchen, a designated washing area that at present had a jiko boiling over with meat Mama Kanono had fished out of the fridge. They'd be lucky if a guest did not lose a tooth to the beef. There was no way the meat was going to soften before the time the guests arrived. Mr. Mathai had gone to the supermarket to buy what he termed as "provisions".

Kanono moved closer to her mother her chubby little hands grabbing at Mama Kanono's wide skirt, a wider comical grin on the baby's face.

'Mummy!' she repeated then gargled in laughter.

'Yes, mummy is busy.' Mama Kanono picked up her daughter and walked back into the kitchen. 'Priscilla! We'll be late. People are coming and this food won't cook itself.'

Priscilla, the Mathais' house-help had disappeared under the pretext of looking for clean tea towels. Now, she was perched on the arm of one of the sofas in the living room watching TV.

From the kitchen window, Mama Kanono saw a commotion taking place outside. Another family was in the process of moving in.

~

Back then, the Karanjas were considered a large family. Having begun a church two years into their marriage, Mr. and Mrs Karanja's home was occupied by a minimum of ten people at any one time. It was a home for their five children and a refuge for relatives, friends and congregation members.

A pickup laboriously rattled towards their gate, piled high with a brown sofa set, coffee tables, cooker, fridge and so many other pieces of furniture that the back of the pickup looked like an abstract painting of chaos.

Mama Kanono, her daughter on her hip, watched the

pandemonium from the solitude of her kitchen.

Mrs. Karanja was the kind of industrious woman born to lead a nation but saddled with a large gregarious family instead. She stood in the middle of the road giving directions to the pickup driver not to back the car up into the wall. It was like a scene out of a rowdy under-budget, but successful film. There were arguments erupting and being foiled every second, people going in and out of the house, children playing on the pavement whilst adults admonished or called out for help or order.

At the fringes of this earthquake of a family, Esther Karanja sat on the pavement sucking her thumb, an expression of unease on her face. She was the Karanja's last born child and worst of all she was born during the short rains, a bad time to be born you must understand. People expect too much from the short-rains season. They hope the rains will make up for the long-rain season's abysmal performance. They hope these brief interludes of warm water spat reluctantly from clouds so light you'd be hard pressed to call them cumulonimbus will bring food. But they are wrong. They are always wrong. No one expects the rains to fail, no one expects the drought to persist, in short no one expects the disappointment of the short-rains season and anyone born in the age of disappointment is a forgotten thing, people too busy bemoaning a year without rainfall to praise the miracle of a new life.

~

Mama Kanono looked at the little girl sucking her thumb on the periphery of her family's life and wondered how parents could be so oblivious. Then she heard the scream.

'Kanono!' Mama Kanono whirled around then realized that she'd absently put Kanono down when her arms got tired carrying her. Kanono must have wandered off.

'Ai ai ai ai!' Priscilla ran in from the back of the kitchen, screaming and holding a screaming wet baby as well.

'Kanono! Oh my God. Jesus no! What happened?' Mama Kanono rushed to take Kanono from Priscilla's arms but Kanono screamed harder at her mother's touch. Behind Priscilla, on the corridor Mama Kanono had stood in not five minutes ago, the jiko was empty, around it was a puddle of water and chunks of half cooked beef. The sufuria the meat had been boiling in had rolled off somewhere after the accident.

Mama Kanono had barely pieced together the accident when she turned and ran outside shouting for Priscilla to follow her. 'Help—help us!' Mama Kanono waved down the crowd of people before her. 'My daughter—please help me! We need to go to the hospital—she's been burnt by boiling water!'

Mrs. Karanja sprung into action, 'Julius, Julius! Remove that pick-up from there. We'll take those other things out later.' Mrs. Karanja gave short succinct orders and for a crowd that appeared chaotic, everyone responded with military precision. Two minutes later Mama Kanono, Kanono (knocked out by the trauma of the event), and Mrs. Karanja (driving after a split second assessment that she'd be faster than Julius the pickup owner), were in the car, speeding out of the estate to the nearest hospital, Mater Hospital. Mrs. Karanja intermittently punctured the fearful silence in the car with 'Jesus!', a prayer unto itself.

CHAPTER FIVE

The Kiosk, February, 1991

When Ng'ang'a had opened his Kiosk just outside Malaba Estate three years earlier, he had not expected business to be as good as it became. For that, he had the country and its newspapers to thank. When customers came to buy milk or majani, their eyes would settle on the newspapers he hung inside the Kiosk on a rope secured with brightly coloured pegs. The day's headline alone would elicit a "Where is this country going?" from one person and this question was enough bait to draw in and keep a hearty debate going which led to customers lingering at The Kiosk longer than they'd intended.

An observant man, Ng'ang'a moved the newspapers from inside The Kiosk to just outside, next to the window where customers made their purchases. Over time, he invested in small wooden stools and two plastic chairs that he set outside The Kiosk so that those who wanted to buy and chat could do so in comfort. From here, he expanded his stock to include mandazis, weak sugary tea and uji served in tin mugs with floral patterns. For the beverages he charged five shillings per cup and the mandazis went for another five bob a piece. At just ten shillings for a drink and a snack, Ng'ang'a's Kiosk became an informal congress for Malaba Estate, rivalling the real estate association in power and scope. It was at The Kiosk that Malaba's residents decided to oust one set of askaris because there was a rumour they were in cahoots with petty thieves who'd been plaguing the estate. It was also at The Kiosk that the same same residents decided to open an investment fund together (this fund is still being litigated as I write). Wasn't it also at The Kiosk that the Karanjas found out that their eldest son had run away with a girl from the neighbouring, Karibu Estate?

The real winner for The Kiosk was when Ng'ang'a introduced a little red transistor radio with a long antenna that would break on the same day the country did, eight years later. He would switch it on immediately he opened the Kiosk and leave it on till his last customer of the day had walked off into the night. The radio livened up conversations and provided a backdrop of music for hot afternoons when Malaba residents would drift out of their homes, bored and restless, in search of willing conversationalists. Conversations were often and readily punctured with impromptu sing-alongs when say Super Mazembe's *Kasongo* came on or the darling of the radio waves, *Sina Makosa* by Les Wanyika.

A concentrated hush would fall around the Kiosk during the one o'clock news as customers listened for any new announcements from the President's administration. In those days, President Moi was in the habit of firing Cabinet Ministers over the lunch-time news. It was, one imagines, an efficient way of dispensing of prominent politicians who'd receive the news of their unemployment through this radio waves as well.

There was an ongoing argument between Ng'ang'a and his patrons because the moment six p.m. hit, he would switch radio stations from K.B.C.'s National Service to its General Service and the music now termed zilizopendwa would be replaced with the General Service's English 'Golden Oldies' on 'Sundowner'. Nothing but nothing could beat the musical excellence of Jimmy Reeves' rendition of *Take My Hand Precious Lord* according to Ng'ang'a and most Kikuyu men of a certain age group. Ng'ang'a would sooner lose customers than miss an opportunity to hear Dolly Parton crooning her country tunes as the sun set behind the Kiosk.

Overtime, the other kiosks around would copy Ng'ang'a but Malaba's residents, for all their gossip, were loyal to him. At any rate, his Kiosk was conveniently opposite their estate gate.

CHAPTER SIX

Wedding Guests, August 4th, 2012

There were only four unexpected guests at the intimate wedding.

Mr. Mathai's sisters arrived just as the reception was winding up. Beatrice saw them before they saw her. After Mr. Mathai went missing, they went missing in action too, as if they too had been snuffed out of existence.

'Can you believe them?' Mrs. Mutiso was at Beatrice's side the moment she saw the sisters too. 'Wait, did you invite them?' she asked Beatrice. Beatrice shook her head. She hadn't spoken to them in so long, she couldn't remember which one of the sisters she'd spoken to last. 'So then what are they doing here? And then these guards! Nkt! What are they here for if it's not to check that everyone coming in has an invite? They think this food is being paid for by money that fell from a tree?' Beatrice hesitated to remind Mrs. Mutiso that the main reason they were spending a fortune on the menu was because she insisted on expensive caterers.

'It's fine. They are here now. Let's go and welcome them,' she said, resolving to be polite.

'What, with me? No! I don't have patience for stupidity and those four are stupid.' Mrs. Mutiso swayed away before Beatrice could convince her otherwise.

~

'Mama Kanono, Bwana asifiwe.' The oldest of Mr. Mathai's sisters took Beatrice's hands into her much smaller ones. She leaned in and kissed the air around Beatrice. The Mathai sisters were delicate creatures. If Beatrice was thin, she was a sturdy thin, muscles taut against her skin. The Mathai sisters were an unhappy thin, the kind of thin that suggests years of bitterness and strife. If you looked at them quickly, you'd be forgiven for assuming they were quadruplets. They had the same pinched face, the same large forehead, the same flared nose, the same decided frown.

I must have forgotten to add, they were Mr. Mathai's step-sisters from his father's first marriage. Mr. Mathai's father raised all his children within the same homestead. Food was not apportioned depending on the superiority of a wife but on the number of mouths each wife had to feed. This system saw great harmony between all the families except the first wife and her children. But then, can you imagine being duped into believing your husband will never marry again because he has gone twenty years without showing any inclination to add to his home then waking up one morning to find a new hut next to yours for your new mũiru and then two more similar huts within the short and exhausting space of two years?

'What a surprise!' Beatrice bristled at being called Mama Kanono. 'It has been many years.'

'Eema, biũ biũ you can get married and not ask your family for permission?' another of the sisters said as she arched a thin, overly plucked, overly pencilled eyebrow.

'Sorry?' Beatrice couldn't help noticing the chalkiness of her complexion. Powder. In the wrong shade.

'Ati sorry? Sorry ni nani? Did you forget you are ours? When you married our brother we paid for you. Since it seems you have forgotten your traditions and culture, we came to remind you.' This was spoken by the third of the sisters. Beatrice was beginning to think they sounded rehearsed, down to who got to say what. She idly wondered if they had fought over who got to deliver that line.

'And me personally—' the elder Mathai sister placed her hand across her chest. The other sisters looked at her sternly. It appeared she'd broken off from the script. '—I don't remember anyone coming to request for our sister's hand in marriage.' She looked around at her sisters, seeking their nods of agreement.

They stared back wearily. The Mathai sisters could only focus and stay in harmony for short amounts of time before remembering just how annoying they found each other. They'd never managed to launch a sustained attack on anyone long enough to yield results. This did not mean they ever forgot the people they were squabbling with. The sisters kept an up to date list of relatives and friends who'd wronged them, remembering to add to it regularly. Inevitably they would regroup and attack again.

'Do you remember how much we paid for you?' The sister who hadn't spoken yet recovered the script after a snippy whispered argument between them. Beatrice watched the performance, knowing better than to interrupt them.

'It is the *height*—' she stretched the word with her tone and pulled at it with her fingers, '—the height of disrespect to your family. You didn't invite us and we took you in and when Mathai, God rest him, di—'

One of the sisters caught sight of Nyambura in the distance, looking around as if she'd lost sight of someone.

'Oh! Is that Kanono? My God! Ebu mwangalie! She is even bigger now. I told you her body is one of those ones that likes weight. But someone needs to tell her she can't—'

'Alice, Alice, my God Alice is that you?' Mrs. Karanja came up to the little gathering, hands held out in joyful greeting. Her presence so entranced the Mathai sisters, their jaws went slack and their mouths curved into an O. In the time they'd been away, Mrs. Karanja's church ministry had grown into one of the largest churches in Kenya. Her face graced their TV screens every Sunday afternoon. The sisters forgot their mission and began vying for Mrs. Karanja's attention with stories about what miracles God had performed recently in their lives, what they were praying for, how they'd always known her church would be successful, how no man could come against God's calling.

Mrs. Karanja winked at Beatrice. She was free now.

Beatrice smiled a terse thank you as she stepped back from them. She looked around feeling lost and unmoored, she blamed the sisters for this but she didn't quite believe they were the reason for the feeling. No, they were a reminder of something far worse, something she'd tried to impeach and then bargain with, and then when none of that worked, live with.

Mr. Mathai was the antithesis of everything Beatrice stood for, this much we know, but that didn't mean he was any worse or better than the next person, he was just—Beatrice shut her eyes. It was unfair, she'd walked into a marriage with a man she could barely stand just to tick off a checkbox in life and (no surprises), it had turned out so badly that when he went missing, above all the emotions she'd felt, there was one that broke free from the maelstrom to reign above the others, one that scared her so much she'd hated herself for it: relief.

Beatrice felt a wave of heat creep up and engulf her in her wedding dress. Mrs. Mutiso had insisted she buy a proper wedding dress, 'second chances are precious,' she'd reminded her.

~

Mrs. Karanja navigated the Mathai sisters towards a table that was neither too far from the gathering nor too near. She offered them refreshments and ensured they were comfortable and at ease (as far as these women could relax), before moving on.

'For a pastor, she's really nice,' Mrs. Mutiso observed. She was once again at Beatrice's side, the caterer next to her.

'She's always been like that.'

'I don't know, I always got the sense she didn't like me,' Mrs. Mutiso tilted her head. The caterer tried to interrupt their conversation with a question but Mrs. Mutiso waved him away. 'There's no point hiring all these service providers when they keep asking you questions, you end up doing all the work and they get paid for it. I'm not going to use them for the next wedding.'

'You got another customer?' Beatrice turned around in surprise and joy.

'Yes. One, though I am waiting for them to confirm. They will, but people like to keep you on your toes,' Mrs. Mutiso said in a firm voice.

'When is that wedding for?'

'I don't know yet, we are still talking but I've given them a good offer. It will probably be a Christmas wedding. Those are beautiful. They're very wealthy as well.' Mrs. Mutiso nodded vigorously as she spoke, her eyes widening with each word. This unsettled Beatrice who prodded further:

'Oh? Do I know them?' she asked.

'I don't know, maybe. Nairobi is small.' Mrs. Mutiso appeared to be losing interest in the conversation, her eyes were on Mrs. Karanja who was now speaking with Steven and his parents who laughed generously at whatever she was saying. 'When did you stop going to church?' Mrs. Mutiso asked. Beatrice was surprised by the question.

'I didn't, I still go, when I'm not busy.' Beatrice steered the conversation back to Mrs. Mutiso's business. 'So the wedding you're planning…'

'Hmm…I don't go anymore.' Mrs. Mutiso continued to watch Mrs. Karanja. Beatrice watched Mrs. Mutiso.

'Why?'

'I think God has seasons.' Mrs. Mutiso finally turned and gave her attention to Beatrice. She kicked up her mouth into a half-smile. 'I'm waiting for my season to begin, again.'

Beatrice opened her mouth. She closed it.

'Sometimes, I think He likes these games He plays,' Mrs. Mutiso continued.

'What games?' Beatrice couldn't shake off a feeling—she knew this feeling—she couldn't name it either but she knew this shadowy thing.

'So now you're going into the wedding planning business full time?' Beatrice asked again.

'Full time?' Mrs. Mutiso repeated. 'Full time—yes full time. Business is good. Lots of customers. People like my work. You know Mr. Mutiso always said I had an eye for design.' Mrs. Mutiso spotted the beleaguered caterer packing up the buffet table and stalked off to stop him.

Beatrice wanted to follow after her friend, to ask her, 'But I thought you said you don't have customers yet?' but then, as it happens in these things, she was, once more, accosted by a guest, eager to congratulate the second-time-around bride.

CHAPTER SEVEN

Bible Study, April, 1991

The Karanjas settled into their new life in Malaba quickly. So quickly in fact that within a month, they'd confirmed what they'd suspected was their primary mission in Malaba Estate: to start a Bible Study group as the estate did not have one.

It hadn't taken long to establish this fact. Mr. Mutiso seemed distracted when Mr. Karanja bumped into him the first morning after they'd moved in, but not too distracted to reply, 'No, I don't think so,' when asked about the status of a Bible Study group in the estate. Janet from house forty-four assured Mrs. Karanja that whilst there was one it was only attended by herself as the rest of the residents in the estate were either new to the estate or actively backsliding.

On the first Bible Study, three rules were set:

1. Bible study would take place on the first Wednesday of the month from seven p.m. to nine p.m. (so that people could get back home in time for the news).
2. The regular Bible Study goers would alternate hosting duties.
3. The hosts were only expected to offer tea and perhaps one or two snacks. Dinner was not expected.

~

At that first Bible Study hosted by the Karanjas, their living room overflowed with their neighbours. In total, forty-nine of the fifty-seven households in Malaba had at least one representative in attendance that night. The age limit Mrs. Karanja suggested was twenty-one because kids would be too much of a distraction. This did not stop a few of the residents from dragging along their children who snored on their laps or played outside in the backyard with the Karanja children. Never again would there be so many households represented at Bible Study.

'Where are the Mulis?' someone asked.

'Oh, I saw Justus earlier, he said they can't come because their pastor hasn't sanctioned it. They are worried about the doctrine that will be taught,' someone else volunteered.

'Ah, Mrs Mutiso! I was just talking about you today.' Baba Sally of house number three flagged Mrs. Mutiso down as she walked into the house. 'You remember Angela Maina—the one who married that lawyer from Narok?'

Mrs. Mutiso was surprised that her neighbour was speaking to her. The Mutisos kept to themselves and their neighbours (who revered them for their wealth but also mistrusted them for it), made it easy to do so as they too avoided the Mutisos. Mrs. Mutiso's reasons for avoiding her neighbours were motivated by self preservation. At least when they thought she was the luckiest woman in the world to have married into a wealthy family, it was with envy that they spoke about her. That was better than the alternative if they were to find out the truth.

Mr. Mutiso had pursued her relentlessly after their first meeting. He appeared in her life one day dressed in khakis and cowboy boots unironically. At first, she'd refused to recognize his advances. What good could possibly come from a wealthy man dating a poor girl like her? And anyway, her friends warned her, 'Men like that only want one thing from girls like you—and it's not marriage.'

Girls like her. Girls who had to send part of their university boom back home to their parents who were still living in a mud hut. Girls who didn't wear a pair of shoes for the first thirteen years of their lives. Girls whose English was so heavily accented it sounded like a lumbering train whose engine was about to fail. Girls like her.

'You remember Angela?' Baba Sally was still enquiring. 'She said you used to go to the same church.' His tone made the sentence sound like a question. Mrs. Mutiso knew what he was doing. It was what her neighbours all tried to do when they did deign to speak to her, he was fishing for information about her mysterious life.

If Baba Sally continued down this line of conversation, there would be questions like "She told me you stopped going to that church. Why did you leave the church?" and "When did you say you got married again?" These questions were like a formula, adding up the year she left the church with the year she got married subtracting that from the age of her twins all in a bid to calculate if the rumours were true: did she get her children out of wedlock? Had she trapped Mr. Mutiso into marrying her?

'She told us you used to be a world class singer in the choir.' Baba Sally nodded in the direction of his wife, the other party in the "us". Mrs. Mutiso turned to look at the lady whose eyes bore down on her venomously.

'Yes it was a long time ago. Have a good evening Baba Sally.' she moved away to ensure she didn't hear his follow up question.

~

'Uh…hello?' Mr. Karanja voice didn't rise above the din as he had hoped it would. 'Good evening everybody,' he tried again, nodding along to his words, his voice not reaching further than Mr. Mathai who looked up when he realized Mr. Karanja was trying to get people's attention.

With a wink, Mr. Mathai stood up and began to talk as if Mr. Karanja had asked for his assistance.

'Everyone! Hello! Okay, okay this is very good. *Waow* look at that. We have been here for three months and I was beginning to think this estate was full of ghosts only. Thank you to the Karanjas for creating such a wonderful institution for us to meet one another.' The room went silent as Mr. Mathai spoke.

'My names are John Njoroge Mathai and this is my loving wife—' here he beckoned for Mama Kanono to stand up. She did so reluctantly and only because he would insist she stood up if she tried to refuse. Mama Kanono was not the only person wishing Mr. Mathai would sit down. Mr. Karanja watched Mr. Mathai delivering his little speech as if this were his house with what was, at first, bewilderment but by now had metamorphosed into irritation.

'Eh…okay, thank you Mr. Mathai for the introduction. Thank you, I hope there is somewhere for everyone to sit.' Mr. Karanja tried to steal back the spotlight from Mr. Mathai.

'No no, not at all, thank you for inviting us and what a lovely home. You can really feel the spirit of God in this home.' There was a wave of "amens" uttered with deep feeling.

'Mr. Mathai, we are only doing God's work,' Mr. Karanja said, not displeased that his neighbours had noticed how spirit filled his home was.

And now here was Mrs. Karanja standing next to her

husband. Her appearance by his side shifted everyone's attention from Mr. Mathai to her. The Karanjas were, as it was becoming evident to Malaba's residents, an interesting mismatch. Mr. Karanja was the kind of person you'd keep meeting throughout your life and each time you would do the right thing and introduce yourself always forgetting you knew him already.

Mrs Karanja on the other hand!

Where Mr. Karanja's features were bland and made him indistinguishable from any other light-skin, port-bellied, Kikuyu man, Mrs. Karanja was striking. To start with all the hair on her head that made up the bouffant she wore for the better part of that decade was all hers. She was the kind of woman people stopped on the street just to tell her how beautiful she was. She could easily have been a TV ad model and she was on track to becoming one when she met the Lord at a Billy Graham crusade at Uhuru Park and never looked back.

I am merely speculating here, but the only way Mr. Karanja landed Mrs. Karanja was because she was on the look-out for a man willing to build a church with her and he shared the same vision as she did. Chance is a wily bastard, let no one deceive you.

~

Mrs. Karanja opened the Bible Study with a short prayer. In the natural order of things, a worship song came next. It took a few minutes for the gathered to pick a song, as would be expected from a multi-denominational gathering. *Amazing Grace* was thwarted because it was too sad. Someone suggested *The Old Rugged Cross*. Someone else shot it down because it wasn't Easter so there was no point singing it. Another suggestion, *Tunakushukuru Mama Maria* was received with enthusiasm from the Catholics but was dismissed by the other denominations. Finally, a song was picked, a song universally loved and claimed by all denominations: *Baraka Za Mungu.*

'Mrs. Mutiso was a choir master once. I think she should lead this one,' Baba Sally piped up before his hand was slapped by his wife.

'Oh really? In high school? We got to the regionals. Which school did you go to? We might have competed against each other,' A bold voice asserted.

Mrs. Mutiso's tongue felt heavy in her mouth. The attention on her made her feel claustrophobic.

'I…uh…'

'I can lead it if the honourable madam doesn't want to,' Mr. Mathai offered and he proceeded to do so though he didn't know all of the words.

~

'My fellow brothers and sisters in the Lord, thank you once again for coming today.' Mr. Karanja's voice was an arduous monotone. From the second he opened his mouth to speak, minds began to wonder. After the song, a few minutes passed where he explained how the Bible Study would work. They would read through the entire Bible over one year, using a study guide to assist them.

'Eh…this guide…don't you think we should be studying the Bible using the Bible itself not a study guide?' Mama Sally interrupted him. This observation got a few nods, a few grunts of approval and even an "amen". 'I mean, why are we using another book to study the word of God? What if the person who wrote it is wrong in his interpretations?' More people were swayed by her thinking.

'Eh…' Mr. Karanja had not anticipated a challenge to his plan.

'I think we should vote on the matter,' Mama Sally continued.

'Wait! Wait just a minute.' Mr. Mathai got up to intervene. 'Mr. Karanja, I mean, *Pastor* Mister Karanja here is the *ordained* pastor. If he has read the book and thinks it is in line with the word of God, then we should do as he says.' Mr. Mathai knew only too well that a vote would end in acrimony and to think this could be the end of such wonderful get-together with his neighbours. He wouldn't have it.

'Eh...' Mr. Karanja resented Mr. Mathai's interjection even more than he did Mama Sally's challenge. He'd also not found the words to defend his decision yet—

'Yes, we have been going through the Bible using this study book with our church Bible Study and we can personally attest to the fact that it is in line with God's word,' Mrs. Karanja said standing up as well to assure her neighbours.

Mr. Mathai and Mrs. Karanja had a pull on their neighbours who preferred to side with them over Mama Sally. They were the popular kids of this particular high school. The matter was dropped and Mr. Karanja was given over a subdued crowd which stayed that way until Mr. Mathai interrupted to say '—but the words in this book are very small.'

'In which book? The Bible or the study guide?' someone enquired only too willing to welcome the interruption.

'The study guide. Mama Kanono can you see this?' Mr. Mathai held the study guide to his wife's face. She tried to pull away, embarrassed by the spotlight. It was one thing that Mr. Mathai adored it but why did he have to keep dragging her into it as well?

'It's not that small,' she said when she realized everyone was looking at her, waiting for her response.

'No, I think Mr. Mathai has a point. The words in this book

are too small. It will strain my eyes,' Someone else agreed with him.

'It's not too small. You people are just growing old,' another voice piped up.

The Bible Study devolved into a conference on eye-sight, who was short-sighted, who was long-sighted, whose family had a history of glaucoma; the fact that diabetes could lead to blindness; the offensive intimation that disability was a punishment from God; God's different forms of retribution; the ultimate retribution—the coming of Christ, which a few people had it on good authority was happening at the turn of the century, a mere nine years away.

'We don't believe in hell.' The room grew still. Mrs. Shah who lived in one of the three homes owned by the extended Shah family, had come along to meet her neighbours. Now, a multi-denominational Bible Study was a challenge on its own. There were the spoken and unspoken biases: Protestants who thought the Catholics were a sneeze away from Atheism, Baptists who thought Protestants to be too liberal and therefore unlikely to be among the chosen few, Seventh Day Adventists who thought—

—And this did not even include the tribal tensions. Yes, the gathering, though friendly enough, was wrought with social, religious, ethnic and cultural tensions but all of these divisions disappeared in the face of Mrs. Shah's statement.

'But your gods are idols. Ours is the one and true living God,' Mama Sally declared. The room held its breath at the harshness of Mama Sally's words.

'Um...I think...I think what Mama Sally is trying to say here—' Mrs. Karanja came forward in an effort to rescue the situation, '—is that we believe that there is only one God.'

'Oh? Which one? The Catholic one?' Mrs. Shah asked

amiably. She spent every day with the same people in the same three houses. Right now, she was just so pleased to be communing with anyone other than her family for a change, she hadn't noticed the uproar her question (born of genuine interest), raised. 'I think he sounds nice,' she added in appeasement when she realised the comment had not gone down so well.

'There's no Catholic God, Mrs. Shah,' Mrs. Karanja tried again.

'It's Mary isn't it? Sorry, I keep forgetting,' Mrs. Shah's apology was sincere as it was off-putting to a certain subset of her neighbours. The Protestants suppressed a chuckle as the Catholics bristled.

'This is why the Bible Study is good. You'll get to learn more about God. For a start no one worships Mary—'

'But we pray through her—' Mama Sally said, interrupting Mrs. Karanja.

'Okay…okay…Catholics pray through Mary, but you can, and you *should* pray directly to God, through Jesus.'

Mrs. Shah cocked her head to the side, confused. 'So it's faster to get to God through Jesus than Mary? But wasn't she his mother?'

'She was, but Mary is not a deity.'

'But she *is* holy, Mrs. Karanja,' Someone else added.

'She is the mother of God but she—you—okay—I think we are going into the details here which will get us a bit confused.' Mrs. Karanja saw no other way to save the situation other than to avoid it. 'Let's get back to the study, shall we?' she expertly steered the conversation into safer waters and handed the floor back to a sullen Mr. Karanja.

CHAPTER EIGHT

Nyambura and the Aunties, August 4th, 2012

'Kanono, Kanono! Come here.' Nyambura had just stepped back into the hall when she heard her aunt (one of the four Mathai sisters), calling her name. There was so much noise in the background, she wasn't sure what direction the call had come from, not that she was interested in meeting her aunties. In fact, she'd purposely avoided them from the moment she spied them walking into the celebration. Nyambura turned to walk back out, pretending she hadn't heard her name, but before she could take a step she felt a cold clammy grasp secure itself onto her left forearm.

Nyambura had known the wedding, really just coming back home, would be challenging for her. Growing up with a nickname like Kanono was traumatic. At first, when her therapist had offered her the word traumatic to describe the experience, Nyambura had struggled to buy into it.

'You've not gone back home in nine years,' her therapist pointed out.

'Yes but that's because I've been busy,' Nyambura countered.

'You don't need to accept that the experience was traumatic if you are not ready to.'

'It's not that I'm not ready, it's just that I don't think it was that bad. It could have been worse, worse things have happened to people in their childhood.'

'Would you say it impacted the way you view yourself? Your identity? Being called the fat one every day?' Nyambura kept quiet. 'Nyambura?'

'Look, it wasn't ideal but…'

…

'...I wish, sometimes I wish my mum or dad would have just told them to stop.'

'They also called you that?'

'In Swahili it doesn't sound as bad as it does in English…but yes they did. Everyone did.'

'Your mother's wedding is in a few weeks?'

'Three.'

'How do you feel about that?'

'Well, it turns out it's unacceptable for me to attend over Facetime.'

…

'...scared I guess?'

…

'...no one's called me that since I left for A-levels, and I just know that when I go home everyone will.'

'Why do you think they will?'

'I'm still Kanono,' she'd said, gesturing to her body.

'Does it bother you?'

'When I'm here no, I don't…not in the way it used to…but then no one is going around calling me that all day.'

Nyambura's self-appointed exile had begun with promise. She scrupulously avoided photos, quickly untagged herself from pictures that displayed more than her face and shoulders, learnt to contour away the pounds on her face; all of this so that she could create an illusion of a thinner Nyambura. Ah, but then she rediscovered the stage, her love of comedy and story-telling– the highlight of her childhood in Malaba had been the Christmas Nativity Play after all. Now her entire body was preserved in videos you could search online to ascertain that whilst Kanono seemed to be enjoying some relative success as a comedian (what sort of career was that?), she had not lost the weight.

~

There was one thing she had been looking forward to, seeing her childhood best friend Esther Karanja again. As a matter of fact, when her aunty cornered her upon re-entry to the hall, Nyambura had just come back from the parking lot, where an odd exchange had taken place. She had been under the impression that they were going to go out for drinks after the reception wrapped up. This impression was encouraged by the fact that they'd had a wonderful time catching up over lunch, at least Nyambura thought it had been wonderful.

When the aunties walked into the reception hall, Nyambura had just come back from the bathroom to find Esther's sit empty. When one of the aunties spotted her looking around as if she were trying to find someone among their guests, the someone had been Esther. So when Mrs. Karanja (Esther's mother), took her aunties under her wing and guided them to a table, Nyambura had taken the opportunity of a freed up door to go in search of Esther. Perhaps she'd gone out for some fresh air, or she'd gotten a call and needed privacy to answer it, Nyambura had reasoned on behalf of her childhood best friend.

Nyambura found Esther at the parking lot rifling through her handbag for her car keys.

'Ess?' Nyambura called out.

Esther looked up in surprise then her features distorted into what Nyambura was sure was dismay.

'You're leaving now?'

'Uh…yeah…I have to meet someone…'

'Oh. I didn't realise you were leaving so early. Your mum is still here,' Nyambura said pointing back in the direction of the hall. Esther looked that way as well, an unsettling look on her face, as if she were hiding something and she knew Nyambura was warming up to it.

'She…the driver will pick her later.' Esther shifted her stance. 'It was good seeing you again,' she offered.

'Yeah, I was thinking that maybe we could get that coffee—'

'I don't know, it's a really busy time right now…'

'I get that, it's just...it's been *years*.'

Esther nodded as if she was just now processing how long it had been since they'd seen each.

'Um…okay…maybe let's try for next week… I'll call you.' she opened her car door then remembering to do so, gave Nyambura a quick hug before jumping into the car.

~

Nyambura was still trying to make sense of the bizarre encounter when she ran into her aunt. She tried to shake off her aunt's grip but it only tightened.

'And where is your other sister? I haven't seen Nyambura anywhere here. Or are you people still not taking care of your father's daughter?'

Nyambura pulled harder to back away, but her aunt's vice-like grip did not falter. Her father's daughter. Nyambura's mouth was suddenly dry. Her father's daughter. She bit the inside of her cheek.

On her last visit to her therapist before her flight, Dr. Theobald had asked her, 'Is there anything else that is concerning you about your impending trip?'

'Yes, apparently I have to take anti-malaria medicine to visit my home because I've been away for so long, the mosquitoes won't recognize me.'

...

'...uh...no. I mean no. Nothing really.'

Nothing really had a name: Nyambura. Her father had given the child he got out of an affair the same name as her. Nyambura was named after his mother, like all first-born Kikuyu daughters are named after their father's mother. He had given her name to the other child.

She was fifteen when she found out. Ironically, it was in the middle of a blistering argument with her mother. Nyambura wanted to go hang-out at Village Market with a group of friends from school. Well, they were not friendships so much as they were acquaintances, but Nyambura hoped that if she hang-out with them often enough they'd start calling her to see what she was up to, instead of the other way around where she always did the ringing, and they did the reluctant giving of hang-out details.

Beatrice, to her credit, knew that the friendship dynamics with Nyambura's chosen group of friends was off and in her own Beatrice-like way she was trying to protect her daughter (and atone for all the times she had not). 'You are not going to loiter in the streets as if you are homeless!' she'd exclaimed. They argued all morning and when Kanyi interrupted to ask if Nyambura was going to seek a divorce from her last remaining parent, Nyambura had rather ungraciously, screamed that she wished it was Beatrice who had died not her father.

'Papa didn't die. He got lost,' Kanyi said as he flopped back onto the sofa and pressed play on his Tony Hawk (Pro Skater 3), game.

Beatrice's hand was halfway to Nyambura's cheek when

the doorbell rang. Priscilla, still an employee of the Mathai household, shouted 'kuna mtu kwa gate, somebody go open it,' from the kitchen where she was snuggled in a cosy rattan chair, engrossed in a Danielle Steele novel. Exasperated with having to pause his game, Kanyi got up and went to open the gate. Nyambura and her mother kept talking over one another with no one to do the listening.

The woman who walked into their home must have been in her early thirties, maybe late twenties, yet, she looked as if life had done its best with her and spat her back out. There was a child by her side. You know these things, you've heard these stories. Nothing new here, nothing new here. A little girl of seven years, a replica of Mr. Mathai. Nyambura staggered back. Beatrice's jaw slackened, Priscilla (ever an ear for a story), exclaimed 'Haiya!' the moment she laid eyes on the girl.

Financial agreements (you understand the nature of these things), were made by Beatrice to take care of the child and her mother. Nyambura was also allowed to go to Village Market that day.

That was the month before she was due to travel to the U.K. to begin her A-levels. The month before her nine year self imposed exile. Now, Nyambura wondered, did the aunties always know about this other child?

'My name is also Nyambura,' she said eventually.

'Yes, but Nyambura is the thin one,' Her aunt said as her eyes combed the room, looking for her sisters.

CHAPTER NINE

Beatrice and Mrs. Mutiso, August 4th, 2012

Mrs. Mutiso was walking out of the hall when she passed Nyambura and overheard Mr. Mathai's sister ask her where Nyambura, her step-sister was. She stopped, considering if she should interrupt and rescue Nyambura from her aunt. As she was about to do so, Kelly Brown's *Higher* came on and Mrs. Mutiso breathed in sharply, she brought her phone instinctively to her chest. This used to be her song with Mr. Mutiso.

In the distance, she saw Steven steal behind Beatrice, swooping her into an embrace whilst singing, *'I can't get enough of your love...'* He turned her around, trying to get her to dance with him. Beatrice shook her head, he sang louder, his words carrying to where Mrs. Mutiso stood... *'do you love me or do you want to leave me...oooh please stay, don't walk away...'*

The sight of Steven serenading his new bride had slackened the aunty's grip on Nyambura who bumped into Mrs. Mutiso as she ran out.

'Sorry Aunty Carol,' Nyambura said to Mrs. Mutiso as she steadied herself.

'It's okay dear—' Mrs. Mutiso noticed the tears reflecting in Nyambura's eyes. 'Don't listen to her,' she said, trying to comfort Nyambura.

'She isn't wrong though is she?' Nyambura responded

acerbically. 'All this time I used to think mum was the evil one.'

'Why would you think that about your mother?' Mrs. Mutiso asked confused. Surely, Beatrice had not told Nyambura?

'I just...she was *never* there and he was...or at least I used to think he was. It turns out in between dropping us to school and picking us up he found time to cheat on mum and get a child he didn't have the imagination to name anything other than my name!'

'Your mum might not have been as fun as your dad was, but she tried Nyambura, you have to know that by now. Everyone is doing the best they can with what they have and sometimes it falls short of what you are hoping for, but at least they try. She tried.' Mrs. Mutiso tried to defend her oldest friend. Nyambura's eyes glittered in anger.

'Or maybe they were both just fucked up,' she said and run out.

Mrs. Mutiso knew better than to follow after Nyambura. She turned back to find Beatrice gliding on the dance floor, smiling up at Steven who continued to sing the song. If she had the money to bet, she'd have bet that the reason Beatrice was not singing along was because she did not know the words to Kelly Brown's greatest hit. The Beatrice of the eighties (the decade the song came out), would not have deigned to waste her time memorising popular hits.

A tremble ran through the hand that held her phone. A throbbing pain slide up her neck and settled on her temples. Mrs. Mutiso's vision clouded over. She hated this song.

She heard Mr. Mutiso's version of the song before she heard Kelly Brown's. The first time she heard Kelly Brown perform it, Mr. Mutiso had taken her to Starlight Club. Under the disco lights, as the funky-rock singer performed his biggest hit for the party revellers, she'd turned to Mr. Mutiso in surprise. It sounded like a completely different song to the one he'd been singing to her the past month. Mr. Mutiso shrugged knowing full well he'd been butchering the song, they burst into laughter, collapsing into each other, dancing and cheering Brown on, and that was the night wasn't it? The night of their first kiss, if the dates align. Through Kelly Brown, Mr. Mutiso had finally wooed her.

Mrs. Mutiso blinked rapidly, trying to shake off the cloak of the past. She was cold now. When the news of Kelly Brown's gruesome murder in Germany reached Kenya, she'd mourned the great singer as if he were her family. Mr. Mutiso finding her reaction irrational, had said, irritably, 'It's not like you knew him.'

Unlocking her phone, Mrs. Mutiso looked at the picture of her twins showing their "just-now" engagement rings. Her phone screen was fractured in the middle, not unlike her existence, which right now felt as if it were at a great personal effort and the friction of the years had led to fissures in her spirit that grew wider as the days dragged on.

CHAPTER TEN

Mrs. Mutiso, September, 1991

The week before the school term commenced was always the busiest at the Mutiso household. The twins were in class two. It didn't matter if it was the beginning of the year or the middle of the year, each term required a new set of uniform, new class books, new stationary, new lunch boxes, new rubber shoes and anything else the girls kept losing or ruining during the term.

However, this term was different. They were moving to a new school and having changed education systems from the Kenyan to the British system, they were going up to year three. Only a month before, Mr. Mutisos parents had announced that out of the generosity of their hearts, they were going to take over the education of their only child's daughters. They wanted to give the twins a similar education and access to opportunities as Mr. Mutiso had growing up. Perhaps the twins could triumph where their father had failed to reach his potential. It was widely believed in the Mutiso clan that Mrs. Mutiso and her "unplanned" pregnancy had curtailed Mr. Mutiso's potential.

Mrs. Mutiso tried to suggest that the school they were currently attending was just fine. In fact, it wasn't just fine, it was one of the best schools in the country. A Catholic girls' school, perfect morals, an excellent academic record, it was the sort of school you definitely want your friends to know your children attend. But it wasn't good enough for the Mutiso grandparents who insisted that their granddaughters should get what they kept referring to as an "all-rounded education".

What is that? 'The world is not just about multiple choice questions, the twins need to learn how to play an instrument, they should be part of a drama club, they need to travel more on international school trips, they need to be taught by teachers from all over the world, and it's important that they go to school with the future leaders of this country.'

Mrs. Mutiso pointed out that they were both learning the piano at their current school and one of the twins was even in an upcoming school play. This news was met with a sniff of dismissal. In the end, and of course, the Mutiso grandparents won.

'And they will stay with us during the school term,' Mr. Mutiso's mother added, just as the Mutisos were leaving. 'Making them commute over two hours back and forth from South B,' said with a little sneer, 'is not fair on the girls.'

Mr. Mutiso did not oppose the idea, to be plain about it, he did not say anything for the entirety of the interaction. When Mrs. Mutiso looked to him for support she realised, with a sick feeling of betrayal, that it had all been planned. He was not hearing this news for the first time.

Yet, there was worse to come. Even as she opened her mouth to protest, there was a dawning realization that her prevailing feeling—and my God how she despised herself for this—was one of relief.

~

Mrs. Mutiso sat at the dining table that evening cutting brown paper into neat rectangles that would cover the twins' class books. They were already at their grandparents' home. The Mutiso grandparents had insisted they needed at least a week to acclimatize before school began.

Mr. Mutiso came downstairs, mumbled something, then went back upstairs, taking the stairs two steps at a time. When he returned, he was dressed in khakis, a blue shirt and a brown leather jacket.

'I'll be back a bit late...the Zimbabweans extended the meeting to dinner at the Stanley,' he said, as if he wasn't sure if he'd heard himself the first time. Mrs. Mutiso nodded at the brown paper.

After they got married, she'd walked into Little Red in town, a designer clothes store she used to walk past wondering what sort of money you needed to have to buy even a handkerchief there. She purchased two dresses now that she was on an allowance from Mr. Mutiso (which was part of an allowance his father extended to him though it would be years before Mrs. Mutiso found this out). She was now the wife of a businessman. She imagined trips to Harare, Johannesburg, London by her husband's side, his attentive, caring, smart, witty wife. She'd need to look the part. Thirty-thousand shillings later and two Calvin Klein dresses in hand, she arrived home to find a note from her husband.

Carol,

Emergency trip came up. One of my business interests in Eldoret. I'll be back end of the week.

Abraham

There was nothing about their twins whose first birthday would fall right in the middle of his unexpected trip, nothing to tell you that they were a newly wedded couple who were going to spend their first week of marriage in different provinces. Mrs. Mutiso had never accompanied her husband on a business trip and she had long stopped buying imported designers.

'Did you hear?' he was still standing there. His face was scrunched in irritation, the lines on his forehead exaggerated. He'd added weight, Mrs. Mutiso noticed absently as she watched him struggle with his jacket zipper before giving up and jamming his hands into its pockets like a petulant child. He was still beautiful. His lips were soft and full, his round face still maintained the boyish charm he had when over a decade ago he'd stopped her outside Dumbusters and said, 'I'm not going to ask you to go home with me, but I know one day you will and I will give you my name.'

Those were the kind of bravado lines guys dropped back then. They wooed you with the promise of marriage. Nothing could get you in a car speeding towards Blue Post Hotel, Thika, faster than a whispered, 'You know one day you will be the mother of my children.'

'Yes, I heard you. Do you want me to leave tea for you?' Mrs. Mutiso asked automatically.

'Eh…eh…no…' Mr. Mutiso stammered.

They'd had such a good afternoon together earlier. After dropping the twins at his parents' home in Karen, they'd driven down to Valley Arcade where they drank coffee as they mapped out their back-to-school shopping plans. At his parents' home things had been predictably tense. The twins, his mother always reminded Mrs. Mutiso, were a byproduct of sin but they were still children, they were not to blame. Mrs. Mutiso didn't get off as easily as her kids and her husband. She was still treated with hostility and distrust even after all these years of marriage to their son. On any other day, the hostility would have set the couple on edge but on the way out of his parents' compound, Mr. Mutiso began imitating the way his father talked from the way he pouted just before he spoke to his rheumatoid arthritis that was beginning to win. At one point, Mrs. Mutiso was so overcome by laughter she leaned forward and lightly touched his thigh with her long fingers adorned with her trademark red manicure.

Mrs. Mutiso got up from the dining table and went around the three-seater sofa that separated the dining room from the living room to collect a paper bag. She came back round the sofa and sat down without looking up at Mr. Mutiso who shifted nervously by the door. She removed class books from the bag and placed them to the side of the rectangular brown pieces of paper she'd cut. She took one class book from the pile and began folding the brown paper into the cover of the book.

'Um…okay, goodnight,' Mr. Mutiso said finally, as though he'd been wrestling with something and a winner had been declared. He grabbed his keys and opened the door. Before he stepped out he turned around and looked back to where Mrs. Mutiso sat. He came round the table and gave her a kiss on the cheek before walking out.

Mrs. Mutiso did not react to the unexpected intimacy. Instead, she finished lining the class book then took the next one on the pile and continued to line the books for the next hour at a constant speed as if she were afraid that if she faltered, she'd give herself a moment too long to question what had happened earlier that afternoon.

Being happy had become a delicate balancing act between her reality and her fantasies. She spent her days building worlds in which they were happy and she really, properly knew how to love her children. Some days, she'd get so caught up in the worlds in her head she'd begin to live them in reality. She'd kiss Mr. Mutiso good-morning because she'd either been remembering what it felt like the first time they made love or because she'd been imagining a reconciliation with his family where they suddenly learnt to love her. Some days, she'd see her twins playing outside and try to imagine what it must be like not to feel so bone weary all the time. This was why she'd never engaged with her neighbours. There was always the fear that if they spent enough time with her, they'd realise that she had not made a conquest at all. She was living in a gilded prison decorated with golden chandeliers and wallpaper depicting a sandy beach, palm trees so vivid you could hear the breeze from the ocean rustling through the leaves.

CHAPTER ELEVEN

Mrs. Mutiso, continued

After the Mutisos' purchased the twins stationary and class books, Mr. Mutiso, buoyed by his successful joke earlier, had playfully suggested they catch a movie. 'Like old times,' he'd said with a wink. In all the movies they'd watched together at the cinema, they'd never spent more than a few minutes focused on the screen. The last one they watched at 20th Century had been an action film. There was always someone who'd come for the earlier screening and illegally stayed for the next one, shouting out spoilers as the movie progressed. They'd thrown popcorn at him in between furious make out sessions.

From the cinema, the couple walked their usual route to Mrs. Mutiso's (she went as Carol then so you will forgive me if I indulge the past and switch to Carol here), Carol's halls of residence. Mr. Mutiso suggested they eat dinner together first, so they stopped at a chips joint just off Monrovia Street. Whilst he ordered the chips, Carol found them seats. The chip-shop was packed with people grabbing dinner but she managed to find two high stools at the communal table facing the wall where a long mirror adorned the wall from one end to the other. As Carol idly people-watched from the mirror, she caught a glimpse of Mr. Mutiso paying for their chips and sausage at the counter. He laughed at something the man behind the counter said, then put a few coins into the tip jar before taking the newspaper wrapped chips and sausage. He looked around the crowded chip-shop trying to spot Carol who waved at him through the mirror to get his attention.

'I got some chilli for you as well,' he said placing their food on the table.

'Thank you.' She leaned in to kiss his cheek affectionately. Mr. Mutiso smiled through the mirror at her reflection.

Before Carol could salt her chips, someone came up to say hello to Mr. Mutiso. He was a short man with an energetic handshake and a bounce to his words. 'Boss! Kweli uko hapa? Me, I didn't know you go to these places like the rest of us!'

Carol raised an eyebrow. Mr. Mutiso laughed and shrugged before steering the conversation towards pleasantries. He asked after the interloper's health and family and spoke a little bit about is family. Carol sat up straight, waiting for Mr. Mutiso to introduce her. This would be the first of his friends that she'd met. She felt nervous and excited at the same time. When she was sure he was going to turn around and introduce her, Carol heard Mr. Mutiso bring the conversation to a close. The interloper looked questioningly in her direction but didn't have the confidence to ask about Mr. Mutiso's date.

'Why didn't you introduce me?' Carol asked as Mr. Mutiso returned to his newspaper of chips and ripped open a packet of salt. He began to vigorously shake the salt packet over his chips.

'Huh? Oh him? Uh…leave him alone, he isn't anyone important,' Mr. Mutiso shrugged dismissively.

'What did he mean you don't come to places like this?'

Mr. Mutiso put the empty salt packet down and picked up a tomato sauce bottle. He looked up at the mirror to find Carol staring intently at his reflection. Carol had a softness to her that was evident even without having to touch her skin to feel it. The first time they'd slept together Mr. Mutiso was taken aback by this softness. It surprised and then scared him that he didn't want to get up from her embrace, that he wanted to lie with her and never return to the world outside the hostel room he'd hired for the night.

'I come here, he was just joking.' Mr. Mutiso poured the tomato sauce all over his fries then began to attack them with enthusiasm.

'So is he one of your friends?' Carol's food lay untouched. Mr. Mutiso looked up and gestured for her tomato sauce, when she didn't appear to care either way he took it and poured it on his chips.

'Who him?' he said when he realized Carol was still staring at him through the mirror.

'Yes, that man who just came up to you and asked after your family who I have never met, and who knows your relatives by name, names I have just learnt—him—is *he* your friend?'

'Oh...eh...he is a friend of the family.' Mr. Mutiso must have been pleased with his answer because he smiled and reached out for Carol's hand which he held as he continued to eat his chips with his free hand.

'Ei boss! Mutiso! Don't tell me that's you.' Mr. Mutiso released Carol's hand instantly—

In total, five men came up to Mr. Mutiso that evening. They greeted him fondly, chatted with him like old friends, asked after his family, stared in open question at his companion, but not once did he introduce his companion to them.

~

After dinner, the couple walked back to Carol's hall of

residence at the top of God's corner, named this way because of the preponderance of churches in the area. Mr. Mutiso kept up a steady stream of conversation about the movie they had barely watched in between kissing and assaulting the spoilers-guy with popcorn. Carol kept up a steady study of the ground in front of her.

'Abraham, does anyone…any of your friends or even your family—do they know about me…us?' she finally asked as they arrived at the entrance to her halls.

Mr. Mutiso squinted at the dying sun.

'Us?' he asked as though the word was new to his vocabulary. Carol took a sharp breath, folded her hands in front of her and ventured a glance at Mr. Mutiso's face which was still tilted to the sun.

'They don't,' she answered her own question. The words tasted bitter and came out stale. 'Lie to me and tell me that they do.' Mr. Mutiso still faced the sun. 'Abraham? Who knows about me? Are we even an "us" or is this a joke to you?'

Mr. Mutiso tilted his head slightly as though preparing to lower it to eye level, then thought better of it.

'Abraham?' My God. This can't be real. This is a joke. This is a joke. This has to be a joke.' Carol's heartbeat slowed down first and then, just when she was sure it would stop, it sped up in an erratic and frighteningly fast pace. It *had* to be a joke. Was this man mad? He was the one who'd approached her first, insisting they were meant to be together. He always assured her that he had known from the second he laid eyes on her that he loved her.

What had he said the first time she asked him when she'd meet his family? They were traditional, very boring, old-timers. He needed to give his parents time to come round to the fact that he was dating seriously. And your siblings? He was an only child. Okay then, what about your cousins? Oh them? They are abroad for further studies. All of them? I don't have many. And your friends? They aren't really the type of people I want you to be around. Even me, I'm in the process of severing ties with some of those friends. That's what attracted me to you, you're so different. Really you think so? Yes, with you, I feel like I can be myself.

And when she suggested he visit her family in Meru? He agreed, said it was a brilliant idea, it would be wonderful to meet the people who had brought up the love of his life, said that, as a matter of fact, he had been about to make the same suggestion himself. They day they were meant to travel upcountry to visit her family, she received a phone call from him two hours after he was meant to have picked her up for the road trip they'd planned for a little over two months.

'Baby, I'm so sorry, emergency at work. I can't make it but I'm sending someone with some money for you so you can take the bus home.'

Did he know that her family had slaughtered a whole cow for him? That they had gone out and bought unga for chapati and made rice and other rich people food for him? And what business emergency she'd asked, innocent of the art of artifice. 'Oh it's a thing at work…one of the family businesses.'

~

'Abraham. Abraham, answer me.'

…

'Abraham? You idiot! You stupid, stupid idiot!' Mr. Mutiso was taken aback by her change in character. His Carol always spoke in a soft restrained voice. The tone of voice and certainly the language she was using now was inconsistent with the person he knew. 'This was all a game to you! I was a game to you. You were never going to introduce me, were you?' Carol had suspected…but love was a complex thing…she'd chalked it up to his traditional family values but now… 'What was your plan, eh? Date me then leave me when it was time to marry the rich girl your parents have lined up for you? I thought it was just your parents who were old-fashioned or whatever you call it, but you're the same. Were you scared my poor fingers will taint your money? If that's the case, I'm so sorry to disappoint you, but your already tainted, I'm pregnant!'

Mr. Mutiso's head found its way to eye-level immediately. Carol had imagined delivering the news over a soft candlelight dinner, not right outside her halls where they'd already began to attract unwanted attention.

'What…what did you just say?'

'Nkt! Look at this man. Look at him. Now is when he knows how to talk.' Carol looked around appealing to anyone passing by, as if they were the jurors in her case.

'Woman, don't play games with me. What did you just say?' Mr. Mutiso grabbed her shoulders and though it wasn't rough, she felt the pent up energy behind those hands.

'Games? Play games? You are telling me not to play games? Then tell me what is it you've been doing with me all this time? So you—you can play games, but me I can't?' she said in defiance. She didn't want to have this conversation with him, she wanted to stop right there, take her voice down several notches, remove the anger from her tone, wrap her hands around him, kiss him, but then she also wanted him to stop too, say I'm sorry, long day baby, I should have introduced you and of course, of course I am overjoyed that we—

Mr. Mutiso steered her away from the entrance so that they were no longer within ear-shot of everyone walking in and out of the halls.

'You're pregnant?' he whispered, his grip around her

shoulders had become uncomfortable. Carol tried to shake him off, he held on harder.

'Did you not go to school? What do you think happens when people have sex without protection?' Carol felt the throbbing pain that would become a permanent fixture in her life slide into place at her temples. She reached up to cradle her head with her left hand.

~

Mrs. Mutiso finished lining the class books, cleared the table away and finally, with nothing left to do, sat back and closed her eyes. It had happened again. The anger and helplessness that had overtaken her that day, years ago outside her halls, had visited again. It had began with the sudden onset of the migraine followed by a tingling in her fingers which coalesced into numbness as it creeped up her forearms, by the time it got to her back, she was sweating profusely and her heart was beating so fast she'd held onto Mr. Mutiso to steady herself, then, just as suddenly, she was sure of it, she was sure of it, she couldn't breathe. She'd screamed and screamed, she couldn't get enough air into her longs, and the sweat had drenched her clothes which clang onto her shivering body. Mr. Mutiso, stared in distress at the woman who was clearly breathing just fine, wondering if she had gone mad.

Ever since that first episode, there had been several mini-episodes. Nothing quite like the first one, but there would be times she'd have to steady herself because she felt the migraine calling the trembling which she knew would lead to the shivering, the sweating, the loss of breath, and finally, loss of control. It was the last part she was afraid of. That first time she had touched the end of what it meant to have control over her life. She had lost her understanding of rational will, but she had come back. Mr. Mutiso, feeling embarrassed, had finally waved down a taxi and taken her to a clinic where the doctor ascertained she was breathing just fine it was probably just the pregnancy.

It had happened again today. This time, she was sure of it: it was worse than the first time. Was it the knowledge that she had given up her children without putting up a genuine fight? Or the suggestion of a cinema date, "like old times"? Whatever it was, they never made it to the cinema. The migraine appeared and unlike it's usual routine, it did not call the other symptoms one at a time. They stomped in at once, taking over her faculties, crippling her sense of awareness. It was so sudden, she was sure someone was holding her in a choke hold. She didn't know it then but she'd shouted at Mr. Mutiso, right in front of the other back-to-school shoppers in Text Book Centre to stop strangling her because how else could she explain the sudden feeling that someone was trying to suffocate her?

The clock chimed eight p.m. in the empty house she had worked so hard to make a home. There were the plush rugs, soft sofas, that beach wallpaper that was meant to lighten up the room and make their home look like a tropical holiday destination. The chandeliers hung low enough to create an intimate setting, the reading nook had two identical wingback chairs (for the couple to sit back and catch up at the end of the day), next to it was an antique writing bureau. A house that never became a home.

~

Mrs. Mutiso found her mother-in-law nursing a drink at ten a.m. the next morning when she went to drop the twins' school shopping. They exchanged a hostile hello, as if they were meeting for the first time, but both had heard negative things about each other. She didn't wait to be offered a seat.

From past experience, she knew the offer would not be forthcoming.

'I've brought the girls' class books and other things for the term.' she said, holding up the paper bags she'd brought with her.

Her mother-in-law, the exact likeness of Mr. Mutiso, looked down at the offending bags with an arched eyebrow. 'Books? What books? We've already bought them everything they need. Didn't Abraham tell you?' she asked trying, but not too hard, to suppress a little smile because she knew the answer. Mr. Mutiso hadn't mentioned anything of the sort to his wife.

'Oh.'

'Well, I have some ladies coming for lunch so maybe you can come back another day.' Mrs. Mutiso was summarily dismissed.

'Can I see the twins?'

'They've gone to the club for a swimming lesson. They are so behind in their extra-curriculars.' Her mother-in-law stood up, not to see her off, but to enquire about the progress with her lunch.

~

On her drive back home, Mrs. Mutiso found bumper to bumper traffic on Langata road. Her vision was blurred by tears, the humiliation of the morning weighing heavily on her spirit. Just as the cars began to move again, a matatu aggressively tried to cut in front of her from the left.

'Ma-dam, barabara si yako! Get off the road if you didn't come to drive.' The driver leaned out of the van and shouted. His words produced a snigger from the passengers sat next to him. Mrs. Mutiso gripped her steering wheel, the migraine sliding into place. She inched her car forward, trying to ignore the matatu that was so close to her car they were just about touching. That wasn't a fight she could fight if she wanted to get home without another "episode" occurring. This time, if it did occur, she was alone. They took people to Mathare for the way she'd acted yesterday. She wasn't sure Mr. Mutiso would come and get her from there if she lost her control again. The thought was so distressing, she felt her fingers begin to tingle again and her heart rate hitched up a notch.

A beggar surprised her with his sudden appearance at her open window, reversing the tingling, taking her mind off of Mathare. Her first instinct was to draw her window up but she'd heard horror stories of beggars throwing feces into the cars of drivers who refused to give them money. The beggar was in fact a boy who couldn't have been much older than her twins. There were ringworms tightly weaved onto his scalp. Both of his hands were in front of him which gave her some relief.

In her distraction the matatu had managed to get in front of her and now it was blaring a gospel tune.

'Naomba unisaidie.' The little boy said in a voice that could not have been above a whisper.

She looked around her car. 'I don't have—' she started to say, before spotting the paper bags of books and school materials on her passenger sit.

'Are you in school?' she asked.

He hesitated. 'It starts tomorrow, but no money,' he said. She handed him the paper bags and reached into her handbag. Fishing out several notes she handed him these as well.

'This is for school, okay?' she said. He nodded his head vigorously and thanked her before hurrying off. From her side mirror, Mrs. Mutiso watched as he crossed the road and went up to a lady sitting under the shade of a tree, who she assumed was his mother. She watched as a tense exchange between mother and child took place and when the traffic began to move again, Mrs. Mutiso was not convinced the money would be going towards school fees.

CHAPTER TWELVE

Mrs. Mutiso and Beatrice, September, 1991

Mrs. Mutiso parked her car on the pavement outside her house. She didn't get out immediately, instead after she switched the engine off, she leaned back into her chair and tried to regulate her breathing. The migraine was still there and as she'd pulled up to her house, the trembling in her hands had begun again. Trying to think about calming down often made it worse. She looked around for someone, anything to distract her.

She spotted Mama Kanono standing outside her house in conversation with a lady in a head-wrap. Without giving it another thought, Mrs. Mutiso got out of her car and crossed the road to her neighbour's gate.

'Morning,' she called from the gate.

'Good morning,' Mama Kanono greeted her.

'Hi, I just saw you and I thought I should come and greet my neighbour.' Mrs. Mutiso felt nervous underneath Mama Kanono's steady gaze. 'Oh, and congratulations as well!' she added. Mama Kanono blinked in confusion.

'Mr. Mathai told us you are expecting...' she said cautiously.

'Oh...yes.' Mama Kanono touched her belly. Mrs. Mutiso thought she was going to add to her brief sentence but Mama Kanono had nothing else to say.

'So how has it been since you moved in?' Mrs. Mutiso tried again.

Chance is a funny thing. Mama Kanono had not spoken to her neighbour since that first meeting the weekend they moved in. She would not have felt compelled to carry the conversation on, but as she'd been talking to Priscilla, she'd seen Mrs. Mutiso's Peugeot 504 round the corner to their side of the estate. She would not have given her neighbour another thought (here was a woman who minded her business as though it were a virtue), except that Priscilla broke off to observe 'Na huyo Mrs. Mutiso sometimes ana-shake shake sana.' Mama Kanono observed Mrs. Mutiso closer. By now Mrs. Mutiso had parked her car on the pavement next to her house and was staring at her trembling hands. She passed them through her hair then held them together as though in prayer.

'You've seen her do that before?' Mama Kanono asked Priscilla, concerned for her neighbour. That couldn't be good, the trembling.

'Sometimes when she is sitting at her balcony she shakes until she has to sit on the floor. Once I saw her talking to herself until she began to shake,' Priscilla said happy to divulge the details she'd noted of their neighbour.

Remembering why they stood outside, Mama Kanono steered the conversation back to Priscilla's tasks for the day. The verandah needed a thorough wash before their guests arrived that evening, and the little hedge next to the wall could also do with a trim. Priscilla was disappointed that she'd not managed to distract Mama Kanono long enough for her to forget the chores she wanted completed by the end of the day. As Mama Kanono wrapped up her list of chores, they were both surprised to hear Mrs. Mutiso call out hello from their gate. Neither of the women had noticed Mrs. Mutiso get out of her car.

Mama Kanono knew that it disappointed people that she was not much of a talker, but she didn't like small talk and she was extremely private. The two qualities created a reserved nature that she'd long stopped fighting to change. And yet, looking into Mrs. Mutiso's eyes, she found herself saying, 'Would you like to stay for tea?' She was stunned to see relief in Mrs. Mutiso's eyes. Also, she noted, Mrs. Mutiso's hands were no longer trembling. That must be a good thing.

'That sounds nice,' Mrs. Mutiso responded in a muted voice that didn't do much to hide her joy at the invitation.

'Priscilla, please make us a cup of tea and did the bread get finished?' Priscilla nodded and then shrugged in response to each question respectively then walked back into the house.

'Attitude?' Mrs. Mutiso asked after Priscilla was, mostly, out of ear shot.

'Yes, but it's so hard to get a good house-girl nowadays. You just persevere.'

'Mr. Mutiso's mother normally hires them for us and she trains them as well,' Mrs. Mutiso volunteered without knowing why she did so.

'Really? What if you do things differently in your house and she's trained them the way she does things?' Mama Kanono ushered Mrs. Mutiso into her home. Mrs. Mutiso took a moment to adjust to the dimness inside, and the question as well. The Mathai' house was one of the houses in the middle ring of the estate, they didn't receive enough light during the day. Mrs. Mutiso noted that Annie's furniture was still present, but many of the pieces had begun to lose their lustre.

'His mother is really good at training them. They learn everything from there so that it's easier for me when they come.' Mrs. Mutiso found an answer she could live with.

'Kwani, how often do you get a new one?' Mama Kanono asked as they settled in the living room.

The questions. The questions. She hated these questions. Mrs. Mutiso was already regretting crossing the road to her neighbours home. Mama Kanono noticed that the question made Mrs. Mutiso uncomfortable from the way Mrs. Mutiso's face screwed into an uneasy frown as she tried to think of an answer.

'Uh...Priscilla.' Mama Kanono called out. She didn't like asking people questions about their life. She also didn't like questions herself. She'd been asking Mrs. Mutiso questions to make her feel welcome, but now that it was clear it had the opposite effect, Mama Kanono was at a loss. A silence followed where Mama Kanono smiled vaguely and Mrs. Mutiso tried to come up with an excuse to leave immediately.

Priscilla came out of the kitchen carrying a tray with two cups and a flask of tea. 'And the sugar?' Mama Kanono asked as Priscilla set the tray down.

'Sugar?' Priscilla repeated, looking for the sugar bowl on the tray. 'Oh,' she said when she realized she'd not brought it out. She returned to the kitchen with a purposeful walk that suggested she had gone to get something, but she never returned with the sugar.

'When are you expecting the baby?' Mrs. Mutiso asked after Mama Kanono had served their tea and gone to retrieve the sugar bowl.

'Early next year,' Mama Kanno said, spare as ever with her words.

'How has it been?' and then after a beat Mrs. Mutiso once again found herself volunteering information, 'Mine was hard. And you know the funny thing is, I didn't know they were twins until they came out.'

Mama Kanono wrinkled her nose in confusion. 'You didn't go to the gyno before that?'

Mrs. Mutiso faltered. She'd stumbled again and given information she'd not planned to give. Mama Kanono saw that she'd put her neighbour in a corner again and felt sorry for it.

'Mine weren't easy,' she volunteered in a moment that surprised her too. She'd never spoken about this to anyone before.

'I thought you only had...Ka-Kanono?' It felt wrong calling a baby "the fat one" to Mrs. Mutiso who was accustomed to people labelling her and calling her by those labels instead of her given name.

'What's Kanono's other name?'

'Nyambura.'

'I thought you only had Nyambura,' She repeated.

'I did—I mean I do. She's the only one who survived.'

'Oh...I'm sorry for your loss,' Mrs. Mutiso said. She had more questions but she felt that Mama Kanono had gone out of her way to share with her and she didn't want to push further. Mama Kanono waved her hand to dismiss the story and smiled a thin distracted smile.

It had worked. Mama Kanono's olive branch of a shared private trauma was what Mrs. Mutiso needed to feel comfortable with her neighbour. It was as though she'd been waiting for this moment her whole life, for a tender exchange between two women that built a bridge out of past traumas neither was ready to speak of, but each recognised in the other.

Mrs. Mutiso carried the conversation thereafter. If she asked a question and Mama Kanono's answer was short and to the point, which it often was, she'd answer it herself, divulging a little more information about herself each time. Encouraged by this, Mama Kanono would offer something up herself, not nearly as much as Mrs. Mutiso but enough to say "your effort is seen". After tea, Mama Kanono knew she should wrap up their conversation, she had a whole day to get on with preparing for Mr. Mathais' relatives who were coming for God-only-knows-how-long.

However, an hour elapsed in which the women talked some more and Mrs. Mutiso ran to her house to grab three beautiful wax fabrics from Ghana which she unceremoniously gifted Mama Kanono because of an offhand compliment Mama Kanono had given her on her dress. 'And I'll introduce you to my tailor! He is a drunk but you won't find anyone else who does work like him in South B!' she said as Mama Kanono stared in bewilderment at the fabric. As the radio in the kitchen announced the lunch-time news, Mama Kanono surprised herself for the second time that day by inviting Mrs. Mutiso to stay for lunch.

'It's just yesterday's food. We eat very simple food here.' she warned, feeling the need to explain the mukimo and cabbage to Mrs Mutiso.

'Traditional food is not simple.'

'It's not spaghetti.'

'But Italians don't think their food is plain. We always rubbish our traditional food when it's actually great.'

And when the mukimo was served Mrs. Mutiso exclaimed, 'This is the green-green one with the leaves? And you call this simple?'

'My mother sends someone with a dish of it every month.' Mama Kanono couldn't help beaming at Mrs. Mutiso's praise.

'Can you ask her to send two from now on? I love this one and there used to be someone in Marigiti who could make it very well but I don't know where they went.'

'Of course. She'd be happy to make more, she makes too much for us already we eat it until we don't want to look at mukimo again and then there's more the next day.'

Mrs. Mutiso stayed through the afternoon, even as as Mama Kanono excused herself to continue preparations for her relatives. She lounged in their living room reading a book she'd gone back to her house to get. Mama Kanono was amused by the fact that Mrs. Mutiso did not operate on normal times. She talked and lounged and ate an entire day away without once looking at the clock or pausing mid-conversation the way a person does when they remember they had something to do.

CHAPTER THIRTEEN

The Christmas Party, December, 1991

Christmas arrived hot and lusty like a newly wedded couple who'd managed to stay celibate throughout their courtship. The air trembled with expectation. It felt, some said, as exciting as the year of Independence. After twenty-two years, the country was once again a multi-party state ahead of the elections next year, which gave people hope that 1992 would be a year of radical progress and change. It felt as if Kenya was outpacing her neighbours in development, and now, politics.

Encouraged by the buoyant hope and excitement in the air, the Karanjas came up with the idea of a Christmas party for the estate. They lobbied for (and were granted), a Christmas party budget during the November Bible Study session. The Christmas party was to be held a week before Christmas. Most of the regular Bible Study goers were enlisted to assist in one area or another to help bring the cost of the party down. Mrs. Mutiso had offered to do the decorations and Mama Kanono offered to help her knowing she'd not really need to put in any work because Mrs. Mutiso enjoyed a good decorating project.

~

It was the day of the Christmas party and Mrs. Mutiso had managed to persuade Mama Kanono to get off work early so that they could buy the decorations together. Shopping complete, they situated themselves in Mrs. Mutiso's closed salon, which was in the community centre adjacent to the estate field, where the party would be held. From here, they would prepare the decorations.

Most of the furniture in the salon had been sold off but there were still dryers and chairs and tables strewn around the dusty shop. Mama Kanono was shocked to find Mrs. Mutiso was still paying rent for the space though it had closed down months before.

'If I let it go and I have another business idea, it might be rented out to someone else by then,' Mrs. Mutiso explained.

Kanono and the twins had come along with them, ostensibly to have a playdate, though the twins ignored Kanono. The twins were eight years old and a nuisance to behold. They'd come back from their grandparents' home for the Christmas holiday with a fresh new attitude on Malaba and its residents. Everyone talked funny according to them. Mrs. Mutiso tried to warn them against uttering such opinions out loud (though it was clear where they'd picked up these and other troubling opinions), so they'd changed tact and just kept mentioning all the rich things their grandparents had like four cars and seven dogs.

'I've been thinking of a new business idea,' Mrs Mutiso said as she set out a packet of balloons printed "Merry Christmas". Outside, they could hear Mrs. Karanja giving instructions to the people who'd brought the tent and chairs on where to place them. There was also a radio playing a Christmas tune about snow and Santa from one of the nearby houses as the December sun blazed in defiance.

'What did you have in mind?' Mama Kanono asked taking out a box of fairy lights and staring at the tangled mess of wires in dread.

'A boutique. I was thinking of importing clothes from

India,' Mrs. Mutiso said, 'And maybe I'll add the products we used to sell in the salon before it closed. Mary Kay didn't do too badly.'

'You'd launch the boutique here?' Mama Kanono looked around in surprise.

'...I was thinking so...' Mrs. Mutiso said, feeling self conscious about her decision. 'It's close to home and...'

'But you'd be limiting your customers to our neighbours.' Mama Kanono's mind was already calculating the potential footfall per month, averaging the potential sales in a month, subtracting the cost of running the shop— 'I don't think that's a wise idea,' she said eventually.

'Yes but you know I am good at picking out clothes,'

'That's not the issue, it's why open a boutique here?'

Mrs. Mutiso faltered... 'I've already renewed the lease for another two years,' she said. Mama Kanono's eyes widened in surprise but before she could say anything a fight broke out where the kids were playing. The twins had broken off the head of a toy parrot that Kanono had insisted on leaving the house with. She stood over the parrot's headless body bawling, her chubby arms covering her soft round cheeks. The twins, upon seeing the tears launched into an argument about who had broken the toy. Mrs. Mutiso got up and separated the twins not even bothering with the usual parental admonitions one would reasonably expect given the situation.

'We can also sell toys, if kids break them this often there will definitely be a demand,' she said with a grin as she sat back down next to Mama Kanono with Kanono on her lap. Mama Kanono burst into laughter but sobered up very quickly.

'Are you sure about this?' she asked as Mrs Mutiso played with Kanono to calm the girl down.

'About what?' Mrs. Mutiso said looking up as if she had no

idea what they'd just been talking about. 'Oh… the boutique? A woman needs her independence. I'll keep trying out the businesses until something works out.' The firmness in her voice convinced Mama Kanono to drop the conversation.

'Hullo!' Mrs. Karanja knocked then entered the closed shop. The women in the shop stood up to greet Mrs. Karanja. Esther, who was Kanono's age mate stood behind her mother, sucking her thumb and peering out from the folds of Mrs. Karanja's long dress.

'How's it going over here? I just came to say the tent is up and the men are still here so they can help you put up the decorations before they have to go.'

Mama Kanono sagged into her chair in relief. Mrs. Mutiso launched into action. She went out to gather and organize the men into groups: balloon blowers, Christmas tree assemblers and decorators, fairy lights hangers—and then when everyone knew what they were doing she went back into the shop and proposed:

'We can organise the treasure hunt for the kids now that everything else is being sorted.' Mama Kanono had never seen Mrs. Mutiso so full of energy. She glowed with a sense of purpose and Mama Kanono would have pointed this out had it not been for Kanono's interruption to ask to go back home for tea time.

~

The Christmas party officially began at six p.m. but guests only started filtering in after seven p.m. The tent glowed with colourful christmas lights. The artificial Christmas tree weighed down with baubles and lights and shimmery paper was the main attraction of the event and it lived up to it's purpose. Next to the Christmas tree was a raised platform where the VIPs would sit. They included the chairman of the estate association (a non-Malaba resident), the guest of honour (a Member of Parliament who was there because the title M.P. sounded impressive to have for a guest of honour. Other than that he didn't have any legitimate reason to be there), and the key organisers of the event.

The Karanjas being the key organizers had disputed this last addition. They saw their work as that of backstage hands. A seat at the high table would be too much. But their neighbours had insisted that they needed to be recognized for the work they had done organising the monthly Bible study, the donations to orphanages and other charities, the blood donation drive in June, and a plethora of other events they'd organized for their neighbours to partake in since they'd moved in. Eventually, it was decided that only Mr. Karanja would sit at the high table as a representative of the Karanja family. Mrs. Karanja insisted she had too much work to do ensuring the party ran smoothly, she'd hardly have time to sit down.

The Christmas party was a raging success. The children of Malaba absolutely loved the estate wide Christmas themed treasure hunt that had them hunting for clues even in people's homes (those who'd been kind enough to allow Mrs. Mutiso to hide clues in their house). Mrs. Mutiso could not remember a day she'd enjoyed as thoroughly as this and looking across at her new friend Mama Kanono, it was clear the usually subdued woman was enjoying herself too. They laughed and cheered the kids on and congratulated themselves on some of the harder hints and riddles in the treasure hunt. It was as if when the clock struck six p.m. and the treasure hunt began, they were ten again and so invested in its outcome nothing of their everyday world could have punctured this beautiful evening.

~

The highlight of the party was the Nativity Play directed by Mrs. Shah. She was a stout yet delicate woman with a high-pitched hearty laugh and a love of people. Though she didn't make it regularly to the Bible studies, when she did, just as in the first Bible Study she attended, she always contributed her thoughts on different passages. When they got to Ecclesiastes, she declared the book to be the most poetic thing she'd read in a long time. 'This could pass for poetry in an English Literature class in schools! And the moral teachings are just—' Mr. Karanja interrupted her in irritation to explain that the word of God was too holy to be taught as poetry.

When the idea of an estate Christmas Party was floated by Mrs. Karanja, Mrs. Shah saw her opportunity to re-live her childhood spent in a prep school in north London through directing a Nativity Play.

'It would be such a shame to have a Christmas party with no play. And when I was in prep school, and mind it was a Church of England one, we never went a year without a play,' she'd argued. Her neighbours did not see why a play was needed or why it would be a shame to go without it. A standard reading of the appropriate verses and a quick sermon would suffice.

'But, it would be *such* fun for the children as well! It used to be my favourite thing in the world!'

'Christmas is not just about fun Mrs. Shah—' Mr. Karanja, ever the pedagogue, launched into an exegesis on the meaning of Christmas. 'I don't want the children to associate Christmas with fun. They need to know that this is the day our Lord and Saviour was born to die for our sins.' He always wore reading glasses when he was preaching or leading a Bible study under the pretext of having a problem with his eyesight. They were too big and kept slipping down his nose as he talked, which led to the unfortunate habit where, as his reading-glasses fell further down his nose, he'd end up looking down at people from the top of his glasses and every once in a while, pushing the glasses back up with his middle finger.

'And I agree with you Mister Pastor Karanja. We can show them all that and more with a play because studies show that children remember best using activity.' Mrs. Shah would not be deterred. Finally, the Bible Study members agreed to sanction the development of a Nativity Play which brought on the next issue: there was a general disquiet about a non-Christian directing a Christian play. Mrs. Shah, prepared for this, assured her neighbours that she would be "strict-like" with following the events of Jesus' birth exactly as they were written in the Bible.

Mr. Karanja asked her if her family was okay with her directing the play to which Mrs. Shah responded with a "why wouldn't they be?" that so flummoxed Mr. Karanja, he had no further questions at the time.

'Besides, if I don't do it, is there anyone else who has the time, not to mention, I will cover the production costs of the play if I direct it.' That settled the matter. No one else had the time or the interest and certainly no one else was willing to put their money towards something as frivolous and arcane as a play.

'I request that we change the name of the play from Nativity Play because it sounds a bit...' Mr. Karanja middle-fingered his reading-glasses as he thought of the word, '...a bit secular.'

Mrs. Shah blinked, taken aback by this new turn of events. Even when you thought you'd prepared, nothing could prepare you for Mr. Karanja's unyielding nature. 'Okay...' she said tentatively, trying to regain her sense of the room and what to say next, '...I like that, yes I like that.' Mrs. Shah's mind worked furiously to think of how to appease Mr. Karanja. 'We're getting into the creative spirit I see! It's all about creativity. What were you thinking of for the name of the play?' She was not going to let a disagreement about the name of the play get between her and her dream of writing (a little writing would be required here and there because acting out the verses exactly as they were written would make for bland entertainment she reasoned), and directing a play.

'Eeeh...ehh...well, of course it needs to be something biblical.' Mrs. Shah hesitated to point out that Nativity was biblical. 'I like Behold the Son of Man.' Mr. Karanja nodded in approval of his own creation, Mrs. Shah blinked again and bit her lower lip to suppress a bubble of laughter.

'Well, it's certainly apropos.' Mrs. Shah said.

They waged a silent war for eleven years where Mrs. Shah referred to the play as the Nativity Play and Mr. Karanja printed it as *Behold the Son of Man Play* on the Christmas party programmes each year.

~

The Christmas Party in it's inter-faith, inter-denominational, inter-tribal communion warmed the hearts of Malaba Estate residents and reminded them that even after a tense last few years, they were first and foremost Kenyans bound by a national anthem that ranked as top three in the world for it's fantastic and soul-stirring lyrics. It was a glorious way to end the year. Even though alcohol was not served at the party, a few residents bought some crates of beer and packet wine from Ng'ang'a's Kiosk, and under Mr. Karanja's steady frown, drank deeply, enjoying each other's company and dancing the merry night away.

They heard the gunshots first and seconds later, a high-pitched scream pierced through the music and merriment and went straight to the ear-drums of every resident in attendance at the Malaba Christmas Party. At first the tent went completely still, as residents pieced together the gunshot and the scream. then it was chaos. Hands, flailing, Malaba's residents ran helter-skelter across the expanse of the field, some into the community centre, calling out for their children, begging the Lord to spare them others into the homes closest to the field.

~

Ng'ang'a woke up at five a.m. every day to be at the Kiosk by six a.m. He was always one of the first people to walk the dirt road off Mombasa road which led to the estates beyond. The day after the Christmas party, he was the first to come across the bodies of Baba and Mama Sally, piled one on top of the other in a ditch that ran the course of the dirt road. Their blood had intermingled then semi-dried into a red and muddy sludge.

Unlike Malaba's residents, Ng'ang'a was a man of action. He sprinted back to the main road. To his left was a petrol station whose attendants were just clocking in for the day's work. He tried to explain to them that he needed a phone to call the police immediately to report two bodies, but hearing the word bodies, the attendants shrunk back. They did not want to get muddled with a murder case and everyone knew the police gave a person who reported a murder hell. Frustrated by their unwillingness to help him, Ng'ang'a looked around for another solution. Just then, he spotted a police Land Rover speeding down Mombasa Road. He ran onto the road to hail it down. The car slid to an abrupt halt and the policewoman driving the car shot her head out of her window and shouted in anger 'What do you think you are doing?'

'Sorry, sorry, there's a body—bodies over there,' Ng'ang'a said panting from the adrenaline that pumped through his body. He pointed back to the dirt road as he tried to catch his breath. A car passed him, nearly missing his body and the driver hooted in anger.

'Well then get in you show us,' the policewoman said. In the backseat Ng'ang'a found two policemen who stared at him curiously as they drove to the scene of the crime. By now, the bodies had attracted a bit of a crowd, flies were buzzing around them and the air was beginning to turn with the distinct stench of death.

'Here, stop here, that's them over there…' Upon seeing the police car, the crowd dropped back, trying to distance themselves as much as they could from the bodies, taking care to put especially vacant looks on their faces.

By seven a.m., news had spread throughout Malaba that there were bodies lying in a ditch just outside the estate. The homes overlooking that part of the road had a direct view of the action from the two bedrooms at the back of the house. Within the hour Malaba residents had made their way into these homes and many stood peering out from the bedrooms as more police cars arrived and the bodies were carted away and the road to their estate became a crime scene. A feeling of guilt pervaded the air, and this unspoken question disturbed Malaba's residents greatly: did they die immediately or could they have been saved?

Baba and Mama Sally lived in house number three, next to the gate. Their obituary in the newspaper read that they were survived by four children. It didn't add that in the next month, the children would be split apart, taken to different homes because no one relative could afford to take care of all of them at once. It didn't add that even before the burial day was announced, their relatives came and ransacked their home of anything of value leaving behind an empty house and four destitute children.

After the bodies had been moved to the mortuary, the police officers took reports from everyone who had something to say, which was mostly hearsay:

'But why were they out so late? Two parents at the same time? That was irresponsible.'

'Ngai! Now can you imagine akina Sally are orphans!'

'Somebody told me there was a high-speed chase.'

'I heard it was because they resisted. You know, in these things you cannot resist. You're not even meant to look the thugs in the eye.'

'Maybe it's because of that big deni they had with that businessman from Kiambu who runs the cement factory in Athi River.'

There were so many opinions flying around that the police officers soon gave up writing their reports and just took part in the opinionating.

The effect of the murder on Malaba was a tightening of security. Everyone copied the Shah's and added broken glasses to their backyard walls to deter thieves from jumping in through the back. Some homes went as far as replacing their bougainvillea fences at the front of the house with glass-topped stone walls and bigger gates. However, in what was customary Nairobi attitude, the matter was forgotten before the New Year, replaced by other pressing and mundane issues like school fees and rent.

CHAPTER FOURTEEN

Wedding Speeches, August 4th, 2012

Just as the wedding guests were beginning to get restless, the MC took hold of the mic and the DJ dialled the music down. 'Alright! Everyone, hello, please excuse me. Eh...the men still adding food at the buffet as if where you have come from your wives were starving you, kindly take a seat.' The men lining up at the buffet table booed and jeered and laughed as the rest of the guests sat at the nearest available seat they could find.

'Time for the speeches.' he said, to which a cheer rang out. 'But before we begin, I wanted to see how many people remember their Form One days.' A groan rolled through the guests who burst into laughter surprised by their collective reaction to that first year of secondary school. 'Kwanza, ebu tusimame, we are going to perform *Badi of Autsaidi* for the couple today!'

Badi of Autsaidi was the English translation of a Kikuyu nursery school rhyme that told the story of a bird that fell down with laughter when it was asked where it had been. The song, like any nursery school rhyme worth the name, had neither rhyme nor reason. The song was one of the milder forms of hazing that took place in Form One where the older kids would get the new kids in school together and make them perform the song, including making the sounds of various instruments in a chaotic a cappella performance that sometimes ended badly for the Form Ones.

The MC split the guests into groups. The table's furthest to the stage would be the drums, another table was the piano, yet another the guitar, he threw in the trombone which led to a lively debate about just what sound a trombone made. Was it a *"mboop, mboop"* or a *"boom, boom"*? After the instruments were assigned, voice types, from soprano to bass, were duly designated. The challenge set forth was to sing *Badi of Autsaidi* the whole way through with each table making its assigned instrument's sound and singing it's assigned voice type without laughing.

The challenge began. The guests tried to sing the song but someone in the drums section began to beat box which tickled the entire drum section until they forgot to keep up the beat. The second round barely made it past the first line of the song because there was a revolt in the trombone trenches: they wanted to be trumpets, trumpets made more sense. The third round was off to a promising start, but the bizarre tangent of the story where the bird said it had failed to bring home banana leaves because it fell into a grandmother's lake, proved to be the undoing of the guests. They tried five times and gave up on the sixth attempt when in tears, the MC said, 'Now I know there is a God in heaven. None of you would have survived secondary school singing like that and yet you are all here.'

When everyone had settled down and more crates of beer and soda had resurfaced, the speeches began.

One after the other, friends and family stood up to congratulate Steven and Beatrice, to express their joy at such a blessed union, to wish them good luck in their future.

The years prior to their meeting were glazed over as if, all those years were just a comma, which suited Beatrice just fine because the past had no business in the present. Just when they thought the speeches were done, Mrs. Mutiso stood up and made her way to the stage. Microphone in hand, she cleared her throat nervously, Beatrice's heart sunk. They locked eyes as Mrs. Mutiso introduced herself as Beatrice's long time friend, past neighbour, wife to prominent businessman Mr. Mutiso, mother of twins who were just engaged. A silence followed the introduction and Mrs. Mutiso stared at the guests with a blank expression as though she'd forgotten how she'd come to be on the stage and what she was doing there.

'I…' Mrs. Mutiso choked on her next words. Beatrice who'd been holding hands with Steven, squeezed his hand. 'Um…' Mrs. Mutiso looked out at the guests, many of whom she knew. She'd heard the snigger that went round when she introduced herself as Mr. Mutiso's wife. She wasn't stupid. She knew what people said. He hadn't lived with her in over ten years. Not since.

'I…' she felt her heart flutter. A familiar migraine materialized. Mrs. Mutiso clenched the microphone. She'd been so taken away by the joy in the room she'd managed to forget herself long enough to get on stage with the good intentions of delivering a maid of honour speech. Strictly speaking, she thought, she wasn't a maid of honour because Beatrice didn't have bridesmaids but if she'd had…

Steven looked at Beatrice, baffled by Mrs. Mutiso silence. Beatrice watched Mrs. Mutiso in trepidation.

'Well…as many of you know.' Mrs. Mutiso seemed to have collected herself just in time. 'Beatrice and I, are very good friends. She's my best friend after all, and you may look at us and wonder just how on earth that is the case.' The guests laughed lightly at this, they did indeed wonder. 'But what you don't know is how similar we are.' Beatrice's fingers dug into

Steve's hand, he had to gently remove his hand from the painful grip.

'*Ouch*! Don't worry I'm not going anywhere,' he whispered with a little laugh. Beatrice didn't hear him. Her heart had stopped beating. Mrs. Mutiso's eyes scanned the room and came upon Nyambura who sat next to her brother a few feet away from her. Beatrice saw the progress and final destination of Mrs. Mutiso's eyeline.

Recently, only very recently, Mrs. Mutiso had started forgetting things, people and places. She'd also began forgetting what was meant to be said and left unsaid. Beatrice only noticed this because they'd spent a lot of time together during the wedding planning process. Mrs. Mutiso would divulge something personal to a room full of decorators or caterers and then her eyelids would flutter in surprise and embarrassment. Once, she told the tailor altering Beatrice's wedding dress that she'd not had sex in a decade then, remembering herself, she said '...mainly because Mr. Mutiso travels a lot.'

'For example—' Mrs. Mutiso began. 'We both adored Princess Diana didn't we Betty? And we both are successful business women, and we both have two wonderful children. Mine just got engaged!' Mrs. Mutiso's mouth curved into a triumphant smile but just before it's apotheosis it collapsed. Beatrice's chair scraped back in an ugly screeching sound. 'No, no...that's not quite right is it.' Mrs. Mutiso was lost in her own thoughts. Lost in her own world. In this state anything could come ou—

'No, I have three.' She lifted her left hand up and counted three fingers as she said aloud, 'One, two, three,' then stared vacantly at the guests who stared back in shock. This was news to everyone but Beatrice.

'Three children,' Mrs. Mutiso repeated. 'So no, we are not alike there Betty.' She sounded disappointed then breathed in as if to fortify herself. Her eyes were glassy and her hands trembled, she mumbled words that were lost to the guests and then, her voice rising she said: 'Mmm...no we are not...' Her breath hitched as if she'd just recalled something. 'Oh! But Betty, our children, they have something in common!' Beatrice was by Mrs. Mutiso's side so fast, in the wedding video that was produced thereafter, she looked like a blur as she ran to save herself.

'Th...th-thank you, Carol,' Beatrice said taking the microphone from her. Mrs. Mutiso let it go without a fight. She looked surprised to find Beatrice by her side. Beatrice's guarded stance told Mrs. Mutiso she'd done something wrong though she couldn't figure out what error she'd made. This thought, coupled with the realization that she was standing in front of over a hundred people increased her trembling. Beatrice was sickened to find herself thankful for these familiar signs of Mrs. Mutiso's attacks. She at least had an excuse to guided her friend off the stage.

~

Nyambura met them as they took the exit nearest to the stage.

'Hey, let me help,' she offered. Beatrice was taken aback by her daughter's sudden presence beside them. 'Where are we going?' she asked taking over Mrs. Mutiso for her mother whose stiff wedding dress made it awkward for her to guide Mrs. Mutiso out.

'The bathroom,' Beatrice said recovering herself. They walked in silence as Mrs. Mutiso shivered next to Nyambura. When they got to the door of the bathroom, it seemed that Mrs. Mutiso had managed to calm down considerably because she let go of Nyambura and said 'I'll go in alone, please.' Nyambura looked to her mum for guidance. Mrs. Mutiso noticed the uncertainty in Nyambura's eyes and smiled a sad smile realising that her word was not trusted. She was not trusted to know if she'd be okay.

'You know you're not meant to see your mother's nakedness or else you'll go blind.' Mrs. Mutiso said patting Nyambura and moving her out of the way. It took Nyambura a moment to grasp what nakedness she referred to.

'I'll go with her,' Beatrice said following after Mrs. Mutiso who turned around at the door and held her hand up to stall Beatrice. 'No,' her hand trembled but she persisted, 'I want to be alone.' When she realized her friend wouldn't be so easily shaken off she said, 'You can wait here if you'd like.'

'I want to help,' Beatrice said.

'Help me how?' Beatrice was silent. She hadn't thought about that. Mrs. Mutiso smiled again. 'I'll not be a minute,' she said pushing the door to the women's bathroom open. She turned around just before she disappeared into the bathroom 'Betty?' she sounded younger than her years. 'I'm sorry,' her eyes slide to Nyambura. Nyambura glanced at her mother then at Mrs. Mutiso in confusion.

'No, it's...it's fine. You go in we'll wait for you here.' Beatrice tried to dismiss the conversation nonchalantly.

'What was that about?' Nyambura asked when they were alone in the hallway.

'What?' Beatrice asked looking around for a place to sit. She spied a bench hidden around a cluster of potted palms and made for it. Nyambura followed.

'What was she sorry about? I saw you interrupt her on stage,' Nyambura said, sitting next to her mum.

'I saw her trembling,' Beatrice said, hoping it would be

enough. She tried to keep her tone even, to keep her eyes rooted to one spot, shifty eyes were a tell she was sure.

'Oh okay…you just looked really…scared…' Nyambura shook her head at the memory. 'I didn't know you can move that fast. It's kinda nice to see you being so tender,' Nyambura said.

'What? I'm tender,' Beatrice protested mainly to keep the conversation moving onto safer ground.

Nyambura looked at her dryly. 'When I fell off my bike when I was learning to ride you told me and I quote: don't do things you know you're not good at.'

'Well…it was practical.' Beatrice watched the women's bathroom door.

'And aged nine when I asked if I could sleep in your bed because I had a nightmare you said: then just don't dream then.' Beatrice turned to look at her daughter in surprise. She didn't remember saying that. She would never have said that.

'I didn't say that.'

Nyambura nodded vigorously. 'I'm shocked you left boarding school out till we were sixteen.'

'I would *never* have taken you earlier and you know it was hard to let you go even then! And look what I got in the end you never came back!'

'Fair enough,' Nyambura acquiesced. 'But I'm here now.'.

'I can see that.'

'See! You're doing it again.'

'Doing what?'

'You're just so…literal.'

Beatrice tried to find the issue with that but couldn't see anything wrong in what she'd said. This frustrated her because she knew her words played a huge role in the cavernous gulf between herself and her daughter and yet she didn't know which words did that. 'I think your father was the…entertainer of the two of us.'

'What does this have to do with dad?' Nyambura sat up straight her back rigid, defensive.

'No,' Beatrice put her hands up, 'I'm not…he was this larger than life character and I just couldn't compete. I'm sorry I wasn't tender or that I was literal but I couldn't…I didn't know what role to play with you kids because he played them all…really well.'

'You could have played mum?' Nyambura's voice cracked.

'I…' Beatrice looked down at her wedding ring then back up at her daughter. '...I didn't always know how to,' she admitted.

The door to the bathroom swung open and Mrs. Mutiso came out beaming, though when she didn't see anyone in front of her, the smile began to crush. Beatrice jumped up and hurried to her friend. Nyambura didn't follow immediately but watched her mother hug Mrs. Mutiso then walk hand in hand with her back into the hall.

CHAPTER FIFTEEN

Family Matters, 1992

Electioneering, much like dating, is as much about thwarting potential competitors as it is about wooing the person of interest. Nobody understood this more than his Excellency Daniel Arap Moi in 1992. It had, understandably, been a surprise to the country when the man who famously said multi-party politics would be reinstated in the country "over my dead body" revealed that the date would be much sooner in a political rally where his sycophants spent the morning decrying those calling for a change to the one party state. With multi-party politics back on the table, rivals sprouted overnight and not one to be discouraged, President Moi set about sowing discord in his two rival political parties, ahead of the elections that same year, with an enthusiasm that was unrivalled. The result of this frenzied activity was newspaper headlines that once again drove Ng'ang'a's sales up.

Between Ng'ang'a's Kiosk and Mr. Mathai, it was hard to tell who fared better during the heated debates that ensured between Malaba's residents. Who to vote for? Did it matter? Mr. Mathai knew just how to skim read the newspaper to pick out interesting little tidbits that he could repackage in a more entertaining way to share with his neighbours. Whilst they read the newspaper to keep up with the nation, Mr. Mathai read the newspaper to keep ahead of it. When the newspaper reported that donor funding was being pulled out of the country, Mr. Mathai added that it was likely because Tanzania had lobbied for it in a bid to beat Kenya in a race to be East Africa's most developed country. When the newspaper reported that the Tent of the Living God "cult" members had been taken into custody, Mr. Mathai added that it was a conspiracy to take focus away from the fact that churches had become profit making machines

Yes, 1992 was a busy year for the Kiosk and Mr. Mathai. As his demand in social circles grew, his movements became more erratic so that you could not have accounted for a moment of his time that year. He was everywhere and nowhere, attending this party, throwing that party. Their home became famous for his trademark short-notice parties. From graduation parties for distant relatives to birthday parties for the employees of their store, Mr. Mathai was a busy man. In fact, when Kanyi was born Mr. Mathai was late picking Mama Kanono up from the hospital because he'd stopped off at the bar to celebrate his new child with his friends. From the way Mr. Mathai lived his life, you could not tell that just outside Malaba Estate, the country was blistered and bleeding from protests and riots caused by the growing fear of the election later in the year.

~

It happened that during one of Mr. Mathai's innumerable parties, Mama Kanono's brother came to visit and decided to stay on after the party.

'Sis, I knew you were doing well but kweli you are a rich woman now.' Kariuki looked around their home in awe.

'God has been good.' Mama Kanono said noncommittally. She was beginning to begrudge God the praise he got for her hard work. It reminded her of how people always congratulated Mr. Mathai on their business and it's steady growth when the man still did not know how to balance a cheque book let alone ran a business.

'No wonder you don't come home these days. With a house like this why would anyone leave?'

'What?' Mama Kanono exclaimed in defence. 'But I send money…it's been busy.' She'd not been to her parent's home in Nakuru since they'd moved into Malaba a year a go. She hadn't wanted to go back. She had trouble reconciling her Nairobi life to her childhood home. When she was home, so near her parents' genteel poverty, it grasped onto her and threatened to go back to Nairobi with her.

Their poverty was in the details. They had a stone house, yes, but no functioning plumbing. This stone house had a kitchen, true, but no cupboards in which to store crockery. This kitchen had a fridge, of course, but electricity had not been installed in their home. The walls of the home she grew up in were littered with old corporate calendars, gauche art prints with Bible verses scrolled in bold typefaces and layers of peeling paint from dreadful paint jobs using cheap tins of paint. She felt as if her newly acquired and fast-growing wealth could and would be snatched away by the poverty around her if she spent too much time in its arms. There were things she missed, though not enough to go home.

'How's the family?'

'You'd know if you visited us.' Kariuki stretched himself on one of the sofas, his head propped on the arm rest. 'You know who comes home more often than you—Macharia,' Kariuki said as he switched on the TV.

Mama Kanono pretended not to hear.

'That wife of his—we know she has seen an education of sorts but the way she is so quiet you'd think she didn't learn how to talk.' Kariuku carried on as he scrolled through the channels.

'You have you seen any education?' Mama Kanono asked to goad her brother but also to get him off the subject of Macharia and his wife.

'Thiĩ na kũu!' Kariuki dismissed the new line of conversation, unperturbed by the assertion that he was uneducated, and returned to his original one, 'And those children of theirs! They're just like Kanono—they speak English through the nose. *Ngo, ngo, ngo!* You can't hear anything they are saying!

Mama Kanono felt her blood warm then rise. She'd refused to think of Macharia outside of abstract ideas such as them together. Now here he was, being presented as a concrete reality with children other than Kanono and—

'But you remember how boring he was? And then can you imagine akina mum used to think the two of you would get married?' Kariuki shook his head in wonderment as he settled on a channel. Mama Kanono squinted at the carpet underneath her feet hoping her brother wouldn't look up and see the battle raging in her that she didn't know how to hide just then. She had not spoken about Macharia out loud in a long time. Now she knew why. The conversation gave her the distinct feeling that she had breached a contract.

'Sis, kwani you've forgotten how to talk even you?' Kariuki turned around when he realized his sister had gone quiet.

'No…I was just thinking about…work.'

'You know I like Mathai but sometimes I think you work more than him even though it's your business together. If you had been with someone like Macharia, as boring as he is, maybe—'

Mama Kanono got up before he could finish his sentence

and went into the kitchen under the pretext of checking what Priscilla was making for dinner. Kariuki shrugged and settled in to watch an old football game.

~

Kariuki stayed for a month. He spent most of his days lounging in front of the TV, watching out-of-date sports matches and reruns of soap operas. The day he met Mrs. Mutiso, he was in a word: undone. He was lounging on the sofa he'd perched on the day he arrived, a toothpick carelessly dangling from the corner of his mouth, when she walked in. Priscilla had just cleared away his lunch dishes and they were carrying on a conversation as she rinsed the dishes in the kitchen. They had established a camaraderie that was driving Mama Kanono mad.

'Oh, sorry, I thought it was just Priscilla here.' Mrs. Mutiso said when she saw Kariuki sprawled in the living room. He stood up immediately and it would always be a wonder to him how he found the words to welcome Mrs. Mutiso and introduce himself, so taken away was he by her beauty. Priscilla, on noticing her last question had gone unanswered by Kariuki stepped out of the kitchen to ask it again. She saw Mrs. Mutiso and felt immediately deflated. Another one had fallen for the unending sexual charms of Mrs. Mutiso. The woman didn't even need to speak let alone be interesting for men to fall over themselves for her. Priscilla went back into the kitchen exasperated.

'Priscilla, prisci—'

'Eh? I'm here.' Priscilla came to the kitchen door and leaned on it, arms folded in front of her. Mrs. Mutiso hesitated, Kariuki frowned and gave her a "behave" look.

'When Mama Kanono comes please give her these and tell her to come and see me after.' Mrs. Mutiso handed her a bag of clothes she'd bought as samples of what she'd like to sell at the boutique. Priscilla nodded with the intention to do nothing of what had been asked of her. Her place in the Mathai home was secure, there was no need to add on extra work for nothing.

Kariuki insisted on walking Mrs. Mutiso to the door and when he found out she lived across the road from them, he insisted on walking her to her gate as well because, 'it's the only gentlemanly thing to do.' Kariuki sounded anything but gentlemanly as he stole leering glances of Mrs. Mutiso's body whenever he thought she wasn't looking too closely.

He was opening Mrs. Mutiso's gate for her when Mr. Mutiso's car came round the corner. Mrs. Mutiso looked up and it must have been the flash of uncertainty in her eyes that Mr. Mutiso saw for in the next moment, he'd parked his car hastily on the pavement next to their house and jumped out of the car breathing fire.

'So this is how you embarrass me when I have gone to work?' Mr. Mutiso grabbed Mrs. Mutiso's arm, ignoring Kariuki who stood staring stupidly in his old corduroys and dirt-brown t-shirt. 'This woman! You think I work for you to be acting a fool in front of people with this…this…' he glared at Kariuki who shrunk back in fear. Finding no words to describe him, Mr. Mutiso turned his wrath back on his wife.

Mrs. Mutiso's tongue mutinied just when she needed it to defend her. It was as if it too believed what everyone said about her, that she was a lazy whore who abused the privilege of her fortunate union whilst her husband went to work, a verb that was used too loosely to describe how Mr. Mutiso spent his days. Mr. Mutiso was shouting now. Kariuki still stood in stupid silence. Mrs. Mutiso's mouth kept moving like a fish but no sound came out.

From the kitchen window, Priscilla had an unparalleled

view of the drama that ensued outside. She lapped it up, taking note of body language and specific curse words and accusations Mr. Mutiso levelled on his wife. She took in the degree of stupidity in Kariuk's stance. Mrs. Mutiso's posture was now a crumpled version of her normal stature. She'd need the details to retell the story. Needing a witness, she called for Kanono who'd come downstairs seeing her opportunity to watch her after-school TV shows now that her uncle had vacated his spot.

~

Mrs. Mutiso felt the migraine lick at her temples the second she saw her husband's car pulling up round the corner. With practice, he'd begun to sound more and more like his parents when they argued. It was as if he also believed she had seduced him, pursued him and tricked him into marriage. His memory of their time together had been erased and replaced with an alternate story that suited his family's narrative much better. In this new story she was a villain who'd robbed him of his life burning potential. Did he know that even when they'd first met, he'd been up to nothing in particular? That he was the kind of man destined to achieve nothing even though he was born to high-achievers? That he was always looking for someone to blame for his pending failure and Mrs. Mutiso had arrived right on time to be his scapegoat for the rest of his life?

She saw all of this with a searing clarity now. It could have been any other woman in front of him and he would still have found a way to blame her for who he'd become, or not become.

'Is this how you put my name to shame? In front of all our neighbours?' Mr. Mutiso's anger had made him puff up, his tie threatened to choke him.

Mrs. Mutiso was about to ask her husband if they could talk

inside their home when he mentioned the neighbours. She looked up and saw Priscilla and Kanono staring through their kitchen window. Their eyes met before Priscilla turned quickly, pushing Kanono's head down as well.

'Abraham, Abraham, people are watching.' She heard the hopelessness in her voice. It acted as a trigger. She was slipping now into the dark abyss. She always came back, yes and thank God too, but each time one of the episodes happened she found herself closer and closer to the hole, slipping down faster, grasping harder. It was as if her mind didn't know how to support her to navigate her reality. She didn't get to heal and go back to safe ground, no, she began each breakdown exactly where she'd left the last.

Mr. Mutiso, knowing the signs, tried to drag his wife into the house but it was already too late. She began to struggle for air then lashed at him and lost her balance. She fell down writhing and begging to be released so that she could breath. Kariuki stared in a horrified silence as Mr. Mutiso dragged his wife into their gate then kicked it closed. Priscilla and Kanono caught everything from their kitchen window.

~

Mama Kanono had had a long day at work. They were expanding the business. Already they'd rented out a bigger space, still downtown, right next to their old store in fact. Mr. Mathai came and went as he pleased. When he was at the store, he spent his time engaged in drawn out conversations with the employees and customers before abruptly leaving on pressing business which Mama Kanono could never fathom.

True to her resolve, when Mama Kanono arrived, Priscilla did not tell her that Mrs. Mutiso had been by with samples of clothes for her to look at. She'd taken them for herself, sure they would not be missed. Kariuki was still dumbfounded by the scene that took place earlier. He spent the evening in morose silence and even went to bed earlier than usual.

By this time, Priscilla had already shared the saga with the Kiosk patrons on a sunset stroll to buy onions and tomato paste (two items that were in plenty in the Mathai house). As the estate sat for dinner that evening, the news of Mrs. Mutiso's episode had spread through Malaba with frightening speed.

The estate was divided. On one hand, it was agreed that Mrs. Mutiso was a seductress of the first degree, the kind of woman who could steal your husband as you turned to pick curry powder off the shelf in the supermarket. Just like that! On the other hand, her behaviour that afternoon was the kind of thing that got people admitted to Mathare. Surely they could save her before it came to that, after all, the estate was still smarting from the deaths of Baba and Mama Sally and their inaction the day the deaths occurred. Underneath all of this high-minded talk was the realisation that everything that had been spoken about Mrs. Mutiso prior to this event had been conjecture, rumours without sails, but finally, they had something real backed by evidence: Mrs. Mutiso had madness in her.

~

A committee was assembled within a few hours of the event. They discussed the episode then voted for a representative party of Mrs. Karanja and Mrs. Shah to go speak with Mama Kanono about the matter.

Mama Kanono was on her way to bed when she heard her doorbell ring. The committee explained the situation to Mama Kanono, the story already distorted as it had travelled the length and breadth of the estate several times. 'We must do something Beatrice.' Mrs. Karanja spoke in her slow emphatic way—a voice bred for the pulpit. 'We cannot sit and let a marriage be destroyed whilst God is our witness.'

Mama Kanono looked from Mrs. Karanja's earnest face to Mrs. Shah even more earnest face. She didn't know what they expected her to do about the matter. In her brief acquaintance with Mrs. Mutiso, she'd only encountered Mr. Mutiso a handful of times. Despite the fact that the Mutisos had a far more comfortable and luxurious home, Mrs. Mutiso always insisted on coming to visit or if Mama Kanono uncharacteristically chose to visit her, she would contrive a way for them to go back to Mama Kanono's home. Perhaps there was a dish she'd forgotten at Mama Kanono's which she just needed to pick up immediately, or a dress she'd bought Kanono she wanted the little girl to try before her very eyes. They'd get back to the Mathai household and even after the visit came to its natural end, Mrs. Mutiso would not leave for hours thereafter. After the first few visits, Mama Kanono stopped enquiring about the twins and Mr. Mutiso. Both topics seemed to confuse and upset Mrs. Mutiso.

'What do you want me to do?'

'We were thinking,' here Mrs. Shah paused and looked to Mrs. Karanja for her supporting nod to go forward, 'We were thinking that maybe you could...you could...I think someone should go and see how she is doing.'

'But it's ten p.m.' It wasn't that Mama Kanono felt no concern for her friend. She knew how private Mrs. Mutiso was, in fact, it was the quality that bound them together. Even now, after a year of relating with Mrs. Mutiso she knew only the barest of details about her friend's life. Married. Twins. Estranged from in-laws. Possible family back home. Housewife. Aspiring business woman.

'Yes but in case she needs help...' Mrs. Shah gave her a

meaningful look, a look that said, remember Baba and Mama Sally, remember how we all ignored that scream?

'Okay, I'll go check on her first thing tomorrow morning. Okay?'

The women were not too happy with the response but even they understood how late it was and how unseemly it was to be visiting with neighbours so late into the night.

~

Mrs. Mutiso, expecting that Priscilla had passed on her message, waited all evening for Mama Kanono's ring on her doorbell. Mama Kanono had a fast, short ring. The doorbell did not ring that night.

She waited and waited, waited until she saw the lights go out at the Mathais' home. She sat in her living room, regal as ever, waiting. When it was clear Mama Kanono was not coming, Mrs. Mutiso went upstairs to the bedroom she shared with the fast asleep Mr. Mutiso. For one moment, she considered suffocating her husband. In the next she had slipped into their bed, courage gone.

CHAPTER SIXTEEN

A Visitor, August 11th, 2012

Mrs. Mutiso's latest business venture, event planning came to her overnight. She named the business Twin Events, after her daughters whom she saw once every other year or so. After university, they'd both settled in Germany. They made the trip home at irregular intervals. So far Twin Events was buoyed by her sole client, Beatrice Mathai. It was Beatrice who suggested, upon announcing her engagement, that Mrs. Mutiso could maybe be a part of the wedding planning to draw her friend out of the house. Mrs. Mutiso had taken the suggestion and run with it appointing herself as the wedding planner and printing business cards within a week of the engagement being announced.

~

'I have a friend who has three different salons she goes to.' Mrs. Mutiso came out of her kitchen holding a tray with two mugs of tea. Nyambura sat on one of the wingback chairs staring at the beach wallpaper that was ripped in several places. There was mould leaking through the top left corner of the wallpaper ruining the colours, making them bleed into each other. When we grow up, the larger than life memories of our childhood shrink to accommodate the reality in which they were created and existed in. The homes we grew up in become smaller, our parents are now two inches shorter, the branch we fell off, breaking a leg and spraining a wrist doesn't seem so high off the ground after all and yet in the case of the Kenya Nyambura left eight years ago, it was as if the country expanded and stretched like a new dawn. Was she imagining it or had the roads grown wider and smoother since President Moi's departure? But here, in Mrs. Mutiso's home, Nyambura's memory of the grand dame and the grand house did not measure up to the reality of the woman nor the house.

'That seems like such a hassle. Why not just stick to one?' Nyambura took her mug and placed it on the coffee table next to the chair. She noticed the dust on the table and the particles of dust floating through the air, illuminated by the light coming from the window behind her. Mrs. Mutiso had a Miss Havisham quality too her—the old decaying house, the overgrown backyard, the same dirra she'd worn when they used to live in Malaba. Back then, the dirra had looked elegant, holding her curves expertly, now the hem was frayed and the colourful pattern faded until all you could decipher were suggestions of colour.

'They are like men, you know? Come too often and something is wrong with you, not with the way they did the weave. So the first salon is for the weave, the second is to correct any problems with the way the first did it, and the third to remove the weave and put on braids when the itching becomes unbearable.' As she spoke, Nyambura had the impression the friend was Mrs. Mutiso, or rather, it was the old Mrs. Mutiso. This one before her wore a curly-kit on short unevenly chopped hair.

Mrs. Mutiso sat opposite Nyambura and began toying with the lip of her mug, acrylic-nailed index finger (at least a month overdue for removal), swirling around the mug in slow idle circles. She was distracted as she spoke. They had been going this way for the last thirty minutes. Their conversation felt like a stream meandering slowly down the afternoon. A stillness hung over Mrs. Mutiso as if the stream was just about to crest and hurtle into a fast moving river before plunging down.

A week after the wedding, her mother away on her honeymoon, Nyambura was restless and killing time before her flight back to New York when a thought passed through her mind. When she parked her car outside Mrs. Mutiso's house and walked into the compound (the gate was wide open and broken off on one of the hinges), she'd met Mrs. Mutiso staring vacantly at the lot that used to be their home which now had a seven-storey apartment block.

'My dear!' Mrs. Mutiso exclaimed when Nyambura walked into the kitchen. 'Oh, my dear, you should have told me you were coming.' She looked around her house apologetically. 'I'd have told Mr. Mutiso to be here to meet you,' she added looking flustered. Mr. Mutiso had separated from Mrs. Mutiso several years ago though this did not stop Mrs. Mutiso from referring to him as if he'd just stepped out for a coffee with friends and was on his way back home. The last anyone heard of him, he'd married again (in a traditional ceremony), to a girl who looked like a younger version of Mrs. Mutiso though this account of the state of things was unverified. Nyambura smiled and assured her it was no problem at all, she just wanted to check on her mother's best friend.

'So how is the honeymoon going?' Mrs. Mutiso asked as she sipped her tea.

'Well, I think. Steven sent us a picture of mum walking barefoot on the beach—in a swimming costume.' Mrs. Mutiso laughed and Nyambura felt her heart flutter with joy at the reaction. It felt like a personal triumph to make Mrs. Mutiso laugh. As Nyambura sipped her tea, a memory arrived unbidden: an afternoon like this one, standing with Priscilla at their kitchen window, witnessing Mrs. Mutiso struggle for air, lose her balance, fall, get dragged into their home by Mr. Mutiso as if she were a sack of potatoes.

'Oh! But do you remember the Christmas parties we used to have? They were so big. That was my first experience with event planning and didn't I do a fantastic job?' Mrs. Mutiso clapped once at the memory then laughed. 'You know that's when I knew you were going to be a star. You were so good in the plays, and funny too, you always made your mother and I laugh.' Mrs. Mutiso got up as if the memory had breathed life into her. Nyambura tried to recall the plays. Her mother had always appeared to be pensive and distracted whenever she stole a glance at her. Her father was her champion and cheerleader. He'd shout encouraging things from the sidelines as if the play were a sports match.

'I was just looking at the albums the other day,' Mrs. Mutiso said as she went over to her little writing bureau which, like all the furniture, was covered in a fine film of dust. There were two photo albums at the edge of the bureau that looked like they had just been freshly thumbed through.

'We used to hire the photographer for the event so I kept the originals—here, come and look.' Mrs. Mutiso brought one of the albums to the three-seater sofa where they could both look at the photos together. Nyambura got up to join her.

'Oh wow! These are so many. You kept all of them?'

Nyambura had once asked her mother what happened to their childhood photos and Beatrice had shrugged as she read through her bank statements, 'I don't know, your father used to keep them.' This was the evening before she was due to fly out to the UK to join the A-levels boarding school her mother had picked out from a brochure. In his lifetime, Mr. Mathai took a multitude of pictures. He went through a phase where he fancied himself a photographer and bought a camera that he would go snapping away at everyone with regardless of how mundane the activity they were engaged in was. Whether it was Mama Kanono drinking tea in the morning, Mr. Karanja opening his gate, Ng'ang'a doing a stock take, there were thousands of pictures. Except now, no one knew where he'd kept them. 'What do you mean dad kept them? He isn't here so how am I supposed to ask him?' And so began another one of the Beatrice-Nyambura arguments.

'Look at how small you children were.' Mrs. Mutiso was flipping through the album, her hand caressing the polythene photo covers. 'Isn't this that friend of yours? What was her name—the Karanja girl. I've been trying to remember her name since the wedding but I can't.' Mrs. Mutiso tapped a red finger on Esther's cornrowed head in the picture.

'That's Esther.'

'Yes! I knew it was a Bible name. Do you remember what those other siblings of hers were called? They had such hard names it's like their parents went to that chapter in the Bible about Jesus' lineage and picked the hardest names from there.' Nyambura laughed which caught Mrs. Mutiso off-guard. After a moment she grinned and laughed as well.

'Are you two still friends?' Mrs. Mutiso asked as they stared at the photo.

'Who, Esther? Uh…yeah, I guess.'

'She was always so quiet and a little sad.' Mrs. Mutiso tilted her head as she looked at the picture. Nyambura noticed how she didn't talk about the twins who, even in the picture looked like they were not part of the tableau. Her memory of Mrs. Mutiso was that of a solitary woman.

'Um…' Nyambura saw her chance. 'At the wedding, you

said something.' Mrs. Mutiso looked up quickly. 'You said you had three children, not two…'

'I said that?' Nyambura knew Mrs. Mutiso was pretending to forget. 'Oh, I don't know where that came from. There's only the twins. This is your first performance!' Mrs. Mutiso tapped a finger excitedly at another photo. Nyambura as Kanono as one of the three wise men. Nyambura let the topic slide for the moment. 'Do you know, every time your turn to speak would come your dad—God rest him in peace—would insist everyone stay quiet so that he could hear you,' Mrs. Mutiso said as she passed another picture of the Nativity play.

'Aunty Carol?'

'Yes dear?' Mrs. Mutiso said as she continued to look through the pictures.

'Did you also know my father was not dad?' Mrs. Mutiso's hand froze in the middle of turning the page.

'Wh-wh-what?' she asked, the blood draining from her face.

'It's okay I already know,' Nyambura said worried that she'd pushed Mrs. Mutiso to the brink of a heart attack.

'What do you mean you know?' Mrs. Mutiso looked around wildly as if she was trying to find an escape hatch to disappear from.

'I've known.'

'What?'

'I thought I'd bring it up with mum after the wedding but she seemed so happy and I've never seen her so happy, so I didn't want to ruin it for her, but I…you are her closest friend…I thought you'd know and I just wanted to ask you a few questions, if that's okay?'

'Wh-what?' Mrs. Mutiso scooted to the end of the couch.

'I…' Nyambura had to calm her down. 'I found out years

ago. Don't worry, you've not done anything—mum won't know I came here today.'

'How?' Mrs. Mutiso asked, her voice shook.

'I overheard the two of you talking about him…my real father…'

'We never talked about him.' Mrs. Mutiso shook her head vigorously then slapped her hand onto her mouth. Beatrice would be mad, she'd be very mad. Had she betrayed her friend? Oh God, had she let something slip in the conversation this afternoon? She thought back frantically.

'No, aunty, please you didn't know I was there.' Nyambura saw that Mrs. Mutiso was not taking the news very well. 'You didn't know, it wasn't your fault.' Mrs. Mutiso was shivering now. 'I'm so sorry, I shouldn't have asked you now. It was wrong of me.' Nyambura tried to calm her down but Mrs. Mutiso looked as if she'd seen a ghost. She grabbed Nyambura's hand.

'You weren't here. Do you understand me? You didn't come here. I did not see you,' she said.

'Of course, I promise. I'm so sorry.' In truth, Nyambura had done an admirable job over the years of convincing herself she'd misheard their conversation and she'd have continued to convince herself of this if it had not been for Mrs. Mutiso's speech at the wedding and her mother's reaction just as Mrs. Mutiso said '...our children have something in common…'

Mrs. Mutiso's landline rang just then. It was in what used to be Mr. Mutiso's office. Mrs. Mutiso turned to face the sound of the ringing phone and if Nyambura thought she couldn't get worse, Mrs. Mutiso proved her wrong. 'Don't answer it!' she snapped even though Nyambura had not made any move that suggested she was going to. 'I'm not here!' she said as if the person ringing her phone could hear her. 'I *said*, I'm not here.

No one is here. No one is here.' The ringing stopped and silence took over except for the blaring horn of a matatu outside every once in a while.

Then the phone rang again. And then it stopped. And then it rang again.

Nyambura watched as Mrs. Mutiso disintegrated with each phone call.

'I can disconnect it for you?' she offered.

'What?' Mrs. Mutiso looked surprised to see her sitting there.

'The phone, I can disconnect it so that no one calls you.'

'You can do that for me?'

'Yeah, sure, it won't take a second.' She jumped up and went to the office then pulled the plug that connected the phone to the network. 'See,' she said holding up the wire. 'Now they can't call.'

'Th-thank you my dear.' Mrs. Mutiso sank back into the chair and breathed in deeply. 'I keep telling him, I don't know, but he won't listen.' she spoke to herself. From the way the afternoon had gone, Nyambura was becoming weary of asking Mrs. Mutiso questions.

'Let me make you another cup of tea,' she offered, not wanting to leave Mrs. Mutiso but not knowing what to do.

CHAPTER SEVENTEEN

Kevin, January, 1993

Malaba estate grew swollen with new residents the year after the elections. Tribal clashes across the country had people fleeing into the capital city en masse. Some were lucky enough to pack a few belongings, most ran in the middle of the night with the clothes on their backs, hoping their children were just behind them. Many never returned home for what was not torched was repossessed.

The ripple effect for Ng'ang'a was another excellent financial year. He'd doubled then tripled and finally quadrupled the stock he ordered to cater to the new additions in Malaba Estate. His only child, who'd been attending a government high school with fewer chairs than there were students, was promptly moved to a private school near to the Kiosk. Ng'ang'a's heart filled with pride each time he saw his son walking up the little hill to his Kiosk dressed in his uniform (sky blue shorts, grey shirt and red tie with long grey socks adorned with blue strips at the top).

The only thing that threatened his joy was the fact that he'd only been able to afford a good school so late in his son's education. The boy was in Form One for the third time. In this new school, he was struggling to catch up with his peers, the gaps in his government meted education showing like a grin missing its front teeth. The school took one look at his grades and insisted he repeat his first three years of secondary school if he had any hope of attaining anything above a D in his final KCSE examinations. There were whole chunks of the syllabus that he simply did not know. On his first mid-term exam, Kevin came last in his class by so far it would have been hilarious if it wasn't a tragedy.

'Hi dad,' Kevin greeted Ng'ang'a as he let himself into the Kiosk.

'How was school?' This was Ng'ang'a's everyday enquiry.

'Eh! It's killing me, but at least I still go,' Kevin responded already getting to work looking through the day's sales, preparing to take over for his father. He had begun helping out after school since he joined the private school where, much to his father's frustration, the student's were let out very early (four p.m.).

'You should be reading. Why do I pay so much money for you to go to school half- day?' Ng'ang'a complained regularly though he only half meant it. Whilst, he'd have preferred it if his son spent his afternoons in school studying, he'd begun to look forward to their afternoons together at the Kiosk.

They were a small and intimate family of two, Kevin's mother having passed away when he was just seven years old. She was crossing the road. The car that hit her never stopped, didn't slow down, passed over her as if she were just a speed bump. 'Your wife—a demon ran over her!' That's what the little girl who'd been sent to call him from the garage he used to work in said. A demon. Splattered across the road was his wife of eight years, the tomatoes she'd gone to buy intermingled with her organs.

Ng'ang'a passed his son the cashbox to count and double-check the money they'd earned that day. Kevin took it and sat on the little stool at the corner of the Kiosk opposite the door, where no customer could see him counting the money. There had been a few thefts at neighbouring kiosks recently. Just a week ago, one of Malaba's residents was hijacked at the gate of the estate. The Askari manning the gate had refused to open it for the resident who screamed and begged for help. The thugs finally stabbed him, though not fatally. He was being unnecessarily loud.

Kevin counted the money in silence. When he was done he made a record of the amount and put the money back into the cash box. He began rearranging the goods in the store. Ensuring that the ungas and packets of sugar were aligned and the bread stacked perfectly, the chewing-gum in neat rows—

~

'Mikate mbili tafadhali.' A customer had arrived, signalling the beginning of the afternoon rush.

'Priscilla, me, I thought you had left Malaba! When was the last time I saw you?' Ng'ang'a began as he turned to get the packets of bread and found his son holding them out for him.

'Eh! It's been busy. Ata I've not gone to church one Sunday since their relatives came. When I go, will I even remember what God looks like?' Priscilla responded as she took the bread and handed Ng'ang'a the exact change for it. Church was an elaborate affair for Priscilla. She began to prepare for the Sunday service as early as five a.m. when she'd hot comb her natural hair using a Kimbo tin filled with hot coals. The year she relaxed her hair, she added make-up and intricate hairstyles to her routine so that the time spent getting ready was still the same as when she'd been frying her natural hair into straightness. This is to say nothing of the outfits she managed to pull off every Sunday. She bought many of these pieces from the celebrated Inama Boutiques of Nairobi (a neat little euphemism for second-hand clothes sellers who showcased their clothes on spread out gunny sacks on the floor of markets like Kenyatta market so that you'd have to bend to pick up an item of interest), and the dye jobs she did on everything from blouses to rubber shoes. On her way to church, she'd stop for a photo right by the Kiosk where the mtu wa picha was always stationed on Sunday mornings, ready to take pictures of families as they left for church. The next week, as you posed for a new picture, you were handed last week's copies plus the negatives. Priscilla hang the pictures on her bedroom wall in careful chronological order and the extra copies and negatives were stored in a leather briefcase she'd permanently borrowed from Mr. Mathai who never noticed its absence.

'We've had so many of Mathais and even Mama Kanono's relatives come to stay with us since elections, and they can't even bring someone else to help me. I'm washing clothes mpaka usiku!' Priscilla launched into a tirade about the Mathais which was not without merit. It was true, the people who felt the greatest brunt at the mass exodus of relatives into the city were the workers in the homes. There were more mouths to feed, more children to educate, more people to clothe.

As she was speaking, Priscilla noticed the boy in the shadow of the dark kiosk. He worked quietly, arranging products, marking down things in a notebook and from time to time, looking up to mutter something. She'd never seen him before.

'Ng'ang'a! Don't tell me. Is this your son?' she connected when Kevin turned around and the light from the meshed window that seperated the customers from the Kiosk lit his face enough for her to see his features. He was his father's replica, from the high forehead to the wide nose and the broad back. He was his father, except for the height. Already taller than Ng'ang'a he would grow by three more inches to a very satisfying six-foot-one by adulthood.

'Haiya! You've not met my son? Kevin, come out and greet one of my very good friends.' Priscilla, like many before her, nursed a crush on Ng'ang'a because of the way he made you feel important and special. He always had a compliment or a thoughtful word of encouragement for his customers. This glowing introduction to his son made her beam with joy.

'Kevin? And your other name?' Kevin had obediently come out of the kiosk to greet Priscilla.

'Kariuki.' he responded with a firm handshake.

'Ng'ang'a, I didn't know you had a son this big. He is literally a man now!' Priscilla continued to pump Kevin's hand as she spoke to Ng'ang'a. Kevin stood beside her in a shy silence.

'God is good! And now see he is even helping his father in the kiosk.' Ng'ang'a couldn't hide his pride.

'One day it will be his!' Priscilla added in excitement.

Ng'ang'a frowned. 'No.'

'Eh? Kwani who are you leaving it to? Si tunakufa sisi wote?'

'This is not something you leave to your children,' Ng'ang'a said.

Kevin watched his father's reaction with dismay.

'Then what happens to him?' Priscilla had completely forgotten the errand that brought her to the Kiosk.

'He will do better. He must do better. This thing can be blown by the wind tomorrow. It doesn't even have a foundation. If there was nothing in the Kiosk, I could pick it up and throw it with one hand. Is that the kind of thing you bequeath to your son?' Ng'ang'a breathed heavily as he spoke. His dream was to invest in a more permanent space where he'd have a bigger supermarket that people could actually enter and shop in at their leisure. From there, he'd open up more branches all over Nairobi, a Ng'ang'a's in every neighbourhood! But getting a bank loan to start a business when you have no collateral (he was crushed to find out the Kiosk was not collateral and if we are being honest, the words he'd just spoken were an imitation of what the bank's business manager had said to him upon his application for a loan), was a fool's errand.

~

'Habari ya leo?' A new customer arrived and the group disbanded. Priscilla took her bread, advised Kevin not to play in school and walked back to the Mathais' house.

Kevin stooped to re-enter the Kiosk and continued re-arranging the goods meticulously noting down inventory. Ng'ang'a turned to serve the new customer, complimented them on their new hair cut, a perfect box-cut. He shook off his conversation with Priscilla. If he indulged himself in thoughts of what could have been, he knew he'd not wake up and he needed to, to ensure Kevin got a solid future and a chance at a life he could only dream of for himself. Kevin brought Ng'ang'a a cup of tea and told him to go sit down and relax as he took over serving the customers. Ng'ang'a switched the radio to KBC's English Service before he walked out of the Kiosk to sit on one of the plastic chairs he'd bought to host his customers. There was nothing quite like American country music to end a long day.

CHAPTER EIGHTEEN

Bible Study, May, 1995

It was Wednesday Bible Study but from the furore in the room, it was clear the regular program had been abandoned for something far more pressing. Malaba's residents were in an uproar about Ng'ang'a's new business decision to sell condoms in his store. The condom ads were all over the T.V. *'Maisha iko sawa na Trust!'* the adverts proclaimed. The prominent ad featured a damsel in car-distress and her knight in shining armour, a mechanic who fortuitously forgot his tools of trade somewhere so that he was forced to fix the tear on her exhaust pipe with a condom he suggestively (but casually), pulled out of his back pocket.

"We are a Christian nation. We cannot have such filth on our TVs with our children watching!" and "Shame on KTN for selling this nonsense to our children!" and "The Government needs to speed up this investigation on Devil Worshippers they keep telling us they are doing because see now they are taking over our TVs!" These were but a few of the sentiments expressed every time KTN ran the Trust Condoms ad campaign.

'You can't be serious!' Janet, the perpetually unwell, she of house forty-four said. Despite her best efforts, she never fully integrated with the rest of the Bible Study goers. She chimed in loudly hoping that the conversation would swing to her side of the room.

'Well, it's not the worst thing is it?' Mrs. Shah said. Despite it not being her intention, she was in the habit of shocking her neighbours with her liberal views.

'Mrs. Shah, sometimes I think you cannot be serious. If you knew Harpreet was buying those…those…things would you be happy?' Mr. Karanja asked in consternation. Every month, he'd ask Mrs. Karanja if it was wise to let an unbeliever amongst them, especially one as oblivious as Mrs. Shah. A few times, he'd ended the Bible Study with an impromptu come-to-Jesus prayer hoping that Mrs. Shah would choose to receive salvation but whilst she never did, she always clapped for those who put their hand up when Mr. Karanja asked, 'Who is ready to accept Jesus Christ as their Lord and personal Saviour?'. Having never been to church, she did not know that one was meant to have their eyes shut for the come-to-Jesus prayers. If one opened their eyes a crack, because the curiosity was sometimes overwhelming, one was not meant to say out loud, 'Good on you, Mr. Mbiu!' or 'Congratulations, Maggie!' to the lost souls who were trying to seek redemption in private.

'But she wouldn't. She sits at home reading all the time.' Mrs. Shah responded to Mr. Karanja's question in a tone that spoke of disappointment in her daughter's lack of an adventurous teenage spirit.

~

So how did the news of the condoms come to overtake the Bible Study? Earlier that day, Mrs. Karanja had sent her two eldest daughters (Priscilla always referred to them as the witches of Malaba and not without reason), to buy onions for lunch having uncharacteristically run out. They came back sans onions but carrying the hot-off-the-Kiosk-Press news of the condoms. They'd never seen a packed of condoms *live-live.*

It was like staring at the face of sin and living to tell the story. It was exhilarating! When Bible Study convened that evening, Mrs. Karanja brought it up as a prayer request for the opening prayers of the Bible Study. It was already eight-thirty and Mr. Karanja had not gotten to the prayers yet because he couldn't get his neighbours off the topic long enough to concentrate on prayer.

'And he has put them at the window right next to the chewing gum. I thought he was a Christian.' Janet, knowing that information was currency, bartered this piece of information hoping it would earn her their interest.

'And he has his son selling them—exposing him to sin at such a young age.' Someone else had topped her story with a more juicy detail.

'Oh that young man selling is his son? He's handsome don't you think?' Mrs. Shah winked at no one in particular then giggled.

'Mrs. Shah that is not a man he is a boy.' Mr. Karanja corrected her though he'd never met Kevin, or gone to the Kiosk for that matter.

'I always thought Ng'ang'a was not a strong Christian. I've never even seen him pray,' Janet tried again, hoping someone would ask her to expound on her theory.

'We have to force him to stop selling them. For our children's sake, we have to protect the sanctity of this estate.' Mr. Karanja stood up as if he were about to march to Ng'ang'a's Kiosk that moment.

'But surely, we can't tell Ng'ang'a what to sell. He is only selling what demand dictates. If people don't buy them then he won't need to re-stock them, and because our estate is his main source of customers, and most of us are gathered here today, we can all agree not to buy,' Mr. Mathai said, seeing his moment, and like a pro, taking it.

The room grew silent. He had made an excellent point. At any rate, everyone who knew Ng'ang'a was so fond of him, no one wanted to be the person to ask him to stop selling condoms.

'I was about to also suggest that,' Mr. Karanja added quickly, seeing the positive reaction that Mr. Mathai's statement had elicited from their neighbours. He was resentful of how easily Mr. Mathai manoeuvred prickly situations. There was also the fact that (and he wasn't being petty he assured himself), Mr. Mathai received way more "Amens" and "Yes Lords" during his prayers than he did. Whilst Mr. Karanja did not fancy himself a jealous man, it irked him that a man who quoted the Bible wrong and had once said "In the book of Abraham", got more amens than an ordained cleric.

~

It was just as well that Mr. Karanja did not march up to 'Ng'ang'a's Kiosk to tell him to stop selling condoms. It would not have ended well for him. In an uncanny piece of coincidence, the same day the Trust distributor approached Ng'ang'a with a signing-on offer (five packs for the price of four), the newspaper ran an article on the Catholic church's protest against condoms. The image the newspaper chose to go with was a photo of protesters holding up posters with the words, "CONDOMS=ABORTION + HIV". The supercilious tone of the posters, not to mention the misinformation about HIV that the newspaper had effectively spread in running that picture had him shaking as he unpacked the condoms. He surveyed the space inside his Kiosk. Putting the condoms at the back defeated the point. He wanted a potential customer to be able to say, "gimme that one", and point directly to it without having to go through the embarrassment of asking for the condoms out loud. They would have to be placed at the front. But where? He could build a rack for them, but that would take some time. He chose to put them on top of the box that housed the chewing gums and various other sweets.

The task accomplished, he set about preparing for the day, steeling himself for people's reactions to the packets of Trust that had not been there the day before. Most of the people who came to the Kiosk that day were too shy to say anything. Some looked questioningly from the condom box to Ng'ang'a, others still enquired if this was a wise decision—it could chase away customers who were not comfortable being so near sex. That last one made him laugh.

Ng'ang'a's younger sister (and only sibling), had passed away nearly five years ago. She was diagnosed with HIV in 1984, the same year the newspapers reported that the first case of HIV had been discovered in Kenya. He remembered skimming the article in disinterest, chuckling when he read that the government's response to the new and potentially deadly virus was that the case was not of national concern because the patient who'd contracted it was Ugandan. As if sickness was so gracious as to distinguish between nationalities! He put the paper aside as soon as his sister entered the house, ready to do battle.

'Where have you been all night? You think this a hostel you can just come and go? Even a hostel has closing hours!' He raged and rallied against her lifestyle choices. Why was she forever at Sans Chique, where it was a known fact that women who frequented the club were call-girls not patrons? The last detail was inaccurate, because in truth he had no idea where his sister went in the evening, and he'd never been to Sans Chique to know what the demographics of the clientele were. But this was anger and anger is not a relation of rational thinking.

On this particular day, her silence raised his ire. He heard himself tell her he'd washed his hands off her, she could go and live wherever she spent the night for all he cared. He often replayed that day, though he knew it was torturous to do so. Maybe, he'd think, maybe if I'd been less harsh she'd have opened up and I could have helped her. It was no use. She was dead. Now that the opportunity had presented itself, he was not going to let another young person contract this virulent virus because of misplaced morals. He would sell the condoms. No doubt, no debate with Malaba's residents.

It would be too revealing to share the names of the residents present at that month's Bible study who ended up buying condoms from Ng'ang'a's Kiosk. However, in the natural way of things, yesterday's outrage became tomorrow's normal and before long, the condom story had died down. Time was marching on relentlessly.

CHAPTER NINETEEN

Mr. Mathai, June, 1995

The phone booth which stood just inside Malaba's estate gate was often the biggest source of annoyance for the Askaris. The only thing more annoying was the monthly "Denied Services" list. It was a list of Malaba Estate members who hadn't paid their service charge on time. Late payment meant that you could not enjoy the services provided by estate management, the hallmark of which was the Askaris opening the gate for you. It wasn't the residents who were always on the list that annoyed them, but those who periodically forgot to pay on time. This latter group did not know how to behave in the face of what they saw as the ultimate humiliation, opening a gate for themselves or their guests whenever they had to get into or out of the estate, until such a time as their service charge payment was settled. There was also the knowledge that perched on the little hill just behind the gate, sitting around Ng'ang'a's Kiosk, were enough gossip mongers for the rumour of their liquidity crisis to reach their homes before they did. These periodic non-payers would become indignant, throw their favourite curse words at the Askaris, and threaten not to move as they held up the other residents in the cars behind them waiting to go through the gate.

The exception to this performed fury was Mr. Mathai. Mama Kanono had sunk their savings into expanding the spare parts store into a fully-fledged garage just off Parklands road. They'd also invested in their first two second-hand cars the small beginnings of what would become a lucrative car dealership business resulting in the BMW contract later for Mama Kanono. With so little cash to spare, Mama Kanono had decided to delay the service charge payment. When he got to the gate, Mr. Mathai jumped out of his car and opened it whilst shouting a greeting to all who happened to be around.

'Habari ya leo,' he greeted the Askaris. He drove into the estate, and walked back to close the gate, then began to drive off when he heard his name called out. From the rearview mirror, he saw one of the askaris clapping from the phone booth, trying to get his attention. There was a phone call for him.

He reversed and parked the car on the pavement. The phone booth smelled faintly like piss.

'Hello?' Mr. Mathai spoke into the phone.

There was a crackling on the phone then a distant 'Hello…hello…hello…'

'Hello? I can't hear you.' Mr. Mathai's voice got louder to make up for the person's lack of clarity on the other side.

'Mr. Mathai?' At once, his heart leaped and his body froze at the familiar voice. It was her. Kristin. Kristin with the breasts he knew for certain God had taken time moulding.

'How did you get this number? I told you—I'll call you on Saturday!' This was too close for comfort. She was calling at home? Well, practically home. What if Mama Kanono drove in at just that moment? Who would he say he was on the phone with? They run a business together, lived together—there was no one he could be talking to that she wouldn't know. It would raise suspicion.

The soft voice choked and he heard what sounded like stifled tears.

'Mr. Mathai…please we need to meet before Saturday. Please, it's important.' She didn't sound like the confident girl who'd approached him at Njuguna's and said, 'Something tells me you're the one buying us drinks tonight.' Her forwardness had surprised him. With the others, they had to be coaxed and cajoled out of their shells. Kristin came without a shell which led him to believe she understood how such liaisons went.

'No, you know I can't. I have to be at the store the whole week now that Mama Kanono is at the garage.'

'We can meet in town then.' The very thought of meeting one of these girls so close to their store—in the same five-kilometre radius bordered on sinful. He, like many of his contemporaries, did not believe in monogamy. He did not see anything wrong with affairs. They had bigger sexual appetites, they reasoned and he couldn't possibly fuck Mama Kanono from the back and wake up the next morning to sit across from her at the breakfast table eating nduma and ngwache.

That's what these other girls were for. It was never to be misunderstood as a preference for the girls over the wives. It wasn't like in the West where men found younger women and mistook sex for love then threw the towel in on a perfectly good marriage to marry the younger girl. Mr. Mathai and his ilk were the very definition of having your cake and eating it. The faithful wife who stayed home, bore you heirs or insurance policies, depending on your prevailing economic circumstances, as the pretty little things told you mundane stories as they let you finger them in the car before dropping them back on campus.

What was integral, the cornerstone of such affairs really, was boundaries. The most important were that:

1. The girls and the wives strictly run in different circles.

2. A man was never to tempt fate into revealing his cards by entertaining the girls in a place frequented by his wife, or communicate with the girl in a manner that might raise suspicion should he happen to be found by his wife.

In one phone call, Kristin had challenged both boundaries unforgivably. When this happened, as it sometimes did, a man was to do the right thing by his family and let the girl go gently, slowly, to avoid backlash where she'd storm into his wife's workplace demanding reparations for poor treatment. He knew all this and was about to engage the first stage of the pull-back manoeuvre when she hit him with the failure of his first and most important pull back that never happened: 'I'm pregnant.'

~

'Now listen to me. You've been a fool once, you can't be a fool twice. Have you told anyone else?' It was Wednesday evening. Forty-five hours exactly since hearing the news that he had gotten a girl pregnant. Mr. Mathai called his cousin Kamau out of pure instinct. Kamau had come out of pure curiosity.

Kamau looked at Mr. Mathai who was looking rather harassed, then heaved a heavy burdened sigh and swivelled back in his bar stool to face his beer.

'What do I do now? She's threatening to—'

Kamau sighed again. He'd dropped out of school before completing high-school, but he more than made up for his lack of further education in street smarts. He was the man who knew who had what, how much they were willing to sell it for, who had money, how much they were willing to part with it for. He understood and moved deftly within the circles of Kenya's elite and played the role of benevolent intermediary to all parties involved in a transaction, and from that he earned a handsome commission that saw his financial status rise from nothing to tens of acres spread across Kenya, a handsome house in Nairobi and who knows what other assets. This was the first time he'd broker a deal between a man and his mistress.

'Times are changing. Now they get an education and they think they have rights. There's no point in Mama Kanono finding out. Why? You are happy why should you ruin your happiness? This is what I suggest—' They were interrupted by the waiter who set down a board of meat and a dish of ugali and kachumbari.

'Let me talk to her. I will arrange it for you. She will never disturb you again. But Mathai, you understand you will have to pay for this child eh? But don't worry I'll arrange it for you.'

Mr. Mathai was not one to wallow in self pity for too long. He was loath to waste a perfectly good evening ruminating on what had already happened. He was only too happy to drop the subject and join in with the other men in the bar for the laughter and conversation they all came for religiously. In Kamau, he knew he had found a trusted confidant and importantly, a gifted strategist who'd make the whole issue disappear. However, as is often the case when you sweep a matter under the rug, the day the rug is drawn back for a spring cleaning, the forgotten matter is found congealed and decayed under years of dust, but, nevertheless, still there.

CHAPTER TWENTY

Kanono and Esther, August, 1995

The Karanjas did not love food. It wasn't something they thought about often, individually, or as a team, and yet, food was in abundance in their home. By the time the kids rose for school at five-thirty a.m. to beat the traffic, there was breakfast laid out on the table. Boiled sweet potatoes, arrowroot, ginger tea in two flasks, two packets of bread, margarine, jam, honey, Weetabix, bananas and oranges, the occasional apples and a flask with boiled milk and water mixture that could be used to make hot chocolate.

The breakfast items were only removed at ten a.m. to be replaced by late-morning tea. This consisted of fresh flasks of tea and mandazis to feed the guests who always poured in before lunch. Mrs. Karanja had drawn up a menu on the third day of their chef, Samson's, employ and it did not change for over twenty years, until Samson died of a heart attack in the middle of the night.

The menu went like this:

Monday

Lunch

Rice, beans and cabbage

Dinner

Ugali, fish and spinach

Tuesday
Lunch
Rice and minji with cabbage
Dinner
Matoke or potatoes *ya dania*, beef stew and *sukuma wiki*
Wednesday
Lunch
Pilau
Dinner
Ugali and spinach and chicken stew
Thursday
Lunch
Rice and njahi
Dinner
Chapati na ndengu
Friday
Lunch
Rice and beans
Dinner
Chips and sausage
Saturday
Lunch
Pilau
Dinner
Spaghetti (for the kids), ugali and *sukuma wiki* with *maziwa lala*
Sunday
Lunch
Kids duty
Dinner
Kids duty

One of two things happens if you cook the same food week-in-week-out. You either start cutting corners, sometimes consciously, a lot of times not, and a few years down the line it no longer tastes as good as it did the first time, or if you are Samson, you perfect each and every dish so that year after year the food just keeps getting better.

If there is anything of note in this menu or the fact that it was canon for twenty-something years, it is that the Karanjas were not looking for a culinary experience. Mrs. Karanja had her monthly budget down pat, she could tell you before the Central Bank of Kenya when inflation was threatening based on her monthly shopping.

The menu was at once a curse for the family and a blessing for their neighbours. Overtime, virtually everyone, including Ng'ang'a could recite the Karanjas' menu off by heart. Thursdays saw Mr. Mathai visiting with his "brother" Mr. Karanja, ostensibly for a catch up but really because Samson's chapatis were the softest most layered chapatis in Malaba. Hands. Down. Wednesday Bible Studies were always packed when the rotation moved to the Karanjas because the ugali and baked chicken in a coconut sauce (the recipe was tweaked from its original and unimaginative chicken stew) was: To. Die. For.

Samson always cooked to feed more stomachs than the seven immediately represented in the household. It was expected that at any one point, there should be enough food to feed upwards of ten guests without prior notice.

~

Esther Karanja was three years old when she first realised that her home, her family, and most importantly, her mother were never going to be a private affair for her personal enjoyment. It was one thing to have brothers and sisters who fought for their place in the family but it was an entirely different and highly stressful matter to be fighting for a position amongst relatives God-only-knows how many times removed, church members, and strangers. Her parents were generous with their time and home, which sounds great except that Esther often found herself squeezed in a bed with her two sisters, top-tail-top, to fit in a stranded single mother today, a relative running away from someone somewhere, tomorrow.

Everyone always seemed to be in trouble and their troubles were always urgent. Esther's three year old troubles—being bullied by her older sisters, or not being able to find her Barbie doll, or finding it only to realise it had been stripped naked and hang on the avocado tree in the backyard by the big sisters, were not big enough troubles to warrant the attention of Mr. and Mrs. Karanja.

They did try in their own way. For example, when each of the children turned one, they were dedicated to God in a church ceremony. They prayed over them fervently and regularly fasted on their behalf. Still, little things slipped through the cracks. As the church grew from a tent in a parking lot in Langata pitched every Sunday morning and rolled away on Sunday evening, to a proper stone building with stained windows, a huge alter-cum stage and enough sitting space for over five hundred congregants—well—they got busy okay? Not too busy to forget morning prayers with their children before they were ferried to their respective schools by the driver, but too busy to notice that the big sisters were really just mean brats. They also did not notice when their sons began experimenting with miraa, or when they'd sneak in a friend's brother's PlayBoy magazines into the house.

~

'You can play with us, but only if you bring us chapati,' Karen, the unelected but still very much official head of the Malaba kids play group, stood between Esther and the rest of the kids who were playing Kati at Malaba's communal field. She did this all the time. One day, hell, one minute, you'd think you were golden because she welcomed you and let you play with them, but the next you'd find yourself standing on the other side having to prove your fidelity to a kid too high on her ego.

'B-but si-chapati is Thursday,' Esther said with a sinking feeling.

'Basi come on Thursday.' Karen turned back to continue her referee duties. 'Okay, Kanono you're out.'

Kanono was already standing on the sideline so she looked up confused as to why it was being broadcast.

'You're also out for the next game. Uko-slow.' And just like that Kanono was kicked out of the games for the afternoon. At first, she was uncertain what her next move should be. She could sit on the pavement and wait for Karen to look upon her with mercy and admit her into the next round (unlikely), or she could go back home and sit with Shosho, her father's mother, who chewed tobacco and thought that Jomo Kenyatta was still president of Kenya.

~

Kanono had just turned the corner to her house when she noticed Esther standing outside her own gate crying and calling for someone to open the gate. Her feet were shoeless. The afternoon sun had burnt through the tarmac which meant it's surface was incredibly hot. Esther kept hopping from foot to foot. Kanono hesitated, not wanting to engage in conversation with the second-least popular person in the estate after her. It wouldn't help her win Karen over if she was—

Esther had seen her. Now it would look mean if she ignored her and walked passed her to her house.

'Kwani slippers ziko?' Kanono asked half-heartedly. That

produced fresh tears and loud messy sniffling and more frantic jumping from Esther.

'A-a-a-akina Wangu…' More tears, the sentence left unfinished but the meaning fully understood. The big sisters had struck again. Mercy prevailing, Kanono invited Esther back to her house. Her baby brother Kanyi was sitting with Shosho in the coolness of the living room. They kept up a steady conversation, Kanyi babbling away in Swahili and English and Shosho languorously story-telling in Kikuyu. None of them were particularly interested in what the other had to say, though this did not deter their friendship. Shosho loved talking to Kanyi because he was named after her husband who she said was killed in the fifties during the State of Emergency. It was in fact her father who was killed during the Emergency. Mr. Mathai's father fell down the stairs, sustained an injury that needed surgery, and would have recovered if the surgeon had not left a surgical implement in him before sewing him up. When she spoke to Kanyi, she got to call him by her husband's name and imagine it was the man himself that she was speaking to.

'And what have you brought us?' Shosho asked in Kikuyu every afternoon when Kanono returned home from her time playing or trying to play with the kids outside. Every day, Kanono would steal whatever coins she found lying around the house, which, considering Mr. Mathai's scatter-brain nature, amounted to a significant amount of money, and she'd use that money to buy a selection of sweets from Ng'ang'a.

The list of sweets was always the same except when a new one was introduced and she'd buy one to test it out first before making a decision on whether or not to add it to her list. The list included khos (little round mint sweets that were so cheap you could get a full bag for less than five shillings), eclairs, balls of chewing gum, a bar of fudge chocolate, one each for herself, Kanyi and Shosho, and a bag of mabuyu (ovalish seeds covered with sugary, tangy, ruby-red baobab powder).

Today, in a hurry to leave the scene of her most recent humiliation at the hands of Karen, she'd forgotten to pass by the Kiosk to buy their haul of sweets.

'Wacha niende, nili forget.' she said. All of her conversations with Shosho were a mix of poor Kikuyu, some Swahili and the odd English word thrown in when she couldn't remember the right word in either of the other two languages.

It was a source of disappointment to her mother's parents that Mama Kanono and Mr. Mathai spoke only English to their kids. If it wasn't for Priscilla speaking Swahili to them, that would have been down the drain too! Mama Kanono's mother always reminded her that though the country had received de jure freedom from the colonisers, the minds of Kenyans were still colonised. From here she'd quote Ngugi Wa Thiongo's famous essay on language in African literature, but it was useless because her daughter had stopped listening to her the moment she heard the word coloniser.

It had become common practice for Nairobi parents to dispense with their mother tongue as they raised their children in an effort to make sure that when the kids learned English, it was not so heavily accented that you could place the child's tribe just by hearing them speak. The effect was that while Kanono understood most of the things her Shosho said in Kikuyu and could speak a few words, she could not string a sentence together in the language, and her Swahili suffered a similar fate.

Introductions were made between Esther, Shosho, Kanyi and Priscilla who'd stationed herself in the living room to iron as she watched Bold and the Beautiful followed by Tausi.

Slippers were found for Esther's feet and off they went to Ng'ang'a's Kiosk, taking care to avoid the side of the estate where Karen's game of Kati had now transitioned to British Bull Dog.

Little conversation was had between the two girls. Kanono was mulling over the game. Not for the first time, she questioned the efficacy of Karen being the referee and leader of their estate games. No one had given Karen the role of leader, she'd just walked into the void as soon as they were old enough to play on their own, and assumed leadership for her age group as if it were a birthright.

~

Esther had only been to the kiosk twice in her life. Being the last born in a house with at least ten people in it at any one time, there was always someone else to send. She kept looking back, expecting to find a member of her household behind them who would swiftly take her back home to her cloistered life of regimented meals and chores but the estate was silent. The afternoon heat kept most of the grown-ups hiding indoors.

She followed Kanono who marched towards the gate, greeted the Askaris and marched up to the Kiosk. Esther was dumbfounded by such an honest display of confidence. Kanono had barely stopped to check for on-coming cars, she'd looked resolutely forward as she crossed the dirt road to the Kiosk.

'Hi Mister Ng'ang'a,' Kanono greeted Ng'ang'a. She picked up a stool that was on the side of the Kiosk and dragged it to the little mesh window in the middle of the wood structure. From the new height afforded by the stool she could see into the Kiosk far better than before. She shuffled to the side then looked back at Esther. 'Aren't you going to pick a sweet?' she asked.

'I don't have any money,' Esther said, crestfallen.

'It's okay, I'll buy for you,' Kanono said with a shrug. Esther quickly joined her on the stool, warmed by the offer.

Ng'ang'a greeted Esther as if she were an old friend even though he'd only ever met her once (the second time she was at the Kiosk with one of her brothers it was Kevin who served them). He even remembered to ask her how Mr. Karanja's foot was getting on since the accident. It was a four-car collision that was more of a nuisance than an accident. Only Mr. Karanja and been injured, but the other cars and their owners spent the morning and a good chunk of the afternoon at the scene of the accident arguing about who was to blame.

Ng'ang'a turned to Kanono and they spoke fondly, regaling each other with stories about the hours that had passed since she came to buy sweets the day before.

'The usual?' Ng'ang'a asked her after they'd caught up. Kanono counted out her coins.

'No. Esther do you like chocolates or sweets?' Esther was caught off-guard by the question.

'I don't know. Any?' she said feeling disappointed in her own answer. Kanono didn't seem to mind her indecisiveness.

'Sawa, four mint-chocs and the rest I'll get mabuyus.' she told Ng'ang'a. After the sweets were packed and goodbyes and see you tomorrows were said, the pair were off.

Kanono handed Esther her mint-choc and shrugged when Esther said thank you.

'Do they always refuse you to play as well?' Esther asked as they walked into the estate.

'Sometimes, depending on the game they allow me. I'm good at hopscotch. I can jump really far.'

'Oh. I've never played that.'

'Even in school?' Kanono asked in surprise. Esther hesitated.

'I don't have many friends in school,' she said unwrapping her chocolate.

'Me too!' Kanono said delighted to have this awkward thing in common with someone else.

'Then who do you play hopscotch with?'

'Priscilla if she's not busy, and sometimes akina Karen but them not so much.' They became quiet thinking about their largely friendless lives. Suddenly, they heard the sound of kids running in their direction. Kanono turned to Esther in horror. They'd be forced to give up their sweets if Karen's crew found them. Esther grabbed Kanono's hand and together they run behind the hedge of the nearest house and hid there. Esther rubbed Kanono's back. Kanono was breathing heavily, her fear of Karen's crew causing her to hyperventilate and perspire excessively. When the kids run off, bored with whatever game they'd been playing, it took a few minutes for Esther to convince Kanono that it was okay to come out of their hiding place.

CHAPTER TWENTY-ONE

Beatrice and Nyambura, August 14th, 2012

'Madam, the ring will be ready next week.' Beatrice's face fell at the news. The jeweler continued to examine her wedding ring through a jewelery loupe secured to his right eye. He smiled in admiration at the fine craftsmanship. It was rare to see wedding bands that were so simple and which, upon closer inspection held within them a carefully constructed world of beauty and intelligence designed for the private appreciation of the ring bearer alone.

Steven bought the bands from a vintage jewelry store in Istanbul while on a business trip. The ring was too large for Beatrice's finger so a day after their arrival back in Nairobi from their honeymoon in Seychelles, she went to get it resized at the jewelry store at Village Market.

'It can't be sooner?'

'No, this kind of ring needs careful and deliberate work. We can't rush it if you'd like to be happy with the final result,' he said, taking off the loupe and returning the ring to it's velvet box. The jeweler took the box through a little door that Beatrice presumed was a workstation.

'I see you're looking at the Swarovski watch. It's a beautiful piece isn't it?' Beatrice nearly jumped. She'd not heard him come back to the counter.

'No, I'm just—'

The heavy door of the jewelry store creaked open and Nyambura walked in.

'Oh, you're still here?' she asked.

'Just finishing up with her.' The jeweler spoke up before Beatrice. 'That will be forty thousand,' he said to Beatrice whose eyes bulged from their sockets when she heard the amount. The jewler did not blink. He should at least have felt embarrassed about quoting such a high price Beatrice thought.

'Madam, I don't think you recall, but my wife and I came to purchase a BMW from your dealership earlier this year. You can afford forty thousand without the huffing and puffing,' he said, crossing his hands over his chest. Nyambura burst into laughter.

'That, she definitely can!'

'But is it customary to pay so much for a resizing? I don't even think the ring is worth that much.'

'It's worth a great deal more than forty thousand.'

'One hundred?' Nyambura ventured, enjoying her mother's shock. The jeweler pointed upwards.

'Two hundred?' Nyambura tried again. The jeweler's finger went up and up.

'Five hundred?' she asked, not believing it herself.

The jeweler shook his head. 'If we're going up in such small increments we'll never get there,' he said.

'Steven spent more than five hundred on your ring?' Nyambura exclaimed. 'And I can't even get a man to pay for his half of the dinner?'

'Steven wouldn't spend that much money on jewelry,' Beatrice said, aghast.

'Mum just pay we go.'

'Oh no, payment is upon collection. But I'll need to hold the cash so I'll just take your card for that,' he said, stretching his hand out in expectation of a card.

'Why do you need my card?' Beatrice asked, feeling abused.

'We need to make sure you can afford to pay for the resizing,' he said with mirth. Nyambura barked with laughter. 'I'm sorry it's company policy, I really do need your card. Or if not that a 50% deposit,' he said when he realized Beatrice had no inclination to hand over her card.

Nyambura's phone rang. 'Oh! It's my agent. I've got to take this. I'll see you in a bit.'

'Movie star?' the jeweler asked.

'No comedian,' Beatrice said, unimpressed. She reluctantly handed over her Visa card.

'They've transitioned before,' Nyambura said, as she answered her phone. 'Hello? Hello? I can't hear you...' she walked back out of the store to take the call.

'Give her my card. She might need it.' The jeweler handed Beatrice her visa card back as well as his business card.

~

Nyambura must have wandered off as she was speaking on the phone because when Beatrice walked out of the store she couldn't see her anywhere. Instead of standing around, she decided to wait for Nyambura at the coffee shop opposite the jewelry store and wrote her message to that effect. Beatrice felt a nervous energy around her daughter. She'd chalked it up to Nyambura's impending trip back to New York and her fear that it would be another few years before she saw her daughter again.

The coffee shop was packed yet many of the tables for four were taken up by single occupants. Scanning the room for an empty table, Beatrice realized that one of the people on a table for four was Macharia. She would have turned and walked out immediately, and in truth she did try to, but a bus load of tourists had just arrived at the door and the noise they made attracted everyone's attention, including Macharia's.

Macharia looked up and then back down at the bill he was settling. Beatrice thought that perhaps, in the years since they last met, she'd changed so much he couldn't recognize her. But then his face shot up and his eyes fixed on her. He gave a little wave and Beatrice was being pushed further into the coffee shop by the tourists and next thing she knew, she was standing by his table and he'd stood up and he was hugging her, and then he said, 'Ciku, what a surprise!'

'How are you?' he was saying. Beatrice was looking at the door, hoping Nyambura wouldn't walk in just then.

'Uh…' Beatrice faltered. She'd not heard the question.

'I'm so sorry, I heard about Mr. Mathai and I tried to get in touch to offer my condolences then but I couldn't get a hold of you.' Beatrice sucked in air sharply. Macharia's sudden appearance had triggered a thought process and now she was making a connection she couldn't have come to on her own earlier. Mrs. Mutiso had not answered her calls for the last few days. Nyambura had let it slip (she was sure it was a slip because Nyambura looked horrified after), that she'd gone to visit Mrs. Mutiso. Beatrice shut her eyes. My God, she prayed, please don't forsake me.

'Is everything okay?' Macharia asked touching her hand lightly. Beatrice followed the length of his hand to the tips of his fingers where they touched her forearm in concern. She should have expected it but she was still stunned when she realized all she felt was the light pressure of someone touching her forearm. The electric current that once flowed between them, even when they went years without seeing each other, was gone. He seemed surprised by this because he took his hand off her forearm and stared at it in bewilderment.

'I'm meeting my daughter in a bit so I need to find a table for us. But I hope you've been well.'

'Oh, you can take my table,' he offered, regaining himself. 'I was just leaving.' He gestured at the bill. 'Your daughter…I think I met her before, with your son. Kanyi?' He asked giving no sign that he was about to leave. He sat back down and Beatrice sat down too not knowing what else to do.

'Yes. Nyambura and Kanyi.'

'You never met mine I don't think,' Macharia said and the look he gave suggested he was about to pull out his phone to show her pictures. 'They must be around the same age as your kids.' Beatrice nodded and turned back to the door. 'Did she tell you when she'd be here?' Macharia continued.

'Any minute now,' Beatrice said with dread.

'I heard about the good news as well,' Macharia offered after a moment of silence. 'My parents told me you were getting married again. Congratulations.'

'Thank you.'

'I'm really glad it worked out for you.'

'You're glad?' Beatrice levelled her eyes on him.

'Well…' Macharia looked uncomfortable. 'Yes, of course I am, we were friends after all. I wanted the best for you. At least it ended well for one of us.'

'What does that mean?'

'My wife had been applying for Greencards to America for ten years without my knowledge. She finally got one, this year in fact. She's moved there with the kids. Now I'm going to join the ranks of Kenya's malnourished middle-aged men who live alone and don't know how to cook,' he said with a weak laugh.

'Then learn how to cook.' Beatrice's voice was curt.

Macharia looked at her in surprise.

'Mum?' Nyambura stood next to her mother's seat. Beatrice had not seen her coming after all her vigilance.

'Is this her? Are you Nyambura?' Macharia asked standing up. Nyambura shook his hand.

'Hi,' she said. She looked at her mother whose face looked almost lifeless with horror and then back at the man who was shaking her hand.

'I'm Macharia. An old friend of your mother's. Anyway, I'll let you get on with it. Ciku, it was good to see you again. Let's try and keep in touch this time.'

Nyambura noticed how Beatrice couldn't find her words.

'Well,' Macharia said after Beatrice did not respond. 'It was nice to meet you.' Nyambura nodded and watched him walk out of the coffee shop.

'Was that youR agent on the phone?' Beatrice asked as Nyambura took Macharia's seat.

'Yeah.'

'What was he saying.' Beatrice swivelled around trying to find a waiter, but mainly, trying to avoid eye contact with her daughter.

'That I need to be back yesterday.' Nyambura continued to watch her mother's manic effort to avoid looking at her.

'Oh, is there work for you?' Beatrice did not understand how Nyambura earned a living or how the industry worked.

'Might be,' she said. 'I've seen that look before.'

'What?' Beatrice asked finally looking at Nyambura

'The way you looked when you were talking to that man. I've seen it before.' Nyambura continued.

'I don't understand, what are you talking about?'

'When we met him the last time, you had that same look.' Beatrice shut her eyes.

~

The last time that Nyambura was referring to was sometime in 1996. Mama Kanono was packing the shopping into their car when Kanyi brought it to her attention that Kanono had disappeared. 'Nono? Where is Nono?' he tugged on his mother's dress as he asked in worry. She nearly forgot her second child in her hurry to go back to the supermarket which was the last place she'd seen her daughter. Kanono, (Mama Kanono didn't know this because she rarely did the shopping), had a habit of disappearing during shopping trips. She'd always resurface just after her father or Priscilla had gone through the till.

Kanono, at ten years old, was a thief. The petty kind. The shoplifting-chocolate kind. As the price of Cadbury's Dairy Milk chocolate climbed steadily, her parents willingness to buy it declined in equal measure. Her daily sweets habit at Ng'ang'a's was not enough. She was like a drug addict who knows they are buying the cheap stuff. The supermarket is where the class A uncut drugs were to be found. She would pick a chocolate from the candy aisle and stuff it under her shirt then tuck her shirt into her skirt or trousers. If she was wearing a dress, she'd pretend to limp holding the chocolate in place in a folded section of the helm of her dress. None of her clothes had pockets big enough to hide the bulge of a stolen chocolate bar.

Mama Kanono was about to get to the supermarket when she saw her daughter running towards her, face stained with tears, a man running after her.

'Where have you been?' she asked as Kanono hugged her and held onto her tightly.

'Mummy, I'm sorry...I'm sorry...I'm sorry...' Kanono repeated over and over again as she clung to her mother.

The man who'd been chasing after Kanono stared at them in consternation. 'This one is your child?' he asked pointing at her.

'Yes.'

'Madam, you have to come with us. She has been caught stealing. She steals very regularly from here. This child is possessed!' he added with feeling.

'What do you mean stealing? I come here with her and I've never seen her steal.' She didn't come often enough for this statement to be valid, but she felt a need to protect her daughter.

'We have been missing chocolate in the stock take and today we have caught her putting it in her skirt,' The man heaved as he spoke, sweat shining on his bald head, his glasses half way down his nose.

'Who are you?' Mama Kanono asked straightening to her full height.

'I am the manager and this child is under arrest.'

'Don't be silly, you can't arrest a child and for that matter, you don't know who was stealing the other chocolates so you can't blame my daughter.' Mama Kanono looked down at Kanono and found Kanyi consoling his sister, rubbing her back softly.

'You people are the problem! You spoil your children like this then they become a nuisance to society.' The manager's voice rose. They'd attracted a small crowd of onlookers. Mama Kanono bristled at the judgment she found in the eyes of the other mothers at the till whose children stood faithfully beside them. She felt as if everyone had a front row ticket to the shambles that was her attempt at motherhood.

Mama Kanono shifted her stance. 'Listen, you don't know anything about my children and what they can or cannot do.'

The man reared back in laughter. 'But I do! I just caught her stealing,' he said.

'My daughter is sorry she took your chocolate. We will pay for it and go. We don't need to stand around and be insulted.' Mama Kanono took out her wallet and from it she took out a one hundred bob note and waved it at the manager. 'Here!'

'Madam, the price for stolen goods is ten times the value of the good,' he said, arms akimbo.

'Ten times? Are you people mad?'

'Those are called consequences.'

'Mummy…mummy…I'm sorry.' Kanono sniffed harder though the tears had stopped.

'This is a stupid policy. No chocolate is worth more than a hundred bob. That's all I have so that's all I am paying.'

'Then we have to take your daughter and hold her till you can pay more. She is a thief we have to treat her like one.' He reached out for Kanono and both Mama Kanono and Kanyi slapped his hand away. The entire comedy made Kanono howl louder imagining a life in prison with only githeri to eat.

'Madam, you cannot obstruct the course of justice!'

'This is not about justice. She is a child! And never touch her again.' Mama Kanono grabbed both Kanono and Kanyi's hands and pulled them away.

'Where do you think your going? You've not paid your daughter's debt!' The manager said.

'I just did, you have the one hundred bob in your hand.' Mama Kanono continued to walk away, her children scrambling to keep up with her. Kanono kept repeating that she was sorry and even tried to explain the circumstances in which she was caught with the chocolate and how it wasn't stealing really—

Macharia stepped out of the watch store right next to the

exit they were aiming for.

Mama Kanono saw him before he saw them. Kanono was deep into her explanation and Kanyi was listening attentively, so much so he kept repeating some of her sentences. They sensed a change in their mother. Kanono looked up at her and saw that her face was stripped of life, as if her very soul had climbed out of her eyes and gone on a walk. She followed her mother's stare and found its source to be a man, not as tall as her father, in a deep blue suit, looking as if he was going somewhere fancy. The man was stuffing his wallet back into his jacket pocket. He looked up and all three pairs of eyes of the Mathai clan were on him.

'Ciku?' Macharia asked as if it was not her.

Mama Kanono could feel her children's eyes on her and the man in front of her.

'Mum?' Kanono tagged at her hand. 'You're being rude. Say something.'

Macharia looked down at the little girl.

'She is eh?' he stepped forward to greet her. 'Hi I'm your uncle—'

'No you're not!'

'No you're not!' Kanyi repeated after his sister.

'We've never seen you before.' Kanyi repeated this as well making Macharia laugh and ruffle his head.

'Ciku,' Macharia straightened again and came face to face with Mama Kanono.

'That's not mummy's name.' Kanyi corrected him. 'It's—'

'No it's my name!' Mama Kanono rushed to say before her children told her former lover that her name was Mama Kanono. Mama Kanono begged God that Macharia would keep his distance, not bring his hand out for a handshake or worse—far worse—a hug. He did neither.

'So—' she said then aborted the sentence. They had never discussed their families with each other. It was the unspoken rule of these things. The last time she saw him was the day she found out she was pregnant with Kanono. They met at Trattoria as they always did, they went to the Hilton as they always did, they made love as they always did, but this time she was careful to prolong it. She kissed him with an academic's deliberation, wanting to memorize everything about how it felt, let her hands linger and wonder and discover once more the contours of the man she'd never hold again like this.

When it was time to leave, she kissed the spot where his neck met his collarbone, which for nearly a year, on Thursday afternoons, she'd loved above all other parts of him. She breathed him in from this place, trying to capture everything about him so that she could draw on this memory much later, when she got back home, and years from then when she'd sit in the quiet of an afternoon like that last one and remember how it felt to be loved by him.

And the memory? Did it stay or did it prove fallible in the hands of time? Facing him, her children at her side, she knew that it hadn't just stayed, it had grown like a tumour, taken over her consciousness and come to define her.

Words must have been spoken, a conversation must have taken place because eventually, the kids tiring of adult conversation, made it known that they were hungry and they wanted to go home because dad had promised to bring them fried fish today. The mention of Mr. Mathai brought Mama Kanono back to reality.

'How—' Macharia didn't finish. He shrugged because he too couldn't bring himself to ask about her husband. The kids tagged at her hands. He looked down at them and said goodbye even though they weren't paying attention. File this one too under fate's dastardly tricks: Because Kanono had grown to emulate Mr. Mathai, making it impossible to look at her and not see the man himself, when Macharia looked at his daughter his only passing thought was that she'd taken after Mr. Mathai, not *his* Ciku. I suppose if he'd been looking for something else it would have revealed itself but he was only looking for a hint of the Ciku he'd known.

Mama Kanono did not resume proper breathing until they were on Waiyaki Way facing the stream of traffic on their way home. Repeatedly her children asked her who that man, "Uncle Machaira" was, and why she was so rude and spoke so little and repeatedly she said, 'an old friend, an old friend.' Repeatedly they asked, 'from where, from where,' and she sang back with an ache in her chest 'another time, another time.'

None were satisfied with the explanation but their mother, they knew, was not a woman of straight answers. The kids settled into a game of "I Spy" to pass the time until they got home. Mama Kanono vowed never to step into Sarit Centre again, the same way she never went back to the Hilton or Trattoria. Nairobi felt like it was a minefield of memories of Machaira. She expended energy to avoid anywhere, even whole streets, that in any way reminded her of him and the self she would have wanted to be, 'in another life, in another life.'

~

Nyambura was silent. She'd asked for a lunch date with her mother but she'd not expected to bring up the topic in this way. As she recounted the story of how she first met Macharia, Beatrice got paler and paler until, as the waiter came to take their order he asked:

'Is everything well madam? You don't look too well.'

'I'm fine,' she snapped and waved him away. Nyambura waited.

'Did Aunty Carol tell—'

'No it wasn't her. And I'm scared she thinks it was her.'

'Then how did you—'

'Am I correct?'

'Your father—John—Mathai—was your father.'

'I know that mum but that other man?'

'I was so young and I...I've made so many mistakes, just one after the other. I mistook that for love. I wanted to be wanted by Macharia even when I knew he'd never want me, not in that way, not in the way I wanted. And I didn't...' Beatrice looked away from her daughter. This confession felt like a public undressing followed by great lashings of the whip at the market square.

Nyambura reached out for her mother's hand. She'd expected that she would be angry when they had the conversation. It would have been a perfectly suitable response. To grow up thinking one man was your father only to find out it was another? Sure, anger would have worked here. But then her world view of her mother underwent a sudden tectonic shift in that moment and she found that underneath Beatrice's veneer, hard-working, yes, yes, disciplined, of course, of course, was brokenness. This she could relate to because she understood what it meant to look whole but to be made of pieces of yourself that you'd picked up carefully when they shattered and stitched back together in the middle of the night when no one was watching.

Beatrice breathed in. 'Your father and I were very different people who would have made other people very happy.'

'Like you and Steven now?' Beatrice looked up in surprise and the realization that she was happy, stunned her into silence.

'Yes, yes, like me and Steven. I'm sorry I never told you about Macharia, but nothing good would have come out of it. I didn't want him to reject you the way he rejected me. I didn't want you to go through the pain of knowing you were someone else's child and they didn't want you, and Mathai was a great father…regardless of our relationship, which you know was not always good…he really loved you and Kanyi.'

'Are you angry with me?' Beatrice asked after a few moments of silence.

'You know before, I'd have been angry but, there's something about growing older that makes you realise things are never that simple. A part of me understands why you didn't tell me, and that's the part that knows I'd do the same thing if I was in your shoes.'

'Do you want to get to know him—Macharia?' Beatrice asked. Nyambura saw the olive branch for what it was and her mother's sacrifice in offering it.

She didn't have to think about it, she didn't need to. 'No, mum. I had a father. I have a step-father who is very eager to get to know us, and I've not put in much effort with him.'

CHAPTER TWENTY-TWO

Beatrice's Surprise Birthday Party, January, 1996

The year was 1996 to be exact. The dates matter in a way and yet they fall apart and don't in another. But it was 1996 and Mr. Mathai, feeling guilty that his promiscuity had ended in pregnancy, and wanting to make up for it, decided to throw Mama Kanono a surprise birthday party. January is traditionally not a month when people are flush with cash, but once Mr. Mathai got an idea into his head, you couldn't get it out.

Together with Kanono, he came up with a list of everything they thought Mama Kanono liked. It was short and none of the things inspired the party feeling. The list of her likes was scrapped and in its place the committee of father and daughter came up with a list of things they liked. Satisfied with it and feeling like they had the bones of what could end up being a legendary party, they called Priscilla in to inform her of the plan.

Priscilla sniffed and said what they all knew, 'Mama Kanono will not be happy—she doesn't like these ma-parties of yours.'

Mr. Mathai gave his daughter a look of conspirators' exasperation. 'Anyway,' he said remembering he was her boss and it wasn't her opinion he was after. 'We are only telling you so that you are prepared. Si-you can call one of the other house-girls so they help you to prepare things eh?' Mr. Mathai always suggested this whilst planning a party which made Priscilla irate because the suggestion was ludicrous. In the end, the parties involved Priscilla haranguing the guests she could bully, which was everyone south of forty into helping her prepare the food, clean up and so on.

Thinking the matter settled, Mr. Mathai moved on. 'Okay, now, how much do we need for food?' he asked Priscilla who'd taken a seat across from them and was eyeing the mess they'd created with the roasted peanuts they'd been eating. The dry, brown peanut skins were everywhere.

'I don't know, do you have a menu?'

'Priscilla, surely!' Mr. Mathai's voice sounded like a whine. Priscilla raised an eyebrow but Mr. Mathai raised a hand to stop her from going further. 'Okay, fine, how much did we use for the last one?' he asked.

'I don't know,' she answered with a shrug.

'But you're the one who went shopping!'

'I don't remember,' she amended.

Mr. Mathai looked down at his daughter as if seeking her help in mediating this stand-off which was a regular occurrence between himself and Priscilla. Priscilla was perhaps the only person who aggravated and tested Mr. Mathai's patience. She always found a way to make him feel like a subordinate in his own home, whether it was giving him lukewarm tea (a clear message that she'd taken time after the tea was ready before bringing it to him), or ironing his trousers with too much heat so they became shiny, or what he felt was the worst crime of them all: refusing to cooperate in the planning of his parties. 'Priscilla acts as if she's the one who owns the house,' he'd once complained to Mama Kanono. Mama Kanono said, 'You'd better leave her to run it unless you want to look for and train another house-help.'

'Then Kanono we will go do the shopping ourselves,' Mr. Mathai said seeing no way to convince Priscilla to be a little more supportive of their plans.

'No, ni sawa nitafanya—I always do it anyway. I'll just do it,' Priscilla acquiesced with a grand show of reluctance. 'Last time tulitumia ten thousand,' she said. Mr. Mathai grumbled at the high cost but removed his wallet anyway and counted out the money. Instead of going to the supermarket, Priscilla would buy the food at the market in town then save whatever money was left over for her own investments. Mr. Mathai was always too absent-minded to ask for a receipt.

~

Mama Kanono's birthday fell on a Monday but the party would be held the Saturday before. Whilst Saturday was strictly a working day for her, Mr. Mathai had persuaded the garage and shop assistants to abscond duty and join in the surprise party. Infuriated at finding the garage and then the spare-parts shop closed when she went to work in the morning, Mama Kanono drove home to begin a witch-hunt of the architect of this plan to close the stores on a Saturday—

'Saaaprrrizzee!' the words echoed throughout her house as Mama Kanono opened the front door. She took a step back, trying to regain her composure. Her home was filled to capacity. In the mix, were her employees.

~

The party was underway and growing stronger by the minute when Mama Kanono finally managed to signal to Mr. Mathai that they needed to have a conversation—now!

Mr. Mathai followed her to their bedroom.

'You think this is a big joke?' she said as Mr. Mathai closed the door behind him. 'That you can just keep spending money this way when—'

'No, this was a surprise for you. I wanted to make you feel special,' he explained.

'Really? Then why does it feel like another one of your parties? If it's my birthday why are none of my friends here?'

'But Mrs. Mutiso is here, and isn't everyone else our friends?' He asked gesturing to the door.'

'Our?' Mama Kanono pinched the bridge of her nose. That wasn't even the point she wanted to make. Going into whose friends those were downstairs was murky territory. 'Look, you know this, you know how money is so tight and I keep telling you we need to tighten the belt and you keep throwing these—these—' she threw her hands in the air.

'But do you want us to live like we are in a convent?' Mr. Mathai replied in consternation.

'You can't use company money to fund these things,' Mama Kanono tried again.

'But the company doesn't even pay us and we've been working there for how long?'

'We are the company. We've not been working there as employees. We are building something so that our children have some sort of security blanket and don't have to spend their adult lives paying their parents debts and working three jobs to afford an education!'

'I know that. Of course I want the best for my children.' Mr. Mathai was hurt by the assertion that he did not.

'Then why can't you just see that we can't keep spending money the way you spend money.'

~

Kanono stood outside her parents' bedroom door, ear pressed to the door listening as they argued. She had never known them to be friendly with each other but they'd been perfectly frigid of late. She sank to the carpeted floor feeling crushed that her mother was upset about the party they'd spent a considerable amount of time planning. Why couldn't she just be happy with something they did for once? Esther came up behind her.

'Everyone is going outside to play tapo.' she said holding out a plate of roasted goat meat for Kanono. Kanono took the plate and whispered a thank you.

'Karen came and said they need more people to play.' Esther added. Kanono looked up from the plate feeling glum. The kids who'd come along with their parents for the birthday were meant to be her friends and now Karen had taken them over because, who could resist a game of tapo?

'Are you coming?'

'I don't feel like, but you can go if you want to.' She said seeing Esther's crestfallen look. Esther hesitated then got up.

'I'll only play for one round then I come back,' she said, running down the stairs.

CHAPTER TWENTY-THREE

Uhuru Park, February, 1996

Kamau, Mr. Mathai's cousin, stood on the banks of Nairobi river reading the newspaper. He was reading the obituaries, a habit he'd formed years ago when he learnt how profitable they were. When the newspaper announced, 'Death has occurred of...' he read, 'Opportunity has opened for...'

Anyone could be a deal-broker, but it took a certain sensibility to know where the largest, sweetest deals lay: in the dead. Kamau would skim through the list of the deceased and because the obituaries section also functioned as a sort of directory with details about previous work places, institutional memberships of note and so forth, he would glean important pieces of information. He learnt to sniff out the "unexpected deaths" with "unresolved matters" that meant there could be assets that the family either did not know about or were in dispute over.

From here, he would arrange to go for the memorial service, the details of which were helpfully furnished in the deceased's obituary. At the memorial service, he would work the room in much the way you imagine Mr. Mathai would but with a sinister edge to his efforts. The memorial service done, family members met, state of the deceased's affairs understood, he'd pay the land's office downtown a visit to learn which tracts of land the deceased owned, how long their lease was for, et cetera. Kamau was a patient man. He knew not to pounce so soon after the funeral. It would be careless to do so. Instead he invested his time in becoming an indispensable and constant friend to the bereaved family. Sometimes it took years before he saw a return on his investment but he always did and it was usually worth the effort. Usually. There was that one time though, that landed him in—

No, he is only a minor character here, perhaps another time.

Kamau heard a scream that distracted him. The voice was familiar. In the distance he spied Mr. Mathai in a boat, rowing upstream towards him. The source of the scream was Kanyi, who'd just spotted what he thought was a crocodile. Kamau folded the paper and tucked it under his armpit as he waited for the party on the boat to alight. It was half-term and the kids out of school for a week, were enjoying a series of excursions planned by their father. They'd asked and then begged Kamau to join them on the water, but the idea that one of his acquaintances might see him frolicking on a boat was enough to keep Kamau safely on land.

'Uncle Kamau!' Kanono shouted. 'You've missed out!'

And from Kanono and Kanyi's perspective he truly had missed out on a wondrous afternoon, chock full of adventure. As Mr. Mathai steered the boat, he regaled the children with stories of Kenya's history. Years later, in school, they would find out their father's version of the country's history was highly incorrect, but whenever he took them on an adventure, whether it was an impromptu trip to the National Park, or a walk in Hell's Gate or a boat ride at Uhuru Park, he'd switch on his wise old storyteller voice and entertain them with made up stories about their ancestors.

~

Finally, Kamau had Mr. Mathai's attention. He'd been waiting for this moment for over an hour. They were walking back into town to the Mathais' store where, Mama Kanono was certain to be.

'Eh…mheshimiwa…' Kamau began.

'Niambie mkubwa?' Mathai responded as he stopped to buy his children ice lollies from one of the passing ice-cream carts.

'You remember the apartments I am developing?'

'Ah yes, the ones in Syokimau. How is that going? You know, bwana, I really respect you. You always know where the good deals are. Sometimes I even tell Mama Kanono we should try our hands at property.' All of this was conjecture because Mr. Mathai had no knowledge of Kamau's business acumen. He was merely talking to be polite but he'd spoken himself into a corner:

'You're right, the development will be extremely profitable.'

'That's what I said, that's what I said,' Mr. Mathai agreed with a generous nod.

'But I'm having a bit of a problem. My investors fell through last minute.'

'Sorry, these people can make you go mad. One minute there's money and the next they say there's nothing.' Mr. Mathai was thinking about his recent argument with Mama Kanono.

'That's true!'

'But it can't be so bad. The way your accounts must look, I'm sure you'll be fine,' Mr. Mathai said with optimism. Afterall, Kamau boasted a great deal about his financial situation.

'No, not exactly,' Kamau said. Mr. Mathai turned in

surprise. 'I mean, the money I have is all being used for other projects, it's all spoken for,' Kamau added quickly. Mr. Mathai smiled in relief as if it was their joint account.

'Okay, then why don't you just get a loan?' he said, eager to help his cousin think through this small hurdle in his business.

'I can't do that either, I've already got a few loans out for some other projects. You know how these things are, the life of a self-employed business man.' Mr. Mathai frowned. That sounded a lot less impressive than his understanding of Kamau's business empire.

'Okay, so what are you going to do?' Before Kamau could speak, Mr. Mathai run after his children who were about to cross the road without a care about on-coming traffic.

'Kanono! Stop and hold your brother's hand!' He shouted as he dashed to get to them. Normally, Kamau did not mind that Mr. Mathai was perpetually with his children because the kids were quite good at entertaining themselves and letting the grown-ups talk but today, he grew more irritated with every interruption to their conversation. He had a limited time to broach the topic that had brought him to Uhuru Park, on a Wednesday afternoon no less. If anyone he knew saw him walking around at the pace Mr. Mathai and his children chose to experience the world in, they'd think he was bankrupt and that was the kind of news that could cripple your CV in the industry.

Once again, he had Mr. Mathai's attention, though it was clear Mr. Mathai was ready to move on from their earlier conversation. This was the issue with his flighty cousin—Mr. Mathai couldn't stand difficult conversations.

'Well, anyway, as I was saying,' Kamau pressed on. He saw the disappointment in Mr. Mathai's face that they were not finished discussing such depressing matters as money problems. 'Now that my investors pulled out, and I've exhausted all avenues of financing, we need money just so that we can break ground and build the foundation. Once that is up, people will begin to put down-payments for the flats and we will use that to finish the building. And I'm also expecting some money to come although it has been delayed a bit. You know how these government contracts are.'

Understanding dawned on Mr. Mathai. 'Oh.' he said feeling a nervous energy spread through him. If there was one thing he had not learnt how to do it was how to say no. He hated to disappoint his friends and relatives but he couldn't see any other way to manoeuvre this case, if he was correct in his assumption that Kamau was asking for money. For one thing, he definitely did not have the cash to loan Kamau, for another, even if he did, Mama Kanono would finish him for it, and there was the kids debt free education to think about.

'So I'm coming to you my brother,' Kamau explained to ensure they were on the same page.

'I don't know. I'd need to talk to Mama Kanono first. You know after the birthday she wasn't very happy. Things are tight,' he said, echoing her words.

'Mheshimiwa, I'm sorry to point it out because you know I have a lot of respect for you, but I—' The kids had slowed down to stare at a passing vehicle that was pimped out with huge speakers and colourful graffiti. Kamau waited until they were out of earshot. '—I think, Mama Kanono, though she is very good, I just think she is the one running your life. This is an investment decision for a man to make. It is you who controls your family interests and that shop of yours is making so much money, all you need to do is borrow against your cash flow. They will give you a loan like this!' Kamau snapped his fingers. 'And as for me, I'll pay you back with interest so that even you, you can make money from this development. You know, this is why Indians here as so wealthy. Instead of borrowing from other people, they work with each other so that way I make money and you make money.'

'This is all very good, but I can't just take out a loan like that. Mama Kanono would know.'

'Let me teach you something. These things don't need both directors to get a loan. You know I run my businesses with my wife, but am I going to disturb her every day to come to the bank with me to sign this or that? No. I do it myself. I'm sure you can talk nicely to your bank manager and give them kitu kidogo for making it less of a hassle for you. Also remember how I helped you out with that girl and her baby. Are they disturbing you now?'

Mr. Mathai narrowed his eyes at the implicit threat. He and Kristin were getting on so well now and their child was going to turn one soon. Their agreement, brokered by Kamau, saw her get housing allowance as well as an allowance for lifestyle expenditures. He got to see his child every other week. Kamau was threatening to upset this agreement which wouldn't do. If Mama Kanono found out about the other child, it wouldn't just be anger he'd have to deal with, it could be a divorce. No, it wouldn't do at all.

~

Three months later, he transferred five million shillings to Kamau's account. When Mama Kanono found out that Mr. Mathai had taken a loan against their business without her consent, the bank manager of their Co-operative Bank branch was fired along with several other staff members. She struck herself off as director of the spare-parts shop (the company the loan was borrowed against), and removed Mr. Mathai as a director of her garage and second hand car dealership.

'This is your mess. You fix it,' she said handing him the documents that would annul their business partnership.

CHAPTER TWENTY-FOUR

Esther, 1996

Mama Kanono was the first to notice Esther becoming more withdrawn. Whilst Esther had always been a quiet girl, she'd begun to look vacant. Mama Kanono asked Mrs. Mutiso if she too had noticed something different in Esther. Mrs. Mutiso paused from telling her about her new business idea (a bakery: it never took off), and turned to look at Esther who was playing in the backyard with Kanono and Kanyi. No, Esther wasn't playing. Kanyi and Kanono carried on a game of chamama but Esther sat back on her heels staring as if she were in another place entirely.

The twins had made Mrs. Mutiso distrustful of children—the way they could turn on you and torture you with emotional distance. She shrugged and turned back to the Australian Women's Weekly cookbook she had open on her lap. She was about to say she saw nothing different in Esther when something about the expression on Esther's face caught her attention.

'So?' Mama Kanono nudged.

'I don't know—I guess it's that age.' Mrs. Mutiso shrugged again. She was seeing things, she was sure. A child that young could not know anything about pain.

~

Esther Karanja. What can I say? What can I tell you that

will convince you that life is not unfair? That it deals us all cards equal to our strengths? How can I when I don't believe so myself. But once again you must forgive me, I do this, I get ahead of myself.

Esther's family was large, this much we know. Their door was forever open to their large community of friends, family and congregation. People came at all hours of the day and night, some stayed a few hours, some a few days, and some a few years. In the chaotic fullness of their lives it was hard for Mr. and Mrs. Karanja to be vigilant about the characters they allowed into their home.

The first time it happened, Esther was lying down on the couch with her head resting on her mother's lap when the doorbell rang. She was just about to doze off, their home oddly empty of the usual life it had. Up until the doorbell's interruption it had been a delicious Sunday afternoon. Her older siblings were in boarding school, her father was in church seeing to some church business and the guests that normally filled their home were also in church as well. Mrs. Karanja had not been feeling well that morning so she opted to come home immediately after the service. The question of skipping church was not a question worth forming. The only acceptable excuse for missing a Sunday Service when you were a church leader was death. Seeing her chance to spend some time alone with her mother, Esther had asked to go back home with her.

Her parents had a brief disagreement about letting her go home early. Mr. Karanja said it would be sending a bad message about commitment to church. In the end, Mrs. Karanja prevailed. Esther was her little gem, and though she'd never admit it, she preferred spending time with her last born than with her other four children who had strayed away from the church even at such a young age. Mrs. Karanja did not realise that they were reacting to their parents' hectic lifestyles. The children wanted the normalcy of a home that was a private affair, where they didn't have to endure meals with strangers every single day, and share their beds every time their guest rooms filled up with guests and there were more people who needed a bed.

~

Mrs. Karanja surprised Esther when she stopped at the petrol station to fill the car's tank and bought two packets of chips and four sausages from the restaurant at the station. She never bought food from a restaurant for her family when they were out and about because the affair would become expensive very quickly. They always packed leftovers or ate salami sandwiches.

They ate their lunch sitting cross-legged on the carpet in their living room using the paper bag the chips were carried in as a plate. Mrs. Karanja regaled Esther with stories of her own childhood and Esther listened in rapt attention. Mrs. Karanja had grown up in a home that was nominally Christian and that was only to appease the missionaries who'd settled in their community. Her parents had long passed away and none of her siblings ascribed to the faith with the same fervour that she did.

'Mum used to make dad traditional beer and he would drink it every day with his friends out of this big gourd.' This was the first time Mrs. Karanja had mentioned alcohol in anything but a negative light.

'A gourd?' Esther didn't know what that was. Mrs. Karanja was shocked out of her reminiscing at the realization that a ritual that had been part of her every day life growing up was foreign to her daughter.

'You've never seen a gourd?' she asked, knowing the

answer. Esther shook her head and a toothy grin appeared. 'Shosho knows how to make beer?' Esther asked confused. Mrs. Karanja was about to correct Esther's use of the wrong tense but was overtaken by a deep longing for her mother. The use of present tense made her feel like her mother was not as distant a past as she knew her to be.

'Back in those days, you had to know how to make beer otherwise your husband would be very mad,' Mrs Karanja said. 'We used to make it from honey.'

'Haiya, even you mum you used to make beer for daddy?' Esther perked.

Mrs. Karanja laughed at the absurdity of the idea. 'No of course not. We are Christians, we don't drink.'

'And Shosho and Guka?' Esther asked, suddenly afraid.

'I think they were,' Mrs. Karanja said though in the end, she was sure they had died unbelievers. She didn't want to scare Esther with the idea that her grandparents might be in hell. It gave her nightmares and she was an adult.

When they were done eating, Mrs. Karanja cleared away their lunch and its remains. When Esther offered to help her, she insisted that the little girl relax and this so confounded Esther she was unable to speak for some time. After, they'd both agreed to nap on the couch downstairs instead of going upstairs. Had they been upstairs, there is a chance they would not have heard the doorbell, and he would not have entered their home and subsequently Esther's life, but they heard it and anyway there were more to come.

~

Jorum was his name. He was weeping when Mrs. Karanja opened the gate for him. His wife had just kicked him out of their house. He was one of the earliest members of their church. By the time Mrs. Karanja re-entered the living room with the weeping Jorum, she'd switched to Pastor Missus Karanja. She asked Esther to get Jorum a glass of water and after that to give them privacy. Esther felt a sting of resentment for the blabbering man who'd just taken away a precious afternoon with her mother but she was also obedient. She got up without a word, brought Jorum a glass of water and went out to see if Kanono had come back from church as well.

Jorum's estranged wife was called for a meeting to discuss the way forward. Divorce was out of the question. Mr. Karanja assured them that over his dead body was he going to watch any member of his church commit the sin of divorce. Mrs. Karanja, who's even temper was a sorry juxtaposition to Mr. Karanja's irrational outbursts asked them to at least work on their marriage before considering divorce.

'Marriage isn't perfect, we have to keep bringing each other to God every day, praying for each—'

'You think I haven't done that? Since even before I met this…this…this *man* I have been bringing him to God every day, every night. I have fasted for him, I have prayed all night! All night! And what good has that been?' Jorum's estranged wife said. If the Karanjas had only taken the time to ask the right questions, it would have raised significant warning bells for them to know this was not the kind of man to welcome in their home. But they didn't, and anyway, there were more to come.

The assumption was that Jorum cheated on his wife, a common enough occurrence, the type that could be dealt with in the way a patient is given a prescription for antibiotics for a mild infection. The prescription included a few couples' counselling sessions, some one-on-ones to help each party understand the role they played in the infidelity, and a session of prayer and fasting. Jorum's wife refused the prescription and left the church. Jorum, homeless and wifeless spent three weeks as the Karanjas' guest before the church raised money for his rent in a small bed-sitter in Kinoo where he received his divorce papers.

~

Jorum did not waste time at the Karanjas' home. On his first night, still desolate, he opted to have dinner alone in his bedroom. Samson asked Esther to take their guest his dinner, knowing the other kids would not obey his request. Jorum heard a knock on his door and opened it to find Esther standing on the other side holding his dinner carefully between her hands. He took the plate of food from her and asked her to come in and take the glass on his bedside table. He watched her pick up the glass and walk to the door and just before she closed it behind herself, he asked her to bring him another glass of water in ten minutes.

Esther did not have a solid grasp of time. Ten minutes? What did that mean? She went back into the main house and looked around for someone who she could trust to tell her when ten minutes were up. Her sisters were holding court in the backyard with a few of the older girls from the estate. There was an important dispute underway about who a particular boy belonged to. They would have been of little help with the time anyway. Their instinct was to bully Esther. If she asked them to tell her when ten minutes were over, they would have teased her about not knowing how to read time. In the sitting room, her parents and their guests were praying for the dinner they were about to eat. In the kitchen, Samson was busy conferring with Bibi Bwanga from house twenty-three on whether Royco was sacrilegious or if it could be used in the absence of regular spices. Esther was certain a great deal of time had passed by as she moved from room to room, searching for a person who was not too preoccupied so that she could ask them to count down ten minutes for her.

In the end, she sat on the bottom step of the stairs and counted one through ten extra-super-slow before asking Samson for a glass of water. She walked back to Jorum's guest room, taking her time because she was still unsure about her timing. At the door she counted to ten again before knocking twice. Jorum opened the door in the middle of the second knock which pleased Esther because she felt as if she'd got the timing just right. He stepped back into the room and let her in. Esther put the glass of water on his bedside table where his dinner lay untouched.

'You're a good girl Esther. Your parents must be very proud of you,' Jorum was saying behind her. Esther said thank you, feeling the pleasure of recognition.

'Does anybody tell you you're a good girl?' Jorum asked. He moved from the door which he'd shut silently as Esther put his water down.

Esther shook her head. Jorum crouched before her and tipped her chin up. 'Really? No one?' he was whispering now. Esther shook her head again. She wasn't sure why, but she felt the urge to back away. 'Do you know how we say thank you to little girls who do a good job?' Jorum rubbed his finger lightly under her chin. Esther shook her head again, the warm glow from the compliment had faded. 'If I show you, you must keep it a secret. Bad girls will get jealous and then they will be mean.' He didn't have to tell Esther twice about mean girls—just look at her sisters.

~

After Mrs. Mutiso left the Mathais home for her own, the kids were playing upstairs when Mama Kanono overheard Esther tell Kanono that sometimes she had difficulty peeing because it was painful “down there”. She was about to interrupt their conversation when Kanyi run downstairs dressed in one of Kanono’s dresses mimicking the way she talked and walked. The girls run after him and followed him around the house laughing at his antics in the oversized smock.

CHAPTER TWENTY-FIVE

Kanono and Esther, December, 1996

The Karanjas' house was across the road and thirty steps away from the Mathais (as measured by the girls), and two gates down from the Mutisos. It was larger than the other homes in Malaba because of the two-storey guest wing they'd added to the side of their house a year ago. Getting permission from the estate association to add the extension had been a mere formality for the charming Mrs. Karanja. She presented a strong case about their home being a sanctuary for lost souls.

It was the unforgivably (for parents anyway), long December holiday, and it had been uncharacteristically rainy for the past few days. The girls trudged to the Karanjas followed by a pool of water. Mrs. Karanja was surprised to find them at the door. As far as she knew, they were at the Mathais for the day and they shouldn't have been walking in the rain.

'Hi aunty!' Kanono shouted though she had no need to because she could be heard perfectly well. Kanono made a beeline for the dining room table which was laden with hotpots that contained the day's lunch.

'Who let you walk in the rain?' Mrs. Karanja asked in consternation.

'Priscilla,' Kanono said as she began to serve herself lunch.

'First you have to take a bath before you eat.' Mrs. Karanja excused herself from the ladies meeting she was chairing.

'You're going to catch a cold in those wet clothes.'

'Oh.' Kanono's face fell. 'But I don't have any other clothes.'

'You can borrow some of Esther's,' Mrs. Karanja said ushering the kids upstairs to take a bath.

Kanono bit her lip. Nothing of Esther's would fit her. 'It's okay I can wear these ones again.' she said in an upbeat voice.

'No my dear, those are too wet,' Mrs. Karanja insisted as she opened the faucet in the tub and let it fill up with water.

'Esther you can bathe in my room, Nyambura you use this one.' Nyambura was left alone in the kids bathroom as Mrs. Karanja took Esther to her room. She didn't want to face the humiliation of Esther's clothes not fitting. She waited until it was clear that Esther was in the bathtub then she went in search of Mrs. Karanja who she found in Esther's room picking out their clothes.

'Aunty,' she whispered.

'Oh! Why are you still here in those wet clothes! You want to get pneumonia?'

'No, but aunty,' Kanono breathed in. 'I can't wear Esther's clothes.'

'Why not?' Mrs. Karanja asked as she placed a pair of tights and a t-shirt on Esther's bed.

Kanono looked down at herself and then back up at Mrs. Karanja. It took a moment for Mrs. Karanja to grasp the meaning of the look but when she did she cringed in embarrassment because she'd not remembered to consider their size differences.

'Oh, that's okay, don't worry,' she said in a rush to ease Kanono's worry. 'That's okay, then you can wear one of akina Wangu's things. I'm sure those will fit.' Kanono seriously doubted that but felt a jolt of glee at the idea of wearing their clothes. Wangu had these hipster jeans with a fade that Nyambura admired from afar. Maybe those would fit?

They didn't.

Mrs. Karanja ended up rummaging through her wardrobe where she found an old mini-dress with a loose fit that she'd worn in her twenties. The dress nearly grazed Kanono's ankles and it made her look like a stooped grandma, but it was the only thing that fit her.

'That looks nice doesn't it?' Mrs. Karanja tried to sound positive in the face of Kanono's disappointment. Kanono was going to refuse when she heard Esther coming out of the bathroom. She didn't want to have this conversation in front of Esther, so she shrugged and went to the kids bathroom for her bath.

~

After their baths, they sat down for rice and njahi with a mug of cocoa and began planning their afternoon. The afternoon activity was often dependent on what the girls thought Karen and her crew would be doing that afternoon. They'd learnt to avoid Karen because of the number of unfortunate run-ins they'd had with her where they left humiliated and embarrassed about their lack of sporting prowess. It turned out that Karen was quite predictable. If she played roundas in the morning it was unlikely she'd play it again that afternoon which meant the field would be free for them to play in. If she went to the neighbouring estate, Karibu Estate, to swing the day before, she wasn't going to go there the next day. This way they were able to keep out of Karen's way successfully during the school holiday.

Things got harder during the long Christmas holiday that began halfway through November and went all the way into January. After a while, Karen would become less predictable and they'd have more run-ins with her and her crew which led to some nerve-wracking moments for the girls, plus they were both too tall now to hide behind a hedge if they wanted to avoid Karen. This holiday alone, they'd run into her at least five times, which was five times too many for Kanono who enjoyed being alpha in her group. Seeing Karen reminded her that she was a pretender to the throne.

Kanono suggested that they go to Karibu Estate because Karen had been there twice already that week, so it was unlikely she'd still go. Esther's interest in leaving the house was waning as she got progressively warmer. She suggested that instead of doing that, they stay in and read.

'Read what?' Kanono asked bewildered by the suggestion.

'Mum just bought me this book called The Lion The Witch And The Wardrobe'

'What's that about?'

'This lion who can—'

The front door opened and a teenager with angry acne walked in. Esther became rigid where she sat when she saw him. He greeted the girls as he closed the door behind him. Kanono waved hello without looking up (she wasn't interested in the Karanjas' countless guests), but Esther was frozen in her seat.

'Gilbert, my dear, hello,' Mrs. Karanja said coming out of the kitchen to find Gilbert at their door.

'Hi Mrs. Karanja.'

'I didn't know you were coming today,' Mrs. Karanja said. 'The boys are not around, they went on the church camp. Why didn't you go with them?' she asked in concern. 'We wanted to pay for you as well.'

'My mum said no,' Gilbert mumbled.

'Okay, well…' Mrs. Karanja wasn't sure what he had come

to do knowing his friends were away.

'I just came to ask if I can play video games upstairs on their computer. Dad is at home using hours.' Gilbert explained.

'Oh! Yes, sure of course you can and you know you don't even have to ask, this is home.'

'Esther, go and open the boys' room for Gilbert, you know where the key is,' Mrs. Karanja said to her daughter as she re-joined the ladies' meeting again.

Esther appeared not to have heard anything. She avoided Gilbert's eye contact and studied her lunch with knitted brows.

'I'll get it!' Kanono said seeing that Esther was uncomfortable. Perhaps, she didn't feel like being sent, Kanono reasoned. The Karanja kids were perpetually doing chores which was not usual at the Mathai household. Kanono sympathized with Esther over this though normally, Esther didn't seem to mind all the work she did at home.

'Esther?' Mrs. Karanja voice had a warning tone to it. 'Delayed obedience is—'

'Disobedience,' Esther whispered getting up slowly.

'I'll take her!' Kanono volunteered again. Gilbert frowned at this new development as he followed the girls upstairs.

Esther went into her mother's room to get the key. Kanono followed her in but Gilbert waited for them at the boys' bedroom door.

'Why are you so quiet all of a sudden?' Kanono asked as she helped Esther search for the key though no search was needed because Esther knew exactly where it was, she was just stalling.

'Nothing,' Esther said looking sullen.

'Okay, but I know it's something. Is it because I want to go swing?'

'No.'

'Is it akina Karen?'

'No.'

'Is it because your mum sent you? Even me I don't like being sent. You get so tired.'

'No.'

'Is it because of Gilbert?' Kanono was throwing things randomly, seeing what stuck.

...

'Is it?' She said sensing a story.

...

'Ess, tell me! I'm your best-friend.'

'Weeee! I don't have time to waste. Bring me that key.' Gilbert interrupted them.

Kanono glared at him. 'What have you done to my friend?' she stalked towards him even though she was much shorter than him and didn't present a real threat to his safety.

'Nothing!' Esther said quickly.

'But you said—' Kanono turned to her in confusion.

'I didn't say anything.' Esther grabbed the keys and handed them to Gilbert then sprinted downstairs. Kanono was stunned by the speed of events for a moment. She blinked severally, growled at Gilbert than ran after Esther.

'Leave me alone,' Esther said when Kanono finally found her in the backyard.

'But I just—'

'I don't want to play anymore.' Esther said.

'Bu—'

Esther turned away from Kanono.

~

Esther did not show up to the Nativity Play rehearsal that evening but Kanono was too involved in preparing for the second to last rehearsal before the Christmas party on Saturday to pay it much attention. The Nativity Play had come to mean the world to her. It was the only time she out-Karened, Karen. This year, Mrs Shah was working on the most ambitious version of the play ever.

Whilst Mrs. Shah had every intention to follow the Bible to the letter with regards to the play (as she'd promised Mr. Karanja she would), there was a small hiccup—she did not own a Bible. Trusting that her memory of the events surrounding the birth of Jesus were still fresh, she went forth to produce the play sans Bible. As a result, each year, a little extra was added to the play that was not in the original Bible version of the nativity story and a little extra was taken out.

Mrs. Shah had her daughter, Harpreet, act as an assistant during auditions and later on, in rehearsals as well. Harpreet came because nobody took martyrdom as seriously as she did. Whilst she obeyed her mother's every fanciful whim, learnt to cook like a "good-Indian-girl" and scored the highest in her school during KCPE and KCSE, Harpreet harboured a grudge against her family. She wrote letters addressed to the agony aunt in the English teen magazine SHOUT! bemoaning life in a third-world country with parents who, she assured this agony aunt (who never featured one of her letters in the magazine nor responded privately), were plotting to marry her off to one of her cousins. It wasn't true but martyrdom required a cause even if one had to be made up. Harpreet sulked through the "Nativity-Silly-Billy-Play" season in what she would have been disappointed to know was classic teenage anarchy.

By the time Kanono was old enough to audition for bigger parts in the play, it was a revered institution. The play was praised for its elaborate and often genius costumes which had become characters in and of themselves. Mrs. Shah's design notes were legendary: 'I want Mary to look beautiful, but not too beautiful because she's just had a baby in a manger, and poor but not too poor, because that will distract from the miracle of the birth. And don't forget, she's a visionary, but not like Mother Theresa, so don't make her dress too saintly, she needs to have some sass.' This translated to blush pink gossamer fabric over a rose gold satin gown. The costumes became more nuanced and detailed as the years went by.

The costume department was headed by and comprised of Pius, Mrs. Shah's family tailor. He sorely disliked his involvement in "this nativity thing" because Christmas was usually a busy time of the year with people paying "through the nose" to get special dresses and family outfits made for the holiday season. Instead of cashing in on the Christmas mania, he could be found holed up in a spare room at the community centre, sowing plastic baubles onto the sheep's costumes for the princely sum of fifty shillings an hour. Mrs. Shah refused to pay per garment and he had no agency in the matter because the Shahs gave him good business all year round. To refuse the Christmas work was to bite the hand that fed him.

And the play itself? One year, she had Joseph speaking in Sheng, which she didn't know so she got the older kids to write his dialogue. This resulted in one or two of them being banned from the writers' room for life after she found out that they'd slipped some "very naughty" words into Joseph's lines after the play went through its screening with Mrs. Karanja during the final rehearsal. The audience had coalesced into hysteria during the scene where Joseph told Mary the baby could not be his because he had not lungulad her yet.

The next year, instead of being a carpenter, Joseph's character was a matatu graffiti artist. When Mrs. Karanja came to watch the final rehearsals and expressed reservations about this, Mrs. Shah reassured her: 'Darling no, don't worry, it's to make it more relatable. Remember Joseph wasn't your banker type—just a carpenter and all that—' Mrs. Shah paused for effect then asked: 'Do you know any carpenter?'

'No, but I don't think—'

'Exactly! You see what I'm saying.'

'I also don't *know* any matatu graffiti artists. It's not wise to change Joseph's profession like that. It might upset people…we don't want a repeat of last year.'

'You don't know how mortified I was. I should have known those kids would be naughty. Although, if we are being honest, it is a fact that Joseph and Mary didn't…didn't…you know…I don't see what all the fuss was about.' Whenever she retold the story to her friends, Mrs. Shah would tear with laughter at the audiences reaction (particularly Mr. Karanja's), though she tried to keep a straight face now.

'It's not right for the children to joke about sex in that way,' Mrs. Karanja explained.

'But they weren't joking about it at all. Didn't you see that was the scene where…' Mrs. Shah regrouped, coming back to the issue at hand. 'Anyway, this is different. Joseph's profession is just how he makes money. It's not like I'm changing Jesus to make him Jecinta.'

There was the year a horse, a few zebras and a pack of lions were added to the manger (so that they could cast more kids who were "just desperate to be in the play"), and Mary was given a "backstory" that same year I believe. Mrs. Karanja tried to push back on the more outlandish ideas, but there was no denying Mrs. Shah's talent when it came to producing terrific plays year after year. The Nativity Play became the highlight of the Christmas parties.

~

The plays had been an unexpected source of joy for Kanono who was at present putting on her costume. Her role last year as one of the three wise men was such a success that this year, Mrs. Shah stopped by her house one afternoon in early November to give her the part of Joseph.

'We're trying something different. This is show business we are not here to bore the crowd. If we did the same play over and over again no one would pay for the show.' No one did, but Mrs. Shah enjoyed a good spot of showbiz talk.

Mrs. Shah was the second person after Esther to seek Kanono out in her home. It did not escape Kanono that this was a middle-aged woman, not Karen at her door. Kanono often day-dreamed that one day Karen would ring their doorbell and ask her to come out and play.

Still, it was an honour to be sought out for a role when everyone knew Mrs. Shah took auditions very seriously. Just because you were Mary one year did not mean you would get the part next year. Once, Angel Gabriel was switched a day to the play for coming late for rehearsals. Kanono imagined lording her success in the play over Karen, but the thought was quickly replaced with the certainty that Karen would not grant her the audience.

~

'And cut! Cut!' Mrs. Shah interrupted Kanono who'd just strode onto the stage in her Joseph costume. Kanono looked down to see what the reason was, scared she'd done a bad job.

'There is absolutely no way a girl is playing Joseph,' she heard Mrs. Karanja roar (as far as Mrs. Karanja's gentle voice could roar). Kanono looked around Mrs. Karanja to see if she'd come with Esther who was meant to play one of the wise men and had been switched with Karen for her lack of appearance at a "crucial" rehearsal. Mrs. Karanja was alone.

'Mrs. Shah, you know I've let you have fun with this play, but this is now going too far. We have to toe the line somewhere!' Mrs. Karanja's veins popped out on her neck and temples. Kanono watched the battle her heart sinking. She really loved her part as Joseph. Together with Mrs. Shah, they'd worked on some really funny dialogue which they knew would be a hit if they could just get to the play.

Harpreet passed by Mrs. Karanja and bumped into her as if she'd not noticed her there. She apologised, but it was clear it was on purpose because of the smug smile on her face.

'Oh because Joseph is a man in real life?' Mrs. Shah asked as if now was when she was comprehending the issue.

'Yes! We cannot have a girl play Mary's husband. What message will that send?'

'But if you just take a look at the costume, it's clear Kanono is playing the role of a boy playing Joseph and anyway, all these kids look the same. Boy or girl there's no way anyone will know.'

Mrs. Karanja narrowed her eyes. Everyone would *know* it was Kanono.

'Find someone else,' Mrs. Karanja said through gritted teeth. Kanono felt the sting of tears. She'd never seen Mrs. Karanja so icy.

'I can't. It's too late for anyone to memorise all those lines.'

'You changed Angel Gabriel on the last day, last year.'

'That's because he only had one line!'

'Mrs. Shah. If you don't find someone else the play is cancelled.' There was a gasp throughout the community centre hall.

'But Mrs—'

Mrs. Karanja turned and stalked off. Harpreet stuck her tongue out at Mrs. Karanja's back. For once, she was on her mother's side.

Kanono sagged in her costume. She heard Karen and a few of her crew members sniggering in the wings. This had to be the worst day of her life. First, Esther didn't want to play with her, and now she wasn't good enough for the part of Joseph.

Even the normally upbeat Mrs. Shah was stunned speechless.

'Um. I think—let's take ten and regroup,' Harpreet said on behalf of her mother who she'd never seen looking so forlorn.

The kids disbanded and went to sit in their groups. Naturally, Kanono sat alone, without Esther to keep her company.

CHAPTER TWENTY-SIX

Nyambura and Esther, August 20th, 2012

The Karanjas' church, Nyambura noticed, looked exactly the same, but bigger. At least three times bigger! The main church hall had been demolished and replaced with a bigger version of itself as if the Karanjas did not want to jinx their good luck by changing things too drastically. Mrs. Karanja had always had an undercover superstitious nature that slipped out once in a while. If you sneezed, she'd clap in delight and say someone somewhere was thinking about you. If a bird flew into the house, she'd look up frightened and say something bad was about to happen. She'd follow this particular superstition with a call to prayer to ward of any ill spirits.

To one side of the main church hall were two boxy buildings. The first was a five-storey parking lot and the second housed the Sunday School classes and the church offices that Esther had directed Nyambura to. She had finally called to say she was free for a quick coffee, and though her voice was light and airy and would have passed for upbeat, Nyambura knew her, and knew there was something forced about it.

In one of the church offices, she found Esther standing over a pile of papers with a young man, as forgettable as her father, beside her. Nyambura knocked on the open door startling Esther who looked up and smiled a thin, tight smile. Before Nyambura could make it further into the room, Esther grabbed her handbag, said something to the man then joined Nyambura at the door.

~

'So how have you been?' Nyambura asked as they got into Esther's car.

'I'm good. I've been good. Just you know…work…' Esther started the ignition and focused on her rearview mirror as she backed out of her parking spot.

'When did you start working with your parents?' Nyambura asked after another period of silence.

'It's been two years full-time.' Esther's responses were short and to the point. Their entire conversation to the coffee shop was like an interview: Nyambura asked the questions, Esther answered them.

Nyambura's phone buzzed as they entered the coffee shop. She was going to ignore it then saw the caller I.D.

'You got it! You got the part! They loved, *loved* your audition!' Michael, Nyambura's agent sounded like he was trying to keep his voice down on purpose, as if he were in a public space, maybe an airport on his way somewhere as they always were.

She paused mid-step. 'Wait what? What? Stop! Stop! Stop!' Esther slid into a booth and looked at her questioningly. Nyambura made a face that she hoped showed that she was excited and the call wasn't one of those bad calls none of us want to receive but we all will. She put her hand up to mime one second and went back out so that she could talk louder.

'Oh my God! Mike are you serious?' she kept asking even though she knew he was. He'd already moved past the initial announcement and was expounding on their next steps forward. That was their deal. You were allowed five seconds to be happy then you had to get back to work. 'If you dwell on your success you become a one hit wonder,' he always reminded her and then he would proceed to rattle of a list of comedians no one remembered any more.

They first met at a comedy open-mic in East London seven years ago. One of those meetings that you can only chalk up to serendipity. Michael had a quick eye for fresh material, he could tell within seconds of an act if the comedian was going to be any good and he'd only gotten it wrong once. He liked the way she delivered her jokes as if they pained her. Those were the best comedians as far as he was concerned. The ones who looked as if they were being forced to tell you their life story on pain of death. When he first met her, she had a ten minute act on her childhood that included the story of how she came to be called "the-fat-one" for the first sixteen years of her life. Even though you laughed it was sobering to process that a child had been saddled with such a burdensome name without her consent for those formative years of her life. Nyambura's comedy shows were cathartic. You laughed and then you found yourself punched in the gut with the reality of the joke and then she had you laughing again, but this time, with tears you weren't sure were joyous or painful or both.

Mike got her out of the open-mic circuit relatively fast and onto bigger stages. By the time she was graduating from university, Nyambura was a household name in the UK. Michael's first conversation with her after her graduation was two words:

'You're moving.' he said in between texting, giving orders at a clip to his assistant, and stirring splenda into his coffee.

'What?' Nyambura had come to discuss visa options that would allow her to stay in the UK longer.

'New York. I've seen some of the scripts you're writing. We can do something with those, hopefully. In the meantime, we need to get you on the auditioning circuit.'

~

Nyambura rang off and went back to join Esther, excited to share her news. Esther looked up from the menu and said, 'I only have ten minutes.'

'What?' Nyambura was knocked out of her bliss.

'I need to be somewhere.'

'Oh, but I thought you...' Nyambura stammered. 'I officially can afford health insurance, I thought we could celebrate or something.'

'What?' Esther looked bewildered by the statement.

'I got this show I auditioned for just before I came home,' Nyambura explained, her face illuminated with joy. 'Its straight to series which is great and—'

Esther was looking slightly past Nyambura like she was not in the conversation. Nyambura turned back but the spot Esther was looking at was vacant.

'Uh...' she faltered. Esther didn't seem to notice she'd stopped talking. 'Ess? Is something wrong?' Nyambura asked, finally. Esther blinked several times as if coming too herself. 'Is there something wrong? Because since I came back you've been acting...off and I can't figure out why because I've not seen you in such a long time I couldn't have done anything wrong.'

'It's always about you. That's not changed.' Esther said.

'What?'

'Everything, it revolves around you and it's about you.' Esther continued.

'What?' Nyambura repeated herself, feeling hurt by the accusation. 'I don't understand—'

'How could you? You were so oblivious to it. My mum always said you had a streak of your father in you.'

'Sorry?' Nyambura felt the blood rush to her ears.

'Selfish, self absorbed, always thinking about yourselves.'

'Are you ready to place your order?' A waiter appeared at their table, notepad in hand.

'I'll have a hot lemon and ginger, takeaway please.' Esther said as she got some money out and handed it to the waiter. He looked at Nyambura then at the money finding it odd that they'd come together but one had ordered takeaway and was paying, and the other looked like she was about to cry.

CHAPTER TWENTY-SEVEN

The Christmas Party, December, 1996

The news was bleak. The Nativity Play was cancelled.

Mrs. Shah stormed out of rehearsals the night Mrs. Karanja threatened to cancel the play if another Joseph was not found and she'd not been seen or heard from since then. It was now Saturday afternoon, four p.m. to be exact.

Kanono had spent the last few days crying and begging Mrs. Karanja to take back her decision to cancel the play. Her tears were a waste of time because Mrs. Karanja was not having it. There would be no play if a girl was playing a boy. She threatened to tell Mr. Karanja if Kanono continued begging and Kanono feared the man enough to stop pestering Mrs. Karanja at every turn.

'Esther,' Kanono lay on her stomach on Esther's bed as Esther arranged her dolls and books. 'What am I going to do?' she moaned.

'I don't know.' Esther hadn't brightened up since Thursday and though they'd seen each other a lot since then, Kanono had done most of the talking and Esther had listened in distracted silence. Suddenly, Kanono sat up.

'Wait! I have an idea,' she said, perking up. 'We basically all know our parts.' Esther finished tidying up her dolls and books and came to sit on her bed next to Kanono but Kanono had already jumped off the bed.

'We can just do the play anyway! They can't stop us when we are on stage. We have to for Mrs. Shah because she's worked so hard and she needs us to.' And also because Kanono herself wanted an opportunity to perform.

'I don't think so. Mum said no,' Esther said fussing with her the threads of her blanket.

'But Ess, we don't always have to do what they say. Like sometimes my mum tells me to do my homework and I don't. I do it in the morning at school.'

'Doesn't she check your homework before you go to bed?' Kanono wrinkled her nose at the idea of it. 'Maybe you can do that but I can't and I don't want to.' Esther crossed her arms.

'Ess…why do you always have to make things so boring.' Esther gaped in shock at the accusation thought it confirmed what she'd known about their friendship. 'Every time I say I want to do something fun you don't want to do it you want to sit here and read when we could be plotting to do an illegal play!'

'Then you go plot. I'll sit and read!' Esther turned around and went to her bookshelf to hide her tears.

'I don't know why you've become so mean all of a sudden,' Kanono said to her back.

'I'm not mean!' Esther shouted as she yanked a book from her shelf.

'Yes you are. On Thursday you just left me alone and you always do that for no reason.' Kanono also felt a prick of tears.

'Girls, tea is ready.' one of the Karanja guests had been told to let the girls know it was time to come down for tea.

'You stay here and do nothing. I've gone to do a play!' Kanono run out of the Karanja's house in a huff, but once she was out on her own she felt the weight of her loneliness. Esther was her other half, her silent partner yes but nevertheless an integral part of her being. Kanono didn't know how to be without this quiet but vital limb and now she was going to have to convince and mobilize the other kids (who didn't really care much for her), to do a play they could get in deep trouble for. Kanono considered turning back and going to Esther to apologise for her harsh remarks. If she did this, at least she was guaranteed a peaceful afternoon where they'd play together in Esther's room, maybe a round of teacha-teacha and then they'd walk hand in hand to the party and it really wouldn't be all that bad to not have a play. But Kanono was more enticed by the idea of putting on an illegal play or attempting to, even though the possibility that everyone would agree to join her was low and there could be dire consequences if they did. She hit the road without a look back at Esther's house. Esther watched Kanono run-walk from the safety of her parent's bedroom window.

~

Kanono went to the Shah houses first and there was a moment where she didn't know which bell to ring and she did *ini-mini-minii-mo* and rang the third gate's bell. Mir, who was around her age, and one of the Karen crew came out to open the gate.

'Is Mrs. Shah home?' Kanono asked, all business like.

The meeting between Kanono and Mrs. Shah lasted all of five minutes. There was a jubilant, 'Huzzah! That's the spirit! An illegal play, a banned play, oh that will do it! They won't see us coming. We'll be like the books they banned during the witch-hunt!' Kanono didn't know what that meant but she was over the moon that Mrs. Shah was onboard.

'Now I can't go out and get the kids. That will attract too much attention, but you and Mir can. You'll split the estate in half and get only the key actors. We won't bother with the extras they might blabber to their parents.'

~

Kanono run out of Mrs. Shah's house, Mir beside, excitement pulsing through her. She'd never done anything like this before.

'You take that side of the estate, I take this side.' Mir said and before she could say anything else he'd shot off to round up the troops as Mrs. Shah had begun calling them.

Kanono looked at her side of the estate and licked her lips. The first house with a troop member on that side was Karen's. The Karen crew was not scary when you caught them on their own, except for Karen who kept up her persona regardless of how many people were surrounding her.

~

The fence around Karen's home had overgrown bougainvillea and from the gate it looked like a ghost town. Kanono realized just then that she'd never seen Karen's parents. She'd just assumed the girl existed one day and that was that.

Kanono rang the doorbell a couple of times before realising there was no electricity because she couldn't hear the sound of the bell echoing in the house. She was relieved that she didn't have to actually speak to Karen and turned around to leave when a movement in one of the windows upstairs caught her attention.

Kanono looked up and saw Karen staring down at her from her parents' bedroom window. She felt herself shaking. Karen crossed her arms and glared down. Kanono tried to give a weak wave, but she just put her hand up, and then brought it back down. Karen turned and went back into the recesses of the house leaving Kanono standing on her own outside.

'Is that a guest for you Karen?' she heard someone at the

open kitchen window say.

'No,' Karen said firmly.

'But I think she looks about you age.'

'She's not my friend.'

'Don't say things like that.'

'I can say whatever I want.'

...

...

'I'm just going to go and see what she wants.' The front door opened and a lady in a kitenge dress walked out. Karen followed behind her.

'Hi dear,' the lady said. Kanono tried to say hello but no sound came out of her mouth. 'Does she speak?' the lady turned and asked Karen. Karen shrugged.

'Hello, are you looking for someone?' the lady tried again.

'Uh...' Kanono licked her lips again. 'Um...I need to talk to Karen...alone.' she managed eventually.

'Oh, oh, of course. Some important business?' the lady winked then turned to Karen, 'Karen, darling come out here and talk to your friend. Such a lovely girl...' The lady walked back into the house talking to herself. Karen didn't move from her position, but Kanono knew she'd hear her all the same.

'The play...we are doing the play, it's back on,' she managed to say. Karen perked up and ran to the gate.

'Really? But it's been cancelled.'

'We decided to do it anyway.'

'Who did? How comes I wasn't there?' A credit to Kanono, her mind was fast and she took in the shift (ever so slight), but a shift nonetheless in their power dynamics and knew exactly what to do with it:

'I did—I came up with the idea. Then I convinced Mrs. Shah and we've decided we are only going to call the main people in the play and we will stage it just when everyone is being served dinner. But no parents can know.'

'You did?' Karen was re-assessing her.

'Yeah. I said we should stage an illegal play because it's not fair that Mama Esther has cancelled it.'

Karen run back into the house. She was there for a few minutes in which Kanono thought she'd lost her but then just as Kanono was about to give up and walk away, she came back out wearing shoes and with the key for the gate. She opened the gate, threw the key in the direction of the main house and then asked Kanono, 'So what's the plan?'

Kanono was flabbergasted at the casual way Karen left her gate open and threw the key. She looked back at the key and asked, 'Won't your mum mind that you just threw the key?' Karen shrugged.

'That's not my mum that's my aunt, my mum's sister. My mum is at work.'

'Oh like mine,' Kanono offered.

'Like everyone's,' Karen said and Kanono felt her hold on Karen dissipating so she swung the conversation back to the play.

'Right the plan,' Kanono began, Karen's eyes twinkled.

'Yeah tell me! What do we do now.'

'We assemble everyone. Mir has gone to call Mary and the other wise men and we've just got a few people on this side of the estate to go.'

The day felt like it was a dream come true. They walked together and talked like friends as they went from house to house, convincing the other cast members to assemble at Mrs. Shah's house. Kanono thought her heart would simply burst with excitement until they reached her side of the estate.

They were just about to turn back and head to Mrs. Shah's

house when Kanono spotted Esther sitting outside her gate on the pavement. Esther had come out to wait for her, Kanono realised.

'Oh we don't need her because I took her place,' Karen said. 'And you said we aren't getting any extras.'

'Uh…' Kanono.

'Let's go back. We have to be there now to do a final rehearsal.'

Esther looked from Karen to Kanono.

'But she can…'

'No extras,' Karen said and turned to walk away. Kanono hesitated.

'I'll come see you after rehearsal. Please don't tell your mum,' she begged Esther then ran after Karen.

'I will!' she heard Esther shout back as they got to the corner.

'Sissy!' Karen hissed.

'Sissy!' Kanono repeated. Esther shrunk back as if she'd been slapped and run off to her house.

~

'What are we going to do? She's ruined it for us,' the kids complained. They were at Mrs. Shah's house for their final rehearsal.

'Now relax. They'd have to lock us into my house to stop us from doing it.' Mrs. Shah took command of the fearful troops. 'Harpreet! Go and show face. Mingle around, I'm sure some people have began arriving, tell us what people are saying incase anyone has gotten a whiff of what's to come.'

Harpreet was more than happy to do so, the illegality of the play had ignited the outlaw in everyone.

'Right. Here's what we're going to do. We're going to do one run through then we're going to go back and join the party and act all normal-like. We don't want to raise any suspicion and if all of you are not at the party that will definitely raise suspicion.' A hand shot up.

'Yes Ian?'

'Can I tell my sister?'

'No, absolutely no one else can know! Everyone is to be assumed to be a blabber mouth.' Several more hands went up.

'What's a blabber mouth?'

'That's the problem with homeschooling an only child. They grow up not knowing what a blabber mouth is,' Mrs. Shah muttered. The child blinked in confusion 'A blabber mouth is someone who goes around telling stories they have no business telling.'

'What time are we going to do the play?'

'Ok no more hands up. No more hands up. Put them all down. I'm not taking any more questions at this time. If you listen to me you will have all the answers and more.'

The kids obeyed which was unusual during a rehearsal, but this was different, it felt important and no one wanted to ruin it.

Mrs. Shah called Kanono to the front and together they shared their plan with the kids. Kanono was in a state of euphoria when she got back home having walked with Karen till Karen got to her house, bid her a fond see-you-later and then continued on her journey home. She stopped at her gate and looked at Esther's gate. She should really say sorry for earlier, she thought. But now she needed to get ready for the play, she could say sorry at the end of the evening.

CHAPTER TWENTY-EIGHT

The Nativity Play, December, 1996

They were to wait for Kanono's cue, then the kids would casually walk towards the community centre where their costumes were neatly set up by Mrs. Shah and Harpreet. Here, they were to change in strict silence. Very fast. Don't get distracted, Ian! And then, just as the guests were enjoying their main course, Mary would carry the props necessary for her role (the manger, a stool, and a baby doll), and she would be followed by the other actors and their props. The set would be sparsely decorated because they were relying on what a bunch of ten-year old kids could carry in two hands. But that was part of the message. Mrs. Shah was fully on board with the starkness of the set. It would amplify their protest.

~

The kids were changing speedily and silently when they heard two distinct voices. Mrs. Karanja and Esther were talking outside. Mrs. Shah put a stern finger to her lips to warn everyone to keep quiet and not move.

'Why have you been so off?' Mrs. Karanja was asking Esther. 'And why do you keep following me around? Where's Nyambura, you should go sit with her. She probably needs you, she looked very upset this morning.'

'She is—'

There was a collective gasp of fear in the changing room.

'—In the loo,' Esther finished. Kanono had never had Esther lie before. She wanted to run out and give her best friend a big hug and a giant kiss!

'Mum?' Esther called after her mother. 'I don't like Gilbert.'

'What?' Because the kids in the changing room could not see them, they didn't know that Mrs. Karanja was presently distracted looking over the D.J.'s invoice which she was going to thoroughly dispute. How could he charge them for speakers when he had them already? It wasn't like he needed to buy a new set for the event.

'I don't like Gilbert,' Esther repeated.

'Oh, darling, that's not a very kind thing to say. Remember what I taught you? People are broken and need our love and kindness, especially when we don't feel like giving it.'

'But—'

'Go and look for Nyambura okay? We'll talk about this later.' The kids in the changing room heard Mrs. Karanja's sure steps receding in the corridor. Esther didn't pose any real danger, so they resumed getting ready for the play.

~

'An outrage! This is an outrage!' Mr. Karanja was nearly jumping as he spoke.

The play had received a standing ovation from the very entertained guests. When Mary walked out onto the space that would have housed a stage, lugging her props, Mrs. Karanja was not in the vicinity to stop her. By the time the play was in full swing, the Karanjas could only stand on the sidelines and watch in horror. To stop the play halfway would attract too much censure from their neighbours who had abandoned their dinner and were laugh-crying as the kids performed with everything in their little hearts and souls and won the crowd over.

'Well, everyone loved it.' Mrs. Shah was back in form. The play was better than she'd expected and there was nothing the Karanjas could do to stop it, now that it was in the past.

'How could you disobey me?' Mrs. Karanja asked.

'I'm a grown woman, not one of your children. The estate wanted a play and we gave them a damn good play! Those kids acted their hearts out tonight, and if you can't see it because of your funny hung-ups about a girl playing the part of a boy, then I'm really sorry for you. There's real talent in some of these kids and Kanono is one of the most talented. And how is she supposed to know that she is, if she doesn't get the chance to perform?'

'The play is cancelled for good.' Mr. Karanja was not listening to anything Mrs. Shah was saying. Mr. Mathai came upon them just then.

'Another stellar performance! I got it all on my video camera!' He came round and vigorously shook Mrs. Shah's hand.

'Did you see my daughter out there?' he turned to the Karanjas pride shining through his eyes. 'Did you see how good she was? The best Joseph I've ever seen by far! By far!'

CHAPTER TWENTY-NINE

Vacation Bible School, August, 1997

It was Thursday. Vacation Bible School (henceforth VBS), had been a splendid success for the Karanjas' church whose name I've resisted mentioning but here it is, do what you will with it: Church of the Lord's International Truth, acronym CLIT. No prizes for guessing who insisted on this name. This year they had triple the attendance of the previous year. The volunteers had shown up on time, the kids had enjoyed the arts and crafts and no major incidents of vandalism by a kid in a temper tantrum were reported. Everyone was having a grand time—everyone except Kanono.

Shout to the Lord all the earth let us sing—Kanono strained from her position at the back of the crowded age 10-12 class to see where exactly Karen was standing—*power and majesty, praise to the king*—the girl had no shame, Kanono thought, forgetting to clap along to the song they were singing—*mountains bow down and the seas will roar*—

Karen was at the front of the classroom, beaming up at teacher Liz, clapping in time to the music. Right beside her stood Denis, also clapping but looking at Karen in her braids with multi-colour beads in obvious admiration—*at the sound of your naaaaaame*—something in Kanono snapped!

Denis was hers. Or at least it had begun that way on Monday. The Karanjas held VBS at their church on the short

August holiday and most parents took it as an opportunity to relieve themselves of their children for a week. In the previous years, Kanono had really enjoyed VBS. It was a mix of all her favourite things, juice, biscuits with a lovely sugar coating, colouring activities and teachers who were so friendly they'd let her and Esther go for seconds during tea time. Esther would always give Kanono her seconds.

Then there were the prizes for memorising Bible verses. Though Kanono was never able to concentrate long enough to memorise a chapter of anything, Esther always took home one of the prizes: a giant exotic bar of chocolate bought from Monty's at Sarit Centre.

Monty's was the holy grail of candy stores for Kanono. It was the only store she knew that sold jawbreakers like in *Ed, Edd and Eddy,* and their pick 'n' mix section made the supermarket's candy aisle look like a wasteland. Every sweet, fudge, chocolate and gum imaginable was stocked at Monty's. You are perfectly right in speculating that Kanono once tried to steal from Monty's. She did not succeed because the store was too small, and the attendants too watchful, for her to get away with it.

Anyway, each year, Esther would split her prize chocolate with Kanono which was tantamount to winning in Kanono's books. VBS had brought Kanono untold amounts of joy and it had once again began with promise that Monday morning. She met Denis within the first hour of the first day of VBS. He was a thoughtful little boy with a round face and a dimpled chin. This was his first year attending VBS, his family having recently moved back home from Dar Es Salaam. He spoke Swahili in a lyrical accent, and English like it was a distasteful habit.

Kanono found him to be the most interesting creature she'd

ever met. Then disaster struck. Karen, whose parents heard about VBS from her parents after they became friends following the illegal play last year, was also attending it for the first time. Their friendship had lasted until January when Kanono went out to play and found herself summarily banned from whatever game the Karen crew were playing that day. Her friendship with Esther was quickly recovered (at least according to Kanono), and life had been going on at it's usual predictable pace when at tea time on the first day of VBS, a girl was ushered into their classroom and it was Karen.

The whole experience made Kanono relieve a recent trauma she was trying hard to forget.

~

On the last day of the second term, just before the August holiday, Eric, a short boy with a delta in the middle of his head, run into the girls' bathroom after school, grabbed Kanono, turned her round to face him and planted a wet kiss on her lips before sprinting back out. She'd been flustered at first, but then another feeling emerged like a warmth in her belly.

She had always been dimly aware of Eric and the other boys in his group, but over the course of the last term her antenna had increasingly tuned to the frequency known as Eric Wafula. It wasn't until she stepped back outside into the sunlit courtyard of the school square that she understood what the kiss had been about.

The boys were heaving from laughter as Eric spat and kicked his tongue in and out. 'Water, water, I need water! I'm going to die!' he was pretending to gasp for air, rubbing his tongue on his dirty sweater sleeves. The dramatics were met and matched with more raucous laughter that caught the attention of more students who were milling about waiting for their parents or drivers to pick them up from school.

The little crew of boys turned into a crowd and the whispers went up and down the crowd even before Kanono had a chance to grasp what all the commotion was about.

'You guys owe me fifty bob each! I did it!' Eric, with the wide, large eyes and crooked smile (Kanono refused to acknowledge the delta in the middle of his head), had made a bet that he would kiss the last person on earth they would ever want to be with: Kanono. The boys had been working on the list for the better part of the term. Kanono hadn't even known such a list existed.

The final blow came as Mr. Mathai pulled up in his noisy Nissan whose breaks had gone soft and shreeky, crying for a much needed service.

'Kanono! Ebu we will be late to pick Kanyi!' Mr. Mathai shouted from where he stood, by the open boot of the car, ready to throw her school bag into it. All the kids around her turned first to look at the source of the call and then to look at Kanono.

She didn't wait for the sniggering or the kids chant: "Ka-no-no! Ka-no-no!" She grabbed her school bag and run to the car. The tears arrived even before she'd fastened her safety belt. For four years she'd managed to keep that part of her life a secret at school. She was by no means popular but at least at school, nobody called her Kanono. By the next day, everyone in school would know that was her nickname and no one would ever call her Nyambura again.

~

Kanono kissed Denis during the first tea break of VBS at exactly six minutes past ten in the morning. She had earlier contrived to be in Denis's group when the class of twenty-something kids was split into five groups for a task. She waited to see which group Denis would gravitate towards and then barrelled through the room to sit next to him. She saved a spot for Esther who followed at a slower pace.

Esther sat at the fringe of this new friendship with a growing uncertainty about what it meant for her over the next week. After Kanono's kiss with Eric, which Esther had heard no end of, Kanono had transformed, not in public but in private with Esther. All of a sudden she was a fountain of knowledge when it came to boys and kissing and babies. 'If you kiss for five minutes you get pregnant. If you kiss for ten you get AIDS,' Kanono had been telling her that morning as they ate breakfast at the Karanja household. To Esther, if felt like Kanono had grown up on the Wednesday afternoon of her first kiss and she'd not taken Esther with her.

'Have you ever kissed someone?' Esther overheard Kanono ask Denis. She groaned internally and if she was any other child she would have rolled her eyes. Teacher Liz was handing out the sheets with the Bible verses they were meant to memorise that week. Last year, Kanono had been beside herself with excitement, even offering to help hand out the sheets so that she could get a first peak at the verses she had no intention of memorising. This year, she absently took her sheet from Esther as she continued her pursuit of Denis.

Denis surprised both of them by shaking his head and adding: '...but I want to, I just don't know how.' Kanono's eyes brightened. At break time, Denis got up to use the bathroom. Esther watched as Kanono jumped up after him, not bothering with the sugar coated biscuits and juice. Denis had barely entered the boys' bathroom when the door was blackened by the shape of a little girl his height. Imitating Eric, Kanono grabbed him, turned him round and kissed his lips. She'd been practicing for days since her traumatic incident with Eric. Any surface that was kissable was used for practice: her teddy bears, bedroom walls, pillows... She wasn't going to be outdone again. It was all in the hope that should Eric rethink his earlier feedback on the kiss and on the first day of third term he chose to try it again, she would be ready for the challenge.

Denis surprised her a second time that morning by also taking hold of her round shoulders and pressing his lips to hers—hard. They stood this way not knowing what to do next. After a few moments of silence punctuated with heavy breathing, they pulled apart. Denis's eyes held the accusation that she'd sold a lie. She had no idea how to kiss, not like on T.V. anyway.

By the end of tea time, Karen had arrived.

~

Karen stole the show without being aware there was a show to steal. Kanono noticed Denis noticing Karen as soon as she walked into the classroom and she knew right then and there she was finished. When teacher Liz asked the kids to form new groups for the second activity Kanono could have sworn there was a stampede for Karen's group. Once the commotion was over and everyone was settled into their new groups, Kanono was dismayed to find that Denis was now in Karen's group.

If she was dismayed on Monday, she was heart-broken by Wednesday and furious by Thursday. Karen and Denis had become an "item". They contrived to be in the same group at least once every day and they ate their break together and once, Kanono had spotted them holding hands at the parking lot!

It was all too much and it was time Karen was put in her place for all the times she denied the girls a chance to play with her (this was the argument she set before Esther so as to make the vendetta look like a joint affair). She had a plan to knock

Karen down a few rungs of her ladder.

~

'But what if they find out it's us? My mum will kill me. Me, I don't want to be grounded. Kwenyu nobody is ever punished when they do something wrong.'

'Relax. No one will know—ok maybe Karen but she won't be able to prove it.'

The letter was ready by Friday morning. The girls had asked to stay at the church late on Thursday afternoon to draft and then decorate the letter with the Sunday School arts and crafts supplies. They glued a generous amount of glitter on the page obscuring some words, drew love hearts with arrows piercing through them and what were meant to be deciphered as red lips.

As their class reassembled after the morning break time on Friday, Denis found a love letter addressed to him from Karen next to his backpack. Karen was immediately lauded as an artist and a poet. Even teacher Liz thought the letter was kind of cute. She didn't (much to Kanono's consternation), scold Karen for writing a love letter to a boy. Kanono sulked the rest of the lesson and refused to take part in learning the Bible verses of the day. Esther, torn between obedience and loyalty, sat next to Kanono at the back of the class but recited the verses along with everyone else.

~

Mr. Mathai picked up Kanono and Esther that afternoon and his uncharacteristic silence along with the bad mood he was in jolted Kanono out of her own bad mood. When his favourite songs came on the radio he didn't sing along to them. She tried to sing to get him to join her but he wouldn't budge.

'Daddy, what's wrong?' she asked. He gruffly shook his head then a vestige of his former self offered Kanono a half-smile through the rear view mirror. Mr. Mathai deposited the girls at Sno-Cream and asked them to sit tight in the ice-cream parlour for a few minutes as he ran a quick errand down the road. The girls struggled onto the bar stools and made their orders. Esther ordered a chocolate ice cream in a cone and Kanono ordered a mix of the triumvirate: chocolate, strawberry and vanilla in a cup.

As the girls ate their ice cream they played one of their favourite games, trying to see who could come up with the most disgusting ice-cream flavour. There were many contenders that day from grasshopper and mint sundae with a poo sauce to Scott's Cod liver oil, vanilla ice cream omena sprinkles…

As the flavours got more ridiculous their laughter grew out of hand until Kanono fell off her stool. As Esther helped her back on, she realised how much she lived for these moments with Kanono where, the girl was not running after an obsession, or trying to outwit someone, or any of those other ill-advised shenanigans the daring Kanono loved to partake in.

Mr. Mathai came back with Uncle Kamau who looked angry. Mr. Mathai was not faring much better.

'Daddy? Are you okay?' Kanono asked again with concern. She was not used to this stranger. She'd also not seen Uncle Kamau in over a year. Her first instinct was to run up and hug him but the look on his face deterred her from doing so.

'Eh?' Mr. Mathai responded then turned back to Uncle Kamau and continued to talk at a rapid and angry clip.

'Dad?' Kanono tagged at his shirt. He shook her off with a roughness that was foreign to Kanono.

For every child, there is a moment where they look at their parents whom they have held in high regard all their lives and see, for the first time, instead of a parent, a human being, made of flesh and bone, just like them and just as afraid of nightmares as they are. The trick is to keep the charade going for as long as possible but on this day Kanono looked up at her father's great height and saw in the place of his forever smile, a frown so deep she knew he was afraid of something. This was the moment the illusion shattered for her.

CHAPTER THIRTY

Nyambura and Esther, August 20th, 2012

Esther's drink arrived and she was about to stand up and leave when Nyambura finally spoke up.

'Where is this coming from?'

'I've watched some of your shows online. Like the one about Eric and the kiss. Why didn't you just tell me that?' Nyambura was confused by the turn in the conversation.

'You and Kanyi were literally the only people who ever looked up to me. I didn't want—I guess I didn't want to lose points with you,' she said. The last part sounded weak, even to Nyambura, but she'd been caught off-guard, she reasoned. Esther's brows furrowed, she gripped the takeaway cup so hard Nyambura thought the lid would pop.

'But you spent so much time after that making me feel stupid and unattractive, literary the same way those boys made you feel. Did you ever think about that?' Nyambura was about to interrupt her, but Esther held her hand up in protest. 'I get lying about an experience we've all done that but you never let me forget for a single day that I wasn't wanted. And it wasn't just that time it was every—'

'Ess...I...'

'You get up on those stages talking about how your childhood was this and that and painful and everyone called you fat, but you weren't any better you know that?' Esther's voice was brittle. It threatened to crack but she held on.

'Ess, we were kids ok. We were all going through shit!' Nyambura shot back in defence.

'But you have the world thinking it was only you who did. That you were some quiet little fat kid who didn't have a friend in the world, well you did, but you didn't want me. You always wanted to be with the Karens.'

'It's an act. That's why they call it a comedy act!'

'Don't insult me.' Esther stood up and Nyambura stood up with her.

'Look, I'm sorry if I hurt you but you never said anything then, so how was I supposed to know?'

'Did you ever tell Karen she hurt you?'

'No but it's not like I'm holding a grudge about it fifteen years later.' Nyambura regretted the words but they were already out.

'Really? Because it looks like you've built a career talking about her.'

Esther pushed past her and walked quickly to the exit, nearly bumping into a waiter carrying a tray laden with food.

~

Nyambura was dimly aware that her phone was ringing. It rang until it stopped then it rang again.

'I've been trying to reach you.' Beatrice said without preamble when she picked up the second ring.

'Oh, sorry I was—' Nyambura sat down as she spoke, overtaken by events.

'—when did you say you went to see Aunty Carol?' Beatrice interrupted her.

'Uh…I don't know maybe…'

'I need you to know!' Beatrice snapped.

'Okay, okay, calm down, what's wrong?'

'Just tell me, what day was that?'

'I think it was the weekend you were away for the honeymoon. Why?'

'She's not answered my calls and I asked Janet, you remember her? From house forty-four? I asked her to go and check on her for me and she said she rang the doorbell but no one answered and the door was locked.'

'Oh.' Nyambura stood up in a daze. 'Do you want me to go and—'

'No, no, I'm on my way there now. I just—' Beatrice ended the call abruptly. Nyambura stared at her phone for a moment. She tried ringing her mother back but Beatrice cut the line immediately. She walked out of the Java with nowhere in particular to go. She was about to call a taxi when she looked up and saw that Esther had not left. She was sitting in her car staring at nothing. Nyambura marched to the car and tried to open the passenger side door.

'Let me in.'

'No,' Esther said.

'Don't be ridiculous if you were really leaving you'd have left.' Esther hiccuped and a half-laugh escaped. She opened the door and Nyambura slid into the passenger seat.

They sat in silence for several minutes watching people walk into the Java, lovers holding hands, parents taking their kids for an after school treat, business people rushing in for a meeting...

The sun had retreated and dusk had taken over, a full moon hanging low and bright, when Esther finally spoke:

'I'm not saying sorry for what I said earlier if that's what you're waiting for.'

'Fair enough,' Nyambura said.

'But I guess I envied you that.'

'What? Being called Kanono my whole childhood?'

'No, not that but…' Esther breathed in and shut her eyes. 'I envied you the carefree life you had.'

'Because my parents were lenient?'

Esther laughed. 'Too lenient, you became a comedian. The Karanjas would never stand for that.' Esther said, imitating her father. Nyambura's eyes widened in surprise as she laughed. 'But no, not just that, it's you. You got to worry about typical kid things, who was your friend, who wasn't playing with you stuff like that and—'

Esther was quiet for so long Nyambura wasn't sure she was going to speak again.

'You remember Gilbert?' Esther asked finally.

'Gilbert?' the name was familiar but Nyambura couldn't put a face to it. 'One of your brothers friends' right?'

Esther nodded. 'Do you remember that day he came to play video games at home even though they weren't there?'

'Uh…yeah that was the day the play was cancelled.' The face was becoming clearer now.

'He hadn't come to play video games. I…they all used the same sort of language you know.' Nyambura was struggling to understand where this was going but knew not to interrupt. 'Come I show you a game or you're such a good girl, or—' Esther's voice broke. Nyambura was going to hug her but Esther pulled away. 'And each time I tried to tell my mum that…sometimes I convince myself it was me, that it happened to me because I was some sort of—'

It was only dawning on Nyambura now. When she thought of their childhood she thought of shared joys and shared traumas but Esther had carried this private trauma alone for all those years.

'Why didn't you tell me?'

'I didn't know how. I just wanted to be a normal kid, with normal kid issues not this other thing.'

'Does you mum know now?'

...

'Sort of.' Esther settled for this answer. 'She knows about Gilbert, but when I told her there were more, she said there couldn't have been because the other guests only ever stayed in the guest wing so she'd have known if something was going on. She said I was young, and it was traumatic so maybe…maybe I'd begun to imagine other people did it too.'

'Oh my God,' Nyambura breathed. 'Do you still live with them?' she asked.

'No, I…uh…I don't.'

'Are you okay working with them?'

'It's not God or the church I have an issue with. Besides I like my job. I'm heading the Children's Ministry team and every Sunday I see two kids coming for Sunday School that remind me of us. That's why I felt erased from your memories when I heard you talking about all these Karen things in your acts and I kept wondering when does she remember me? You were the best part of my childhood and I wanted to be the best part of yours so I didn't feel like it was all…crap.'

'First, that's amazing that you're teaching Sunday school. VBS was the highlight of my life! Look, I'm sorry, and I get what you mean. They say entertainers are horrible narcissists and I just didn't think of myself that way till now.'

'I didn't say you were a—'

'But I'm saying it. You're right, the world revolved around me and the fact is, as much as I don't like thinking about it, my dad was the same with my mum. He was great so long as you were not relying on him to be an adult and make good adult decisions so that's why he was a great friend, but then I didn't see my mum was a genuinely great mother, even though she let people get away with calling me Kanono for so long. No one is perfect, we all have things we could have done better. And I wish I'd done better by you.'

'You can now by using some of that brand new insurance money to buy me dinner.' Esther said.

'I can definitely do that!'

'So like, what insurance are we talking?' Esther asked as she switched on the car.

'The kind that gets you plastic surgery.'

'Those exist?'

'Yeah if you've had an accident and need massive reconstruction work done.'

'Oh I thought you meant a boob job,' Esther said sounding disappointed.

'Me too. But it's right there in the fine print. No vanity plastic surgery.'

'It's not a vanity when you're still an A cup.' Esther stole a meaningful glance at Nyambura's chest as they drove to dinner.

'You don't know my life!' Nyambura covered her chest in mock indignation.

CHAPTER THIRTY-ONE

Mrs. Mutiso, August 7th, 1998

It was the August school holiday and the twins were home from their grandparents. Karimi, the twins nanny (generously provided by Mr. Mutiso's parents), woke up early out of habit, which wasn't what alarmed Mrs. Mutiso this particular morning. It was her husband, you see. This chronic late riser had begun waking up at five a.m. ever since Karimi and the girls came back home. He was going out for a jog, he'd told Mrs. Mutiso the first morning he woke up early.

Mr. Mutiso did come back sweaty but for whatever reason, Mrs. Mutiso couldn't shake the feeling that running wasn't the exercise he'd been engaged in. This Friday, what had woken her up were sounds not unfamiliar to her. At first, they sounded like animalistic grunts, impatient with energy. In the pin drop silence of a holiday morning the noise was easy enough to make out. Mrs. Mutiso got up to investigate the sounds, softly creeping downstairs. She had barely turned the corner from the first landing of the stairs when she saw that right in front of her, in her very own kitchen stood two people joined at the groin, moving in unison.

Her husband's tracksuit bottoms and underwear were bunched at his ankles. Karimi's skirt was pulled up, her blouse open, bra pulled down to reveal pert little breasts with big swollen nipples that her husband was presently lathering with kisses. The grunts were from Karimi. That's what struck her first. That a girl this petite, this quiet and shy, could grunt at such a low pitch. They didn't see her. Not at first.

Mrs. Mutiso stood towering above them on the top of the first landing. Her breathing was even. She didn't do those things she saw the wives in Nigerian movies doing when they caught their husband cheating. She simply stood their transfixed by the performance.

~

'So, you think you can just fuck in my house?' The question sounded like it came from everywhere at once. The two lovers jumped apart confused. Karimi pushed Mr. Mutiso to the side and pulled up her bra.

Mrs. Mutiso abruptly turned around and took the stairs back up to her room.

'Don't worry, I'll make this okay,' Mr. Mutiso said in Kimeru. Instinctively, Karimi knew he'd walk up those stairs and swear to his wife that Karimi had been the one who pursued him.

'There's nothing to make okay.' The whole encounter felt surreal for Karimi. It was as though it had been lifted out of a dream, it certainly had the texture of one. She didn't notice Mr. Mutiso leaving the kitchen, so deep in thought was she. When he came back downstairs dressed for work, he stopped at the foot of the stairs, started to say something, shrugged and walked out the door. That one is his father, she thought as she watched him back his Peugeot out of the verandah.

~

After her husband left for whatever activities preoccupied his days, Mrs. Mutiso summoned Karimi to her room. The twins were still asleep.

'How long?' Mrs. Mutiso asked from the mirror of her

dressing table where she sat preparing for the day as if it were another normal day.

'Pardon?' Karimi thought it was a trick question designed to trip her up.

Mrs. Mutiso swivelled in her chair and faced Karimi. 'How long?' she asked again.

'Uh…'

'You can tell me.' Mrs. Mutiso's voice sounded gentle, mother-like. Karimi was confused by this

'Since I came.'

'Ah so a week then.'

'The first time—the first time I came.'

'So then, what is that? A year?' Mrs. Mutiso turned to her table and took a tub of body butter which she opened and luxuriously rubbed onto her arms. It smelled lovely.

'I think.' Karmi shifted nervously.

'That adds up.' Mrs. Mutiso spoke so softly, Karimi wasn't sure she'd intended for her to hear this.

'What did he tell you?' Mrs. Mutiso asked.

'Tell me?'

'How did he convince you?'

'He…oh…he was just…'

'Thoughtful?'

'Yes.' Karimi shifted again.

'Remembered things, observant, kind even?'

'Yes.'

'Did you enjoy it?'

'What?'

'The attention?'

'Yes.'

'Me too. When it was freely given. You know, many times I've asked myself would I have done it differently? If I knew how it would turn out, (how boring: loveless marriage, disinterested partner). Would I have run?' Mrs. Mutiso took out a box that contained her earrings. She took out a pair of pearls.

'Seeing him with you today, I now know. I wouldn't have. Isn't that pathetic? The early days with him were…I've never known such happiness in my life. I hope you enjoyed yourself at least. You do understand that now I have to fire you.'

Karimi nodded, thankful at least that Mrs. Mutiso had not chosen to humiliate her which would have been easier.

'Pack your bags. I'd like you out of my house before my children wake up,' Mrs. Mutiso said as she rose from her seat.

'Yes.'

'And Karimi—'

'Yes?' Karimi said at the door.

'You took good care of my children. I won't forget that.' Mrs. Mutiso sounded genuinely grateful. 'You taught them Kimeru. I hear them speaking with you. I always wanted to, but I was too scared I'd get in trouble with their grandparents. But now they know their mother tongue. They can't take that away from them,' Mrs. Mutiso went into her bathroom and closed the door.

Karimi heard a faucet being opened. She stood at the threshold of the bedroom, her mind a turmoil of thoughts but a predominant one forming and surging to the forefront of her mind. Mrs. Mutiso was not whomever she'd thought she'd known and it was too late to get to know this other person she felt a strong kinship with. Karimi felt robbed of an opportunity she didn't even know she'd desired. Mr. Mutiso was a distant thought now, but his wife—Karimi wished she'd met her first, then she realised, Mrs. Mutiso would not have opened up this way in ordinary circumstances. A pity that, the realisation of a friendship lost before it began. I must remember, and you must remind me to tell you what became of Karimi, but this is not her story so we shall not dwell on her too much. But remind me, will you?

~

A few hours later, Mrs. Mutiso was lying on her sofa in the living room when her head began aching. There were degrees to her headaches. Sometimes they led to other things, things you know by now, but sometimes they just throbbed to remind her she was vulnerable. Today's was the throbbing kind. She called for the twins but receiving no response, realised they'd snuck out some time after breakfast to go God-only-knows-where. There was nothing for it. She, Mrs. Mutiso, would have to go to the Kiosk to buy painkillers.

Silence as vast and long as Lake Turukana after the rains (have you seen them by the way? We wait in anticipation for them for the third consecutive year), greeted the unexpected figure of the handsome Mrs. Mutiso swaying—as only she did—up the little hill to Ng'ang'a's Kiosk. Karimi had already been by and though she kept her mouth shut as to why she was carrying a bag with all of her belongings, the rumour-mill had already been at work, speculating on what events could have led to her abrupt dismissal. Chairing the conversation was—as always—Priscilla.

Mrs. Mutiso greeted everyone with a general "habari ya leo" and a nod, though not to anyone in particular, before turning her attention to the matter at hand. Ng'ang'a's son, Kevin stood attentively at the window of the Kiosk, ready to serve her. His head grazed the ceiling of the Kiosk and at twenty-one, nearly at his final six-foot, he loomed larger than the Kiosk.

'Oh, I don't think I've met you before? Did Ng'ang'a sell

his Kiosk?' Mrs. Mutiso asked, though, if that was the case, someone would have mentioned it at Bible study, but sometimes her mind wandered and she missed what her neighbours were saying.

'Nope, he didn't. I'm his son, Kevin. I'm filling in for dad. He went home to check on Guka who hasn't been doing too well.' He smiled and asked her what she'd like. He had one dimple on his left cheek. It was so small, but the realisation was like a veil lifted off Mrs. Mutiso's eyes.

In a matter of moments, the business was done. Pain killer in hand, money exchanged, there was nothing for it than for Mrs. Mutiso to head back home. And then a vestige of her conversation with Karimi slipped into her thoughts. When was the last time she'd been so happy? What had made her happy then with Mr. Mutiso? It was the headiness afforded by the first flushes of love. She didn't hope for love anymore, but the headiness? The rush?

'I have a few other things I need to buy. I've forgotten the list at home. Come and get it from me later.'

Kevin agreed to come once there was a lull in customers. The thought of walking into the famed Mutiso home with it's gold chandeliers that everyone spoke about would be a wonderful if unexpected experience for the day.

~

Back at home, Mrs. Mutiso found she no longer needed the painkiller. She stared at her reflection in her bathroom mirror and was a little surprised to see a glow that was reminiscent of days passed. She showered and changed into her "guests in the house" clothes—a fitting dirra that accentuated her ample curves, a gold set of earrings with matching ring and necklace all glimmering with emerald stones. She did her braids up into a top bun and tied a silk scarf around her head. Thirty minutes passed before she heard the doorbell ring. Thankfully, the twins were still at large.

Kevin had jogged there, a fresh sheen of sweat on his forehead, his shirt wet under the armpits. Mrs. Mutiso opened the gate for him, and walked ahead of him deliberately swaying more than usual.

~

Kevin had seen it in her eyes when she asked him to come and collect the shopping list from her house. It was easily recognizable because he'd seen it in other women's and men's eyes before. But never had it had such an effect on him. Mrs. Mutiso was fable by this point to Kevin. He had heard of her since he was a child, overhearing and eavesdropping on their customers conversation. He'd known, the moment he saw her swaying up the hill to the Kiosk that this was she: the famous Mrs. Mutiso.

Kevin stood underneath the gold chandelier in Mrs. Mutiso's living room (here the stories had not lied), watching her back as she wrote a list of items for him to bring from the shop. She was perched on a small chair at her writing bureau facing a wide open window. Her soft rear spilled over the chair, her manicured fingers, scrawled a list in an elegant cursive hand. He came round so that he could better see her profile. He watched her breath in and out, noticing the quickness of her breath as her chest rose and fell rhythmically.

Everything about Mrs. Mutiso was like looking at a picture in high resolution. She was that much brighter, her features sharper, her movements more deliberate, her face more expressive than anyone else Kevin had ever met. He had been absorbing these features for a time when he found that she was no longer sitting at her bureau but was standing in front of him, list held out, a faint smile on her lips.

'You'll tell me how much it is?'

He nodded, took the piece of paper absently scanning it before he folded it up and put it in his pocket. At the bottom of the list, right next to one litre Coke, Mrs. Mutiso had written Trust x1. If he'd jogged the first time, the second time he fairly sprinted to the Kiosk and back. He didn't bother with Priscilla who'd been waiting for his return to buy salt she'd forgotten to buy earlier. He didn't hear her threaten to tell Ng'ang'a how inept his son was at running his Kiosk. He didn't notice her peeking through the Kiosk door as he grabbed the packet of Trust condoms and put them in a small black paper bag. Years of sending messages to and from Mrs. Mutiso and Mama Kanono had taught Priscilla to recognise that distinctive writing on the list Kevin was reading from.

~

Mrs. Mutiso was sitting in the living room thumbing through a magazine when Kevin returned.

'That was fast.'

'There weren't any customers.'

'So how much will it be?'

'Uh...' Kevin did the mental calculation quickly because he'd forgotten to add it up when he was packing the groceries. 'One thousand and twenty five.'

'Gosh, things are getting expensive, aren't they?' Mrs. Mutiso said without much conviction as she removed several crumpled notes from her purse.

'So Ng'ang'a's son?' she asked idly.

'Yes, only child.'

'What do you do when you're not working with your father?'

'I'm in university. I'm actually on holiday.'

'Oh?'

'Yes, I'm studying law.'

'That's nice,'' Mrs. Mutiso's courage was faltering, 'very nice.'

'I...' Kevin could feel an opportunity slipping from him.

'Hm?' Mrs. Mutiso asked eagerly.

'I should get back, incase customers are waiting,' Kevin heard himself saying.

'Oh, yes, yes, we shouldn't keep them waiting.' Mrs. Mutiso didn't know how to salvage the moment. He turned and walked to the door slowly and she followed to shut it after him.

'Your change?' Kevin asked.

'Just keep it.' Mrs. Mutiso said and they were both disappointed that the conversation had not progressed in the direction they'd both hoped it would.

Kevin opened the door but Mrs. Mutiso miscalculated and bumped into him by mistake as she stepped forward to close it. And isn't that how sparks ignite? An accidental bump? The magic of unexpected intimacy?

~

Mrs. Mutiso found a quality in Kevin that she'd never witnessed in her husband. He was curious, eager and therefore teachable. From the beginning, Mrs. Mutiso had ascribed to Mr. Mutiso a superiority of intellect, spirit and character that he had never and would never earn. To her surprise she found these in Kevin.

It was as they lay in bed, Kevin dozing off, Mrs. Mutiso staring at the ceiling, ruminating on the differences between her husband and her new lover, that they heard the blast.

It was so loud, the windows in her bedroom shook. A thick grey mushroom rose up above the roofs of the houses and buildings beyond, the grey in stark relief against the Nairobi-blue sky.

CHAPTER THIRTY-TWO

The Mathais, August 7th, 1998

Kanono was outside on the verandah playing hopscotch with Esther and Kanyi when they heard the blast. They sprinted back into the house and straight into Priscilla who was watching *Family Matters* in the living room as she ironed and folded clothes. She was so engrossed in the show, she didn't register the blast.

'Prisi! Prisi! Someone is shooting guns outside!' Kanono exclaimed.

'Guns? I've told you people not to cry wolf like that boy. No one came to save him the day a wolf finally came.' Priscilla said as she took one of Mr. Mathai's trousers from the pile and increased the temperature of the iron before beginning to iron them.

'No one said there was a wolf. We said—'

The front door opened and Mrs. Karanja run in, frantic. She'd heard the blast too and, like Kanono, had assumed it was a shooting in the estate. Her immediate thought had been for her last-born child. Though her other children were not in the house and she could not account for their whereabouts, her deepest concern had been for her little girl. Later, she'd reason with herself that it wasn't that she loved Esther more, it was that she at least knew where Esther was so it made sense to go in search of her first.

'My baby!' Mrs. Karanja, swept Esther into her arms. Kanono watched her carry Esther as though Esther were little more than a feather and longed to be carried in that way by her own mother who could not bare her weight and had not been able to since Kanono was four years old. At least her father still could.

'Priscilla did you hear that?'

Priscilla hated to be the last to hear a piece of news. 'The guns? Oh they were very loud! I had to tell the kids to get inside immediately. Do you think it's near here?' Kanono, Esther and Kanyi exchanged looks but Priscilla gave them a stern look that suggested they were better off remaining silent.

News has an interesting way of filtering down. For at least an hour, the party in the Mathai household believed that what they'd heard was a gun. In the Mutiso household, where Mrs. Mutiso had switched on the T.V. in her bedroom as soon as she saw the mushroom cloud in the horizon, it was clear it was a bomb. At Ng'ang'a's Kiosk, where a group of customers had been grumbling as they waited for Kevin to return, there was heated debate about the cause of the blast. When Kevin arrived, at their insistence, he switched on the radio before he served a single customer. They got the tail end of the emergency news broadcast. A bomb blast at the U.S. Embassy in town—

The red transistor radio, as if it had only ever existed for such a day as this, died after disseminating the news. The filtering continued unabated until eventually, Kali, one of Priscilla's friends, stopped by the Mathai household to borrow some sugar and in the process recited the news. There was an addition to the earlier broadcast: 'And apparently, the Co-operative bank right next to the embassy has also been affected.'

'That's where mum and dad go to the bank.' Kanono said. Kali blanched and turned to Mrs. Karanja and Priscilla in horror. Mrs. Karanja, who'd not left because she didn't want to put her child in danger incase the thieves with the guns were actually in the estate, turned to Kanono and asked in a stern voice: 'Are you sure?'

'Yeah, that's where dad opened my bank account and they gave me a piggy bank for savings so I don't buy so many sweets,' Kanono responded struggling to understand why Mrs. Karanja looked so worried. The words bomb blast were new to the kids.

'No, father, God no—please no!' Mrs. Karanja exclaimed. The kids grew more bewildered at this, thinking she was talking about Kanono's piggy bank.

'I can show you? It's not bad.' Kanono offered and got up to get it.

But just as Kanono was about to climb the stairs, Priscilla shrieked. 'Yes, she's right! She's right! That's where they bank.' The hot iron fell face first on the carpet and singed it before Priscilla could pick it up and switch the iron off. Kali stood on the side. Feeling like she was trespassing on something private, she let herself out quietly.

~

It was midnight now, and no one had left the sitting room. Mrs. Karanja kept switching between T.V. channels looking for whichever channel had a more recent update. They had tried calling the spare-parts store and the garage but lines were engaged so nothing went through. The kids had by now seen enough of the news to understand that something horrible had just occurred and somehow Mama Kanono and Mr. Mathai could be connected.

They didn't hear a car pull into the verandah (the gate had

been left open by Kali as an oversight). When the front door opened they turned in relief. Mama Kanono came through the door, dirty, caked in soot, cheeks black. She stepped further in and they held their breaths. A moment passed and then another. Mr. Mathai was not behind her.

'Where's daddy?' Kanono asked looking past her mother.

'D-da-da…' Mama Kanono was fatigued, she couldn't make out the words. She began to sway back and forth like a bridge about to collapse. Mrs. Karanja jumped into action and came to hold her then guided her to a seat. Mrs. Karanja asked the kids to go upstairs and asked Priscilla to get Mama Kanono a glass of water. No one moved, no one wanted to move. No one could take their eyes off Mama Kanono who was the only person who could tell them about Mr. Mathai's whereabouts.

Mama Kanono stared straight ahead to where the T.V. sat in the middle of a black cabinet. Guarding the T.V. on both sides were her Princess Diana plates. The news presenter said something and then the screen went blank for a moment before blinking back to life with footage from earlier in the day. The cameraman was not steady, the journalist talking to the camera kept turning back to look at the rubbled distraction, forgetting to address the camera. Mama Kanono felt dislocated from the present moment.

What do I tell you? Mama Kanono was at her dealership/garage, having dropped Mr. Mathai at the spare-parts store (they were sharing a car because his car had gone for service), when she heard the blast. He had been falling late on the bank loan payments from the money he lent Kamau (who'd disappeared and all efforts to contact him were in vain). Earlier that morning, Mr. Mathai had asked her for a helping hand with the loan for the first time since his folly. She had refused. 'That's your mess. I keep telling you to be more careful with how you use money. Maybe go and talk to the bank manager and see if he can give you a grace period. If you're running the store properly, you should be able to repay that loan.'

Mama Kanono drove downtown as everyone was running away. She saw the scar that minutes before had been the American Embassy and knew, just knew that Mr. Mathai was somewhere within the banking hall at the neighbouring Co-operative Bank which had also been decimated by the bomb.

Even before the dust settled, she was pushing her way through the crowds of people running away from the heart of death to get to it. On her bare hands and knees, Mama Kanono began to pull out stone after stone. She spent the entire afternoon searching the ruins, helping the other civilians who'd stopped to lend a hand to victims and the Red Cross, carrying people to ambulances, and all the while looking for Mr. Mathai.

~

'I need to go back.' Mama Kanono got up.

Mrs. Karanja tried to restrain her. 'You're too tired. Rest tonight. You won't find him in the night.'

'If he is there—if he is there, then I'm not going to let him sleep there alone.' She picked up her car keys and walked out. For a moment, she debated asking Mrs. Mutiso to go back with her but she got into the car and drove off. The vigil was hers and hers alone.

~

It was a year, it was a second, it was a day. Mama Kanono lost track of time. Every time a person or a body was found, Mama Kanono, along with everyone else who'd not recovered their family, hoped it was their person. Some tried to spark up conversation to comfort each other, Mama Kanono rebuffed these attempts.

'You've been here every day since Friday…' one of the Red Cross volunteers observed. '...have you checked the mortuaries?' The last person to be rescued from the rubble alive had been brought out a full twenty-two hours before. Since then acres and acres of bodies had been recovered but there was no longer any expectation that there was anyone alive in there. It was no longer a rescue mission. Mama Kanono stared ahead and ignored the question.

#

Mrs. Mutiso, it turned out, didn't need to be told how to help. When she heard that Mr. Mathai was missing and Mama Kanono was camping out at the scene of the tragedy, she rounded Mrs. Karanja, Mrs. Shah and a few other women from the Bible study group, split them into groups and gave them each a list of hospitals and morgues to search for Mr. Mathai in. Mrs. Karanja tried to suggest a strategy, but Mrs. Mutiso denied her the opportunity to take over the search. From morning till afternoon, the women set out to their assigned locations looking for Mr. Mathai. In between her search, Mrs. Mutiso would stop by the site to bring Mama Kanono a flask of uji and a change of clothes, none of which she accepted but distributed to the other volunteers.

~

Families waited for their loved ones to come home or call or something—to let them know they were okay. Not hearing from them, they, like Mama Kanono, went to the site of the blast in search of their people. There were families that camped at the morgues of Nairobi waiting for each wave of new bodies to be carted in and permission to be granted to go round and check if any of the bodies were their family members. There were some bodies that were burnt beyond recognition. There were bodies that two or three different families would identify as their sister, niece, aunty. The grief of the moment was diminished by the torture of the weeks that followed: to have to debate whether a dead body is yours, mine or theirs?

~

Mr. Mathai was never found nor was his body identified. In the aftermath, there were rumours about families that claimed bodies that were not theirs, just to have a body to bury, someone to say goodbye to. Who's to say…who's to say, if one of the bodies was his?

CHAPTER THIRTY-THREE

Mrs. Mutiso and Mama Kanono, January, 1999

'My God, a boy? Are you mad?' Mama Kanono exclaimed. Mrs. Mutiso had sent a message asking Mama Kanono to come to her house. This was different. They almost exclusively never spent time in Mrs. Mutiso's home.

'This is why I didn't tell you before. I knew you'd judge.'

'What is there not to judge?'

'He is nearly twenty-two.'

'Listen to yourself Carol! Nearly twenty-two?'

'Betty, if you have nothing constructive to say please shut up.' Mrs. Mutiso got up and paced her living room. Mama Kanono stared at her in shock. 'It's not like we are blind!' Mrs. Mutiso began. 'It's not like we don't want sex. They think they are the only ones with these uncontrollable appetites they keep talking about. Do they know how often we go to bed early just so we can give ourselves a bit of pleasure before they come and heave themselves on us?'

'They? Who is they and who is we? Don't speak for anyone but yourself!'

Mrs. Mutiso, stopped pacing and met Mama Kanono's gaze. She looked at her for several moments then let out a short, bitter laugh.

'You're not serious. Surely, you're not trying to lie to me?'

Mama Kanono shifted in her chair. 'Lie to you about what?

This isn't about me? I'm not the one who's pregnant.' she folded her arms tightly in front of her and straightened her back in silent challenge.

Mrs. Mutiso deflated like a punctured football and sunk onto her carpeted floor. This was the carpet she'd bought with Mr. Mutiso after he came back from his business trip to Eldoret that first week of their marriage. He'd taken her furniture shopping to apologise for leaving on such short notice. The carpet was heavily patterned and just now, her gaze on the carpet, she realized that what she'd always thought were abstract weavings of people and place, were stories, tied together with a rope pattern that weaved each rectangle of story to the other. Each little rectangle showed a different scene, lovers, cooking, children…the daily life of a family.

Mr. Mutiso brought in workmen to install the carpet and the other furniture he'd bought despite her request that they do it together. Mrs. Mutiso caressed the carpet as her eyes travelled the length of it. On the edges, she saw bald patches where rats had been feasting on it. The clocked ticked and then tocked. Outside, a car passed by, window down, radio on full blast playing Freshley's *Stella Wangu*. Mrs. Mutiso took up the tune and began to hum it. The song told of Freshley's heartbreak when he went to pick up a lady (whom he loved and had sold his worldly possessions to raise money for her education abroad—this is relevant), from the airport and he saw her walk off the plane, hand in hand with another man. His agony was so great, he wanted to cry in Kikamba, in Dholuo, in Kihindi just to find another way to express it, but his frustration was doubled when he remembered he only had Swahili.

'So what now?' Mama Kanono asked eventually.

'I don't know. Those backstreet clinics are not safe. You

always here those stories of women who bled to death after a botched abortion. I'm too scared to go to them.'

~

At the Mathai household, Kanono and Kanyi were watching *TaleSpin* when the phone rang. Priscila picked it up, listened for a few beats then told Kanono to go and call her mother from Mrs. Mutiso's house because there was a phone call from her car dealership and they were insisting it was urgent. Kanono grumbled because she'd just arrived from school and wanted to watch T.V. in peace, but she left the house all the same. Disagreeing with Priscilla was a futile activity. She was about to cross the road to Mrs. Mutiso's house when a car with one of Esther's brothers hanging out from it nearly hit her as the driver sped past. Flustered, Kanono took time to gather herself and even considered stopping by Esther's house to see what they had for tea but she heard Priscilla shout from the kitchen window, 'Haraka, basi!'

Mrs. Mutiso's gate was open. Kanono let herself in and walked up the verandah to the house, finding it open, she walked straight through and was at the threshold of the open door when she heard Priscilla shout: 'It's okay don't bother. They said it's not urgent anymore,' which is why for years she had been uncertain if in the distraction she'd misheard her mother say:

~

'Mr. Mathai was not Nyambura's father.' Mama Kanono spoke the words that had been in her throat since the day Mr. Mathai came to pick them up from the hospital in that silver Nissan of his, singing *Mwanamberi*, butchering the lyrics of the Luhya folk song. This truth was the only comfort she knew to offer Mrs. Mutiso

They heard Priscilla shout, 'It's okay don't bother,' but

didn't know who she was speaking with and accustomed to Priscilla's loud voice, they didn't think anything of it.

Kanono became distracted by the sight of Esther at her gate and ran off to her friend, so when Mrs. Mutiso said, 'I know,' Kanono was no longer in her compound.

Mama Kanono shot up, 'How?'

'It's obvious to anyone who has eyes.'

'But everyone—'

'Don't worry, it appears everyone around you is blind.'

'How long have you known for?'

'Since the day I met you.' Mrs. Mutiso said. The morning they met, Mrs. Mutiso had been observing the new family from her bedroom window. She was ready before the twins and her husband and with nothing to do because their nanny was getting the kids ready, she sat by the window and waited. From her window she could see straight into the Mathais' bedroom window. She observed as a woman rushed in spoke quickly to the man who was getting ready at a leisurely pace then rushed back out. A little girl waddled into their room and the man swept her up into a hug and planted several kisses on her. They came to the window and opened it then he put her down and continued to get ready as she played around him. The woman came back in with a dress for the girl and helped her to put it on. And that was the moment she knew. As the woman put on the girl's dress, she stole a glance at her husband who's back was turned to them as he fished through his cupboard for a shirt. She looked back down at her daughter—really looked—and then back up at her husband. She bit her lip. She was wondering if it was becoming more obvious as the girl grew into her looks that she was clearly not related to the man.

CHAPTER THIRTY-FOUR

Betty and Carol, August 20th, 2012

Without the phone calls, Mrs. Mutiso's home was eerily silent. They had been growing in frequency since the first one. Her answer was always the same:

'I don't know Kevin. It was a closed adoption.'

He didn't believe her.

'But I'm sure the great Mutiso name can open anything,' he'd said.

'No. Mr. Mutiso doesn't know. I can't drag him into this.' She continued the pretence that her husband was a part of her life because she liked the way it sounded, it felt like an armour of sorts though it wasn't one she trusted in.

'If you won't, I will,' Kevin had threatened the last time they spoke. Since that was the last time she had answered his calls and Nyambura had unplugged her landline and her phone was off, she wasn't sure if he had reached Mr. Mutiso. She wasn't sure if it mattered anymore.

Mrs. Mutiso got up from bed. It was going to four p.m. The sleeping pill had just worn off. She'd make a cup of tea then take another pill. After Mr. Mutiso left, she'd dispensed of a househelp. The allowance he gave her barely covered the cost of keeping the lights on in the house. If it hadn't been for the pay from organizing Beatrice's wedding, she'd have had to beg for money, Mrs. Mutiso thought as she walked downstairs.

There were no tea leaves left to make tea. Ng'ang'a's Kiosk had long been demolished along with the other Kiosks in their area and though there was a shopping centre there, Mrs. Mutiso was not up to the task of walking. It would have to be cocoa. Mrs. Mutiso poured milk and water into a pan, added a spoonful of cocoa and set the pan on the stove. She looked out of the window as she waited for the cocoa to boil.

Annie, like most of the other homeowners of Malaba, had demolished her house and put up hastily built flats modelled after the leaning tower of Pisa. Only the leaning part, mind you. The estate association had been the province of the Shahs, and once they moved out, no one took over the reins to continue managing the estate. It showed in the speed with which the once beautiful Malaba deteriorated. Many of the bougainvillea fences were replaced with stone walls and those that were still there were overgrown and choking on weeds. The potholes were no longer getting filled regularly, the pavements the children used to play on were cracked and losing a battle to wild grass. Large black water tanks, raised on ugly metal stilts took up people's backyards and verandahs.

Mrs. Mutiso's cocoa boiled over as she looked out of the little window in the kitchen to the house that had been the Mathais for nearly ten years before they moved. By the time she gave her attention back to the tea, half of it was all over the stove.

'Shit!' Mrs. Mutiso put the gas off. She looked around for a cloth to clean up the mess with. Finding none, she went out to her backyard to look for one there. Hanging on the clothes-line was a solitary, torn rug. She yanked that off and the clothes-line twanged in protest at the unexpected aggression.

After cleaning up, Mrs. Mutiso dumped the rug on the floor in the kitchen then poured the remaining cocoa into a mug, it barely reached halfway. She took the mug into the living room and sat at her writing bureau where she forgot her cocoa as she stared out of the window.

~

The child then.

Mrs. Mutiso quickly realized she did not have the strength to carry a child, bare a child and then mother this child. She knew Mr. Mutiso's parents were shrewd. If Mr. Mutiso could be duped his parents could not, and call it self-preservation, but to be found with another man's child was to be thrown out of the only home she had. So she made decisions.

At four months pregnant (and not showing), she said to Mr. Mutiso, 'My mother isn't doing so well. She has requested that I go back home to take care of her'. At six months: 'I can't come back just yet, my sister just delivered and needs help with her home'. At eight months: 'Dad's diabetes flared up, mum is in recovery and my sister has a baby and the rest of my siblings are in Nairobi, no one can get leave so I have to stay'.

The baby—a baby girl—was born on the 15th of July 1999. Where? Allow me to tell you one more story within a story.

~

Lillian Odere was the consummate business woman.

She run a home for pregnant girls, sometimes women, who found themselves in the precarious position of carrying an unwanted pregnancy in a country where abortion was illegal. The girls, sometimes women, called her Mother and she let them stay (no fee, but please donate), from whatever date they wanted until the due date of their child. Here, Mother helped organize the adoptions of these babies into loving homes but because, as she told the girls, sometimes new parents were often very skittish about a birth mother having a change of heart and knocking on their door to get their baby back, or worse—far worse—stealing into the adoptive parents' home in the dead of night to take their baby back, the parents expected—demanded—complete privacy: closed adoption.

When the girls, sometimes women, woke up the next morning after they'd given birth, Mother would inform them that their baby was now in a loving home. That was fast. I didn't expect it to be so fast. A waiting list, decades long of families desperate for a child, you know how these things go. Yes Mother, thank you Mother. Now drink up, we must get you up and ready to leave so we can free up space for the next desperate soul. Yes Mother, thank you Mother.

Sundays were the only day Mother took off. She was a devout Christian and attended a church in Dagoretti. The pastor, her brother, visited with the girls, sometimes women, every Monday and he prayed with them. Mother told them that he dedicated each and every baby to God before the baby was taken to a new home which filled the girls, sometimes women, with relief. Maybe now, their child would have a better life than they did because they were anointed with the holy oil.

Some of these new parents were very very particular. Oh, she's too black and you can tell she's going to get darker. A black girl like that? We couldn't take her, we're too light, people would know? What's wrong with his lip? Do you have another child without a cleft lip? We prayed for a boy with curly hair, mine is kinky but my husband's is curly. Can you help us find one like that Mother? And Mother, the consummate business woman would say, 'Not a worry dear, you prayed for a miracle and it's my job to deliver a miracle. I am expecting more children next week, come back next week'.

And what happened to the too black girl and the cleft lip

boy? Mother, the consummate business woman, knew a woman in Manchester who took discards and trained them for a lifetime of serfdom (you need to get them started early Mother, send them over as soon as you can), and Mother's brother the pastor, spoke with his wife who agreed to help them take these children to their new home in Manchester.

~

After Nyambura left her house, Mrs. Mutiso had gone to the supermarket to buy more tea leaves (ah yes! That's why she had left the house!) when she saw a picture of a familiar face on the front page of the Daily Nation. Below it was the headline: MIRACLE BABY SCAM. She dropped the packet of tea leaves which burst open and she didn't hear the attendant shout at her to pay for the damaged goods as she hurried out of the supermarket, a copy of the newspaper in her hand.

Here it was now, lying on her writing bureau, Mother's face staring back at her. Mrs. Mutiso read the copy of the article again. She tried to remember (but of course she couldn't, because she never got to see the baby girl), if her baby girl had a cleft lip or any other "defect" as Mother called them. What good was it anyway? It was a closed adoption and according to the newspaper, Mother was poor at record keeping so it was impossible to trace the children to their new homes.

Mrs Mutiso looked back outside. Her backyard was overgrown, the soil choking on weeds. The adoption, the ultimate sacrifice, had still not saved her marriage, she thought. When she came back, Mr. Mutiso was frothing at the mouth because his parents were frothing at their mouths that a woman they had paid dowry for (they hadn't, they refused to), had left their son to go gallivanting who knows where: I told you I was with my family. Lies. Lies. Lies. They have not seen you in years! When she came back home he had moved out and her twins were no longer allowed to visit their mother. In the five months she was away trying to save her life, it had gone up in flames.

'What did you do with the baby?' Beatrice asked, the first time she saw Mrs. Mutiso again.

'I went to a home and they delivered the baby and gave her away for adoption.'

'Why didn't you tell me where you were going?'

'I wanted to make my own decisions for once. I can't keep relying on you, I'm a grown woman too.'

'Kevin knows.' Beatrice had said.

'How?'

'His smarter than anyone gives him credit for being.'

'How do you know?'

'Priscilla. And don't ask how she knows but I gave her a huge pay rise, and a plot of land near her parents' home to keep her mouth shut, so no one else has found out.'

Despite everyone's best efforts, Mrs. Mutiso's life was hanging in tatters and the newspaper article was the last significant tear. She continued to stare into the backyard and her eyes passed over the weeds, the untrimmed hedges, up and up until they were on the clothes-line where the rug she wiped her spilt cocoa with had hung.

She stared at it, really stared it, then looked away. Mrs. Mutiso got up, suddenly restless, and went to put the mug of untouched cocoa in the kitchen sink. She saw that the kitchen door was open and the rug on the floor. Best to go hang it, she thought. She picked it up and walked out to the backyard. As though carried by a will beyond her she dropped the rug, untied the clothes-line on one end of the pole and walked to the other end to untie it. She walked back into the kitchen with the clothes-line, taking care to close the door behind her. Best not to make it so easy for thieves, she thought. She walked into the living room and looked around it. Best to change the bulbs on that chandelier, she thought. She picked the chair she'd been sitting on at the bureau and brought it to stand underneath the chandelier. Best to tie the clothes-line around the chandelier, she thought. She tied the rope around the chandelier. Best to check that the chandelier is safely secured she thought, and yanked hard at the clothes-line. The chandelier swung and clinked against itself but the clothing-line was secure. It would hold. Best to—

~

Beatrice hang up on Nyambura because a police officer had stepped onto the road and stood right in front of her car. She came to a halt.

'Hi officer?' she said, trying to contain her nerves.

'Madam, talking on the phone? At this your big age you should already know that it is an offence punishable by law.'

'Yes officer, I'm very sorry.'

'Sorry never brought anyone back from the dead,' he said then walked around her car, sizing it (expensive, new model), checked her insurance (up to date), her tyres (new), and then came back round to her window.

'Haya, driving licence please.' Beatrice reached into the glove compartment for it. She pretended to search for it for a few moments then said:

'I think I left it at home.'

The officer reared back as if she had slapped him in the face. 'So not one but two offences?'

'I'm really sorry.' Beatrice said as she checked the time. Six p.m. The officer appeared to be a talker. She didn't have time 'Could you just write me up and then I'll deal with court and everything later?'

'Waow! So you run this country now? How do you think it works when a woman is caught driving recklessly without a driving licence?'

'A woman?'

'Is this even your car? How do I know you have not stolen it and it is about to be—'

'Look, I know my rights. Write me up. I will pay bail on Mpesa and then go to court on Monday.'

'Your rights?' he laughed and leaned into her car from the open window. 'Madam, you are my prison—'

The traffic light turned orange. Beatrice gripped her steering wheel and surprised the officer by swerving back onto the road. From her rearview mirror, she saw him stumble back but catch himself in time before a passing car could hit him, as she flew down the road.

~

Beatrice banged on the door but there was no answer. 'Carol! Carol it's me, Betty, open up!'

...

'Carol!' Beatrice tried to open the door but the effort was in vain. She went round and tried the kitchen door. Closed. She went further into the backyard, brushing against the stinging nettle bushes that grew wild in Mrs. Mutiso's garden. The curtains were open. Beatrice peered through the window and saw an empty living room. She was about to turn back and head to the front of the house when the blue clothes-line tied to the chandelier caught her attention.

'Carol! Carol!' Beatrice screamed as she banged on the window. Even if she broke the windows, the grills would deter her from entering. Beatrice looked around the room frantically. 'Carol!' She screamed again.

~

Mrs. Mutiso had just finished getting dressed when she heard the screams. These days, she could get so into her mind, the world dissolved into an endless blur. She listened now. There was a banging somewhere in the house. Probably Janet again. She was just going to wait it out. Mrs. Mutiso walked back into her room and closed the door waiting for Janet to tire and leave. She'd put her best dress on. She liked this one. The sunflower yellow. It suited her complexion. She went to sit on her bed and looked out of the window one last time to where the Mathais' home used to be. She spotted a familiar car.

Betty? Mrs. Mutiso blinked. She also saw what she wanted to see sometimes. Like the twins. Sometimes she swore they were here with her. No, but that was Betty's car for sure. It had to be there because a group of boys had come to admire it. Unless she was imagining them too. Could be she was, Mrs. Mutiso reminded herself.

'Carol! Please, I'm begging you if you're still there please open for me!' Oh! Carol stood up at once. It was Betty! She beamed with joy. Fancy that. A chance to say goodbye.

Mrs. Mutiso sprinted downstairs but didn't see Beatrice at the window that faced her backyard because she wasn't expecting to see her there. She ran to the front door and opened it but there was no one there. Seeing things again! I told you, you were seeing things! She cursed herself. It was just as well, just as—

'Carol! Carol, I'm here!' Beatrice banged frantically on the window when she looked up and saw Mrs. Mutiso staring at the closed front door. Mrs. Mutiso jumped and turned in surprise.

'Oh Betty! What a surprise. You should have called I would have made you tea.' Beatrice was hoarse and crying and it reminded Mrs. Mutiso of the last time she had seen her that way—

'Is everyone okay? Is everything okay?' she asked hoping that none of Beatrice's family had come to harm but fearing the worst, because the last time it had been the worst.

'Please let me in,' Beatrice asked in a whisper that was barely audible.

Mrs. Mutiso rushed to the kitchen door to let her in.

Beatrice stumbled into the house and immediately took hold of Mrs. Mutiso's body and turned her around and around as if she was searching for something on Mrs. Mutiso's person, then she hurried past her to the living room. Mrs. Mutiso followed bewildered but remembering how distant Beatrice had been that time Mr. Mathai went missing.

'Betty? It's not Nyambura is it?'

Beatrice ignored her and stood on the chair underneath the chandelier, untied the clothes-line, walked back to the kitchen, Mrs. Mutiso following, opened the kitchen door, violently threw the line out then turned to her and said:

'Were you going to do it?'

'What?' Mrs. Mutiso was flustered.

'If I hadn't gotten here now, were you going to go through with it?'

'I…'

~

Beatrice, we know, had always thought that life was a poker game and the cards were what they were and you were just supposed to get on and play a damn good game of poker. This belief was shattered the day Mr. Mathai went missing-presumed-dead. Comparing life to a game of cards was to trivialize its importance. When the dust had settled and the grief had taken centre stage, Beatrice found that what she grieved most was the lives they could have had if they had realized early enough they were not meant to be together. She'd never told anyone about the conversation they had that morning on the way to work. Their last conversation. She could have easily paid off the loan in six months but she was determined to teach him a lesson. Maybe—and this maybe was like poison drip fed slowly over the years—maybe if she had agreed to do so, he'd not have made the trip to the bank, her children who still have a father. After he died, Beatrice kept thinking about divorce. It had never come up for them and she obsessed about this fact. Divorce broke families yes, but was there a way it saved them too? Was a broken home sometimes better than one held together by the skin of its teeth?

'He's gone now and there's nothing I can do about that, but Carol is still here.' Beatrice told herself. 'She's still here. She's still here.' Her eyes did not believe it and it appeared neither did her heart because it hadn't resumed a more natural pace.

It was Mrs. Mutiso's turn to walk out of the kitchen and for Beatrice to follow. Mrs. Mutiso picked up the newspaper from her writing bureau and gave it to Beatrice to read. Beatrice was confused, she wondered if her friend was even lucid anymore. How had she not known how badly off Carol was?

Then she read the headline. Of course, the story was not news to her. ' It's very sad,' Steven had said. 'Can you imagine the desperation women need to be in to give that woman their child?'

'This…this is where you went?' Mrs. Mutiso stared back but didn't nod nor shake her head. Beatrice read the article again. 'Oh, my God, why didn't you tell me?'

'Because I didn't want to believe it either. I got it so wrong, so, so wrong.'

CHAPTER THIRTY-FIVE

A Historian Conjured

This is not the end but when I consider it all (pictures, diary entries, recipes cut out of magazines, old receipts—I was thorough), it is this clipping from the newspaper that Mrs. Mutiso framed and kept in her room that calls to me most. It speaks of fate and a character trait people don't know she possesses: her ability to relent, to ease, to abruptly change course, because she too knows what it means to yearn for and never know peace. Very well then, to honour her, we will end here.

~

The women grew silent as the judge walked back into the courtroom. She was a young judge. 'How can she possibly understand our plight?' the women wondered. 'But still, at least she is a woman not a man' the fact did little to console them.

'All rise for Judge Anita Mwaura.' The women and the rest of the court and the journalists and the defendants stood up. The judge did not make eye contact with anyone as she sat down. 'How can she know the pain? She has borne no children,' the women lamented. 'From a good family, well off parents, great education. How can she know the desperation?' they asked one another. The judge sat down and the women and the court and the journalists and the defendants sat down after her.

'I am ready to give my judgment but before I give it, do the defendants have any last words they wish to say?'

Lillian Odere surprised the court when she accepted the offer.

'I have the records,' she said, 'I know my future is already spoken for and this will not change it, but I have the records.'

Lilian, the consummate business woman, had kept record of mother and child using a code for each pair. She had a record of each home the children went to and of the children that were trafficked, though the trail went cold once the babies reached Manchester.

Now you want to know don't you?

~

I was on my way to my morning lecture when I saw the newspaper headline: "MIRACLE BABIES FOUND (SOME)". I didn't think much of it and continued on my way to class.

'Why would they print the list of the parents names?' I overheard a student in the row in front of me in class say as she read the article on the Miracle Babies online. We were waiting for a lecturer who we didn't even know was passed out drunk at his local at that very moment.

'I don't know. Maybe to shame them. Those people should be shamed. Everyone follows the strict rules on adoption but these rich people think they are better than that?' Her desk mate responded.

I leaned in and idly read the article from the girl's computer along with the rest of them. They didn't seem to mind. I glanced over the names, then our class rep stood up and said he'd just received a message from our lecturer's wife saying that seeing as her husband had not made it home that night, it was unlikely he was going to make it to class that morning.

The student in front of me shut her laptop, but not before I saw my last name (not very common), right next to the first names of my parents.

~

This is the newspaper article that hangs in her room in the home we share, where fate has been merciful and love abounds, laughter too, and though we've just gotten an eviction notice from Mr. Mutiso, we have each other, and that's got to count for something.

ACKNOWLEDGEMENTS

I'd like to thank Dr. Nyairo. Without you this book would not exist and I'd still be talking about my some day novel. Nyokabi, thank you for reading the ugliest first draft known to man. Ropa, my heartbeat, you make me dream larger than I could on my own. Agnes and Bernard, you're my lifeline, thank you for supporting me. South B, thank you for weighing on my spirit until I had to write you down. The cast of Malaba, thank you for graciously allowing me into your lives.

ABOUT AUTHOR

Makena Maganjo grew up in Nairobi. She studied Economics at the University of London. Soon after she graduated, she returned to Nairobi with a bag full of optimism and a few short stories including, *The Months of the Mango*, which was later published by The East African. She shrugged off the pull of creative writing and started *Bintis,* makers of fine honey and nut butters. The unhealthy relationship between manufacturers and local supermarket chains brought *Bintis* to its knees around the same time as a well known supermarket was sinking.

Makena picked herself up and got a job at a digital logistics platform. As engaging as the short sting was, what kept Makena awake at night was the voices of Kanono, Mr. Mathaai, Mrs Shah, Mr. Karanja, and the entire cast of *South B's Finest*. She heeded their call and quit her job to become a full-time writer. This is her first novel.

You can reach out to Makena at:
makenamaganjo@gmail.com

JUST A KA-QUICK ONE

Dear Reader,

I'm writing this in a coffee shop. It is the last thing I will write before this book is published. I am indulging myself in a spot of imagination, trying to imagine the faces, lives and loves of the readers who'll have arrived at this last page. How many of you are in matatus on your way to work at this moment? How many of you are sitting in a coffee shop much like I am, a cold coffee by your side. How many of you are in a distant city, thinking of the South B you left some ten years ago, the one you've never seen, or this one that I painted?

First of all, thank you for purchasing and reading *South B's Finest*. You truly could have picked any other book at the bookstore or online and you picked mine. I am eternally grateful for that.

If you've got a little time, it would mean a lot if you could review this book on Amazon. If you enjoyed the novel, a review will help other readers discover it and if you have feedback it will help me improve my craft.

From one reader to another, until the next novel and the next world and the next cast of beloved characters, I bid you a fond farewell.

Yours sincerely,

Makena